SHREDDERS

MICHAEL COLE

SEVERED PRESS

SHREDDERS

Copyright © 2021 Michael Cole

WWW.SEVEREDPRESS.COM

ISBN: 978-1-922551-19-1

CHAPTER 1

He felt the bite.

"Son of a bitch!" Will slapped his shoulder, squashing the mosquito against his skin. The bastard must've had a proboscis like a freaking drill for it to hurt like that. Alas, he got his revenge, though he would have to suffer the itching.

Will didn't sweat it. After all, he had another itch to scratch, and he could hardly wait to get started. He was a quarter-mile away and he could hardly contain his joy. He didn't want to display it too much.

Gotta be suave.

Will was twenty-seven years old. It wasn't his first time hooking up, but on the other hand, this wasn't a simple hookup. He was grateful for feeling unhindered excitement. The last couple of times carried a little weight from guilt. But the taboo of cheating was memorable. Intoxicating. Maybe it was the joy of doing something he shouldn't have been. The risk of being caught was thrilling in its own right.

All through the drive, he was thinking out loud, "Oh, I shouldn't be doing this." Yet, he was doing this. Even worse, he wasn't regretting it. Before, he at least felt a little guilty, but was still drawn back. It was like a clean-living person doing an illegal drug and liking it, but wanting to stay clean. He rationalized it as the wedding was not for another six months. Technically, it wasn't adultery. Of course, if Venessa used the same logic to screw around, he would be pissed, but Will deliberately forced that consideration from his mind. What she didn't know wouldn't hurt her.

He passed a long stretch of rural area. Aside from a couple of properties, this whole side of town was nothing but summer green. There were more residential properties on the other end of Lake Carlson, but over here, it was mostly country.

He pulled into a winding dirt driveway which led to a two-story house. With three thousand square feet, its occupant had more than enough space. It was a nice property by a decent-sized lake. To think it was paid off made him a little jealous. The living room light was on. But she wasn't inside.

Will could see a small fire in the front yard, flickering just a few meters from the lakeshore. He saw the silhouette of a trim woman with hair that fell halfway to her back. She stood up as he parked the car. Even in the dark, he could tell she wasn't wearing much. Tight jean shorts and a crop tank top. Their effect was immediate. And knowing Lea Talley, that was by design.

She stepped into the stream emitted by his headlights, an athletically built woman who took pleasure in showing off her figure. Her sandstone-colored hair hung to her midback. She put a hand against the house and leaned, enticing her visitor with that smile.

Will shut the car off then got out. He hesitated only to toss his wallet and keys in the center console. He wasn't worried about anyone robbing his car. From what he knew, there had not been a serious crime committed in this town in over a decade. The cops here loved it. Who could blame them. If he could make fifty grand a year eating coffee and donuts, he would.

"Was worried you were getting second thoughts about coming," Lea said.

"Not a chance," Will said.

She smiled again. The headlights, which Will forgot to switch off, gave him full view of freshly whitened teeth. There was hardly a flaw to be picked out with Lea. Not a stress line, perfect weight, well-disciplined with her diet and exercise. Not worrying about a mortgage and car payment likely helped a little. Will had learned that her dad used to own a tractor supply market a few miles north. Being the only one for several miles, it did great business. A couple of years ago, he got terminal cancer in his lungs which spread rapidly. He sold the business and gave Lea the profits before he died. She had been living comfortably ever since.

Will finally turned the headlights off then joined Lea by the house. He took the liberty of touching her bare shoulder.

"Want a beer?" she asked.

"Won't say no to that," he replied. She led him back to the fire. He sat on a chair next to the cooler. He cracked open a beer and gazed out into the lake. Even with the intoxicating presence of a woman as beautiful as Lea, he still had to take a moment to appreciate the nature around him. The crickets were chirping in the background. The water itself was calm, almost motionless. Something splashed in the distance, probably a fish catching a bug. The best part, in his opinion, were the loons. Right as he sat down, an eerie yet beautiful call echoed across the lake. It was followed immediately by another, originating from somewhere else.

"I bet they're lovers. Calling to each other, craving companionship," Lea said.

"Could be."

"You don't call me much."

"Well, I have to be discreet."

She smiled, but didn't laugh. She pulled her chair next to his. Wasting no time, she casually reached over and undid the first button on his shirt.

"What's Venessa up to these days?"

Will cleared his throat. It was surprising that she would bring his fiancée up. He wasn't sure if she was expecting a serious answer. Especially since she was unbuttoning the next button of his shirt.

"Good."

She reached under his shirt and rubbed his chest. "Enjoying her new job?"

"No complaints so far," he replied. She began planting a series of kisses on his neck. They were gentle at first, but were quickly intensifying, as was her breathing. And his.

"Has she moved in with you yet?"

"Uh, no. Not yet. That'll be in a month." Was this the right answer at this time? Judging by her actions, it seemed to be.

"You excited?"

.   "I suppose so."

Lea pulled away. "You suppose so?"

Will couldn't tell if this was sarcasm or if she was genuinely irritated. He decided to go with the flow.

"Very excited."

That smile returned, and Lea went right back to work. A carnivore, she was. Her hands had become claws, raking at his waist. She planted her lips against his.

"She's a nurse practitioner now, right?"

"Uh-huh." Once again, his answer spurred her on. She leaned back, just long enough to pull her top off and throw it into the dark. Immediately, she threw herself back onto her lover. Will's hands moved up her bare back while he helped himself to the goods in front.

Lea was a goddess. Every answer was like a drug, adding to a high which had no limits. This man chose *her* over his fiancée, who was also an accomplished career woman. Nurse practitioners made six figures, and still he decided to spend this night with her. As he had a thrill from doing something he shouldn't be, Lea was getting a thrill from being the other woman.

"What does she think you're doing tonight?"

It took several seconds for him to answer. He was pulling his shirt off and getting back to work nipping at her tan flesh. "Uh, I told her I had a stomach bug. Didn't want to hang out."

"Oooh," she said. She slid off him and strutted toward the lake. Panting heavily, Will watched her pull her shorts and panties off, her bare ass barely visible in the campfire's glow. She looked back and smiled, continuing on toward the lake. She was feeling especially adventurous tonight.

She had one last question for him, and it had nothing to do with the woman. "You coming?"

Will stood up, kicked off his shoes, and removed his pants. He stood, basking in the glow of the fire like a warrior in Native American times. He heard a scrumptious 'mm-mmm' sound from his lower. She was in the water, backstroking further out. As though just to appease him, the cloud blocking the moonlight finally moved. The glow was just enough for him to make out those breasts cruising along the water's surface like boat sails.

Sorry, Venessa. Love ya, but a guy has needs.

He hustled to the shoreline.

"Oh yeah. Get over here, big guy."

"Think you can handle it?" he replied.

"Only one way to find out."

After wading waist deep, Will dove and swam toward the magnetic attraction which called for him. She was only fifteen feet ahead, eagerly awaiting his approach. After a few strokes, he was past the point of touching the bottom. No way to hit the goalpost like this. Clearly, she wanted to fumble around in the lake before getting to the *really* good part. No problem. This was far more adventurous than anything Venessa ever wanted to do.

He closed within a couple of yards. Lea laughed, bracing to be seized in the mighty arms of this man whom she proudly seduced.

Suddenly, she yelped and ducked under. Right away, she surfaced again, gasping for breath.

Will laughed. "Oh, no. You're not fooling anyone. Get over here, you filthy whore." Lea yelped again and floundered. She thrashed her arms out, sending frenzied laps of water toward Will. She lunged at him, not passionately, but *desperately.*

"Something's biting m—AHH" She writhed in agony, accidentally driving Will beneath the water. He hit the bottom, immediately pushing off with his feet. He rose to the surface like a rocket. Lea was thrashing, shrieking with each frenzied movement. This was no bizarre act. She was truly in anguish, as though she was being stung by a hundred wasps simultaneously.

"Come here!" the naked Will shouted. He reached out and grabbed her hand. He grasped it tight. The fingers were thin. Bony—completely lacking flesh. There was no mistaking the texture of those hands, as they'd been all over him. He pulled her closer, bringing her whole arm into the moonlight. There was no skin or muscle. It was all bone.

Trying not to panic, he pulled her close to him. She was spasming, but no longer thrashing. She hung limp against him. There were no breasts pressing against his chest…they were gone. Stripped away. Her head hung to the side, the meat shredded around her throat, blood gushing from the jugular.

This time, he gave way to panic. He pushed her corpse aside and turned toward shore.

Pain struck.

He jolted. It was like a mosquito bite times ten. Another hit. Then another, followed by another. One became five. Five became ten. Ten became a hundred. His flesh was being pulled every which way at once.

Will struck the water with his hands, simultaneously attempting to swim and fend off these invisible attackers. His efforts only served to give them more meat to peel away.

He flailed, mouth agape. He wanted to scream, but water kept rushing into the back of his throat. His flesh was coming off in golf ball-sized chunks. His toes were ripped from his feet. Ribbons of skin and muscle was peeled from his legs in a matter of seconds. Then they went for his penis and testicles.

Up until then, Will thought he already experienced the worst pain in his life.

He tasted his blood in the water. Even in his crazed state of mind, he was still determined to escape. He reached his arms out. From his fingers and wrists dangled three nine-inch bodies. Skillet shaped, they thrashed their tails, while clinging to him with hook-like teeth.

One fell from his finger and landed on his face. Knowing the scent of fresh meat, it attacked without hesitation. It ripped the eye from his socket with hardly any effort.

Will sank into the weed bed, landing alongside Lea's skeleton, void of flesh.

CHAPTER 2

Nothing is as nice as waking up to the smell of scrambled eggs, fresh bacon, and hot coffee.

Royce Dashnaw knew he had the best daughter in the world. Ellen was probably the only nine-year old he knew that actually liked being an early bird, let alone be out of bed before her old man was. Even on his days off, she was an early riser. Sometimes she'd be reading a book, hanging out on their little beach, or doing chores.

He checked his clock. Six a.m. He could hear the coffee maker brewing.

"God I love that kid."

He took a quick shower, then put on his blue tactical pants and blue uniform shirt. He watched himself in the mirror as he neatened his uniform, then quickly studied his jawline. A day's worth of beard growth… "Eh, I should be able to get away with it." He ran a quick brush over his recently cut red hair then strapped on his duty belt and thigh holster. Last but not least, he loaded his Glock 19 and secured it in that holster.

Now for the important part: eggs and coffee!

Royce found Ellen in the kitchen. For nine-years old, she was tall. She had her mother's blond hair and green eyes—the only good contribution that witch gave to the kid.

"Morning, Dad."

"Hey, kiddo." He sat down at the dining room table. The plate was already set up, the contents smelling delicious. "Kid, how lucky am I to have you?"

"Uh, *very* lucky!" she replied. Royce smiled. How mature and sharp she was. All As in school, reading at a junior high level, and showing up the boys in athletics. "Want creamer this time? Or are you going to be a man and drink it black?"

Royce nearly choked on his foot. *Where'd the kid get that wit?...*

"You're putting me on the spot," he said.

"I'm forcing you to think carefully. That's what you're always telling me, right?"

He smiled. "I guess I better aim to impress and drink it black this time." Ellen filled the mug and handed it to him. He took it, then looked across the table. There was no other plate. "Thanks. Did you eat already?"

"Yep."

"Gosh. Maybe I should get you a job in the department," he said.

"Hey, I'd go for that. Better than hanging out at Jacob's."

Oh boy. Now for the 'Dad' in me to kick in.

"Oh, come on now. Jacob isn't that bad."

"He's not *bad*, per say. Just really annoying. He's glued to that stupid iPad. And…he's a wuss."

"Oh, be nice!" It took everything not to laugh. Jacob was a nice kid, but Royce agreed he was a bit of a wuss. Once he took him along on a fishing trip and the kid couldn't stand the sight of a worm. On top of that, he could barely set the hook. He either yanked on the rod too soon or waited too long. And yes, like too many kids in this generation, he was a little too heavily drawn to his electronics.

Being the dad, Royce couldn't admit that to Ellen.

"I'm not being mean," she said. "I just don't see why you think I need a babysitter."

"Believe me, kid. It's not what I think. It's the law. You're only nine. Gotta be at least thirteen. They're strict on that in this state."

"Oh, stupid government bureaucracies. Think they know better than everyone else. Meanwhile, they go ahead and screw up the budget and everything else they touch. But hey! Gotta look over the shoulder of parents!" She ran hot water over the dishes as she ranted.

Once again, Royce tried hard not to smile. *Damn, I freaking love this kid.* All the lessons he taught her stuck like glue. She knew how to save money, how to cook for herself, had a good grasp on math, and also knew the importance of questioning things. More specifically, not taking things for granted. The only negative personality trait she inherited from him was the sense of ego. Royce had overcome his in recent years. Prior to that, he always had to one-up everyone. The smartest guy in the room, as a previous girlfriend once described him.

"You like Jane, though. Right?"

"Eh, she's okay." Ellen tried to think of the most politically correct answer as she scrubbed the dishes. "She's nice to me. Doesn't treat me like I'm an inconvenience…"

"She better not. I'm paying her pretty nicely to have you over there," he said.

"Oh, no." She laughed nervously, which in turn made Royce a little nervous. Jane was nineteen and was home from college. Royce was starting to suspect she brought the crazy college life back with her.

"She's not having boys over, is she?"

"Just once." Ellen saw the fork drop. "Um, they don't do anything."

I don't care if they do anything, as long as it's AFTER I pick you up. He picked up his fork, sipped his coffee, then continued eating. "That's good to hear." What else was there to say to that?

"You could take me to work. I *should* work in the office."

"Ha! I'm sure you could. But, again, there are laws."

"Ugh! Government! Can't keep its nose to itself."

"God forbid they see what goes on in this house." Royce finished his plate and handed it to her. "Alright, my little child laborer, clean that up for me."

She took the plate, then pointed a finger at him. "I ought to get something for being such a good kid. I vote we watch *Predator* tonight."

Royce walked past her, deliberately hiding his smile. *I'm such a horrible father.* "*Predator*, huh?"

"Yeah. Movie's bad-aaaahh—really cool!"

"Yes. Yes it is." Royce grabbed his ballcap and pulled his vest from the computer chair. "You sure you don't want to watch anything like, I don't know, *Frozen?*"

"Movie sucks! People freak out over it because it has one catchy song."

Royce once heard a coworker describe Ellen as a little Royce Dashnaw with a ponytail. He had to agree.

"Oh, alllllrigtht. We'll watch it later on. I'll even get popcorn. Now, go get your stuff. Gotta leave in a few minutes."

"Yes!" Ellen pumped a fist into the air and ran off to her room. "Better not be the butchered TV version."

"No, I wouldn't do that to you," he said. He finished putting on his vest. As always, he checked his gear. Not once in his police career had he ever been shot at. Half the cops in the little department didn't even wear a vest. But it looked cool, and Royce was willing to settle for that.

Ellen came out with her bag.

"You should take your fishing pole," he said.

"Yeah, I know," Ellen replied, reserved. "Then I'd have to share with Jacob. I'd have to put on the worm, teach him how to cast again, unhook the fish…if he even manages to set the hook."

Royce hesitated before responding. Fact is, he agreed with her complaints. Aside from her, he hated sharing his fishing rod with anyone too. Hell, he sometimes hated letting Ellen use it. That's why she had her own! However, he needed to be a good dad and teach her to be kind and help others.

"Well, why don't you try and teach him? If he catches on, maybe we'll buy him one for Christmas or something."

"I guess."

"Hey, if you wanna watch *Predator*…"

"Cooking breakfast isn't enough for you?"

"I thought you did that from the goodness of your heart."

"I do. But still—" She stuck her tongue out at him.

"Ha. Smart aleck. Go grab your tacklebox. Who knows, maybe you could teach Jane something too."

Ellen went into the back room to get her tacklebox and rod. "*You* ought to be the one teaching her."

Royce swallowed. Hooking up was a subject matter he wasn't quite ready to share with his daughter. She could be thirty and he wouldn't be ready for that.

"Uh," he chuckled as he stalled to figure out a response. "She's a little young for me."

"Heard her call you hot," Ellen said.

"Not interested. Moving on."

"That's good. I'd rather you get together with Pam from work. I know she really likes you."

"Ooookay! If this conversation goes any further, CPS might start investigating me. Let's get outta here."

Ellen smiled. Like any kid, she took great pleasure in driving her old man crazy. She went out the door first.

Royce flicked the lights off. "Definitely my kid."

CHAPTER 3

"Hey, come on little bro! Time to rise and shine."

Jacob lifted his pillow and squeezed both ends against his ears. The whole point of summer vacation was to *not* get up at the crack of dawn every day. "Go away."

He heard the twist of the knob followed by footsteps across his room. With the pull of a curtain came a stream of sunlight so bright that even his pillow couldn't shield him from it.

Jacob tossed the pillow aside. "Come on!" He looked up at her, only to wince. He'd probably be able to find something in his sister's features to poke fun at, if only the sun wasn't blinding him. Too bad his stupid window faced the east side.

Jane was already dressed for the day. Being the college girl, she had to make sure her fit body was on full display, with just the right touch of modesty to not drive away Ellen's dad. Jean shorts, red tank top that showed her abs. At the age of nine, Jacob didn't quite understand the attraction of skin display. He just figured it was the young-adult style.

"Ellen's gonna be here any minute, and you're still in your jammies."

"Why don't you two play and let me stay in here." He put his head back to the pillow, only for Jane to yank it away.

"Jacob. Mom already warned you about your attitude. My word, whatever I tell her, is as good as the truth. If you want that *PlayStation 5*, you need to play your cards right."

Jacob stretched, then sat up. "Don't know why you two want me to get up. Ellen doesn't even like me."

"Aw! You sound disappointed. I think it's really cute you want her to like you."

"What?"

"You have a crush!"

"*WHAT?!* No! Ew! Not that way."

Jane chuckled. "Give it a few more years, you won't be saying 'ew'."

"Sis, you're weird."

"Runs in the family, little brother. Now, get your ass up." She shut the door on her way out.

****

"Look at this. Nice lakefront property. Plenty of space to fish. Maybe I should stay here and have you go to work instead!"

Ellen chuckled. "I could be a cop." Now it was her dad who was laughing. "What? I could!"

"I believe you."

"I really could! I'd use the nightstick and bash a criminal in the kneecap. Then put him in an armbar…"

"Alright, settle down." Royce pulled into the driveway. "I'll give you this—there are plenty of jerks out there I wouldn't mind doing that to."

"Oh yeah! Like the tree-huggers you told me about?"

"I didn't call them tree-huggers!"

"Yeah you did!"

"What?!"

Ellen nodded with exaggerated motions. "And I heard you say you'd like to grill up a steak in front of them, then have them watch you eat it!"

Royce snorted. "I still don't remember saying that to you—were you eavesdropping on my phone conversation with Pam?"

"It's not eavesdropping when I can hear you across the house."

Royce bit his lip. "Alright. You've got me there. That day, I had some unpleasant encounters, was venting to a friend after work, and I might've said a few mean things. Come on, let's get you squared away." They got out of the SUV. "Listen, sweetie. It's okay for people to be passionate about things. Some people tend to be a little overbearing. They tend to have a 'my way or the highway' attitude. They can't accept the reality people have different tastes and opinions."

Ellen collected the fishing rods and followed her dad to the door. "Is that the problem with the environment people?"

"They're called activists. And…yes. At least in the case of this particular group. They tend to get pretty mean when they don't get what they want."

"What do they want?"

"For people to stop fishing, for the tackle and meat shops to be boycotted—shut down, rather. All in the name of animal rights."

"I know *I* wouldn't get along with them." She proudly held up her fishing pole and tackle box.

Royce laughed. "Luckily, I don't think you'll have to worry about 'em."

He went to knock on the door, only for it to open first. Jane threw her arms wide to give Ellen a hug. "HI!"

"Oh!" Ellen made a strangled sound as Jane squeezed her tight.

"Good morning. How you doing today, little wannabe sis."

"I'll let you know…" Ellen sucked in a breath when Jane finally released her.

Royce handed Jane an envelope. "Here you go. Appreciate it, as always."

"Oh, it's no problem Officer Dashnaw. We're going to have fun, as always. I see Ellen brought her fishing gear along."

"You gonna fish with me?"

"I—" Jane forced a smile, "maybe I'll try throwing a cast or two. I'm not good with handling fish. But I'll make sure Jacob tries it."

Ellen would've rolled her eyes had her dad not been standing there. "Yeah, okay."

Royce patted her on the shoulder. "Remember what I told you."

"Yeees, Dad."

"Good. I gotta go. See you when I get off, hon." Royce waved to them as he returned to his vehicle. As he buckled in, he switched his personal squad radio on. As he backed out of the driveway, it started going off.

"Dispatch to any available unit. We've got a call at Monty's Tackle. Owner's informing me that the environmentalists are gathering outside his front door. Chasing away customers."

Royce groaned. "All I had to do was wait *thirty seconds.*" He picked up the mic. "Hey, Dispatch, this is Dashnaw. That's on my way in. I'll check it out. Have someone at the station punch me in, would ya?"

"You got it, Royce."

That wasn't the dispatcher. Royce smiled. "Thanks, Pam."

"No problem. Dispatch, go ahead and log me to that call as well."

"Unit One to Dispatch, I'll head over as well."

Chief Elwood and Officer Pam Nettie. *Everyone* was starting early today.

****

Ellen watched him drive off, then went into the house. Jane was heading for the hallway.

"Jacob? You dressed yet?"

"Almost done."

"Okay. I'll take your word for it." Jane returned to the living room and sat on the couch. "You hungry? I can fix you up something."

"No thanks. My dad and I ate earlier."

"My gosh! You guys really are early birds, aren't you?"

"'Early to bed, early to rise, makes a man healthy, wealthy, and wise.'" Ellen thought for a sec. "I think it was Ben Franklin who said that. I might be wrong."

"Well, maybe he has a point. Be nice if he included women in that statement, but that's beside the point."

"Oh gosh!" Ellen threw her head back. "He meant *both*. Everyone's so sensitive these days!"

Jane laughed. "I just said that to get a reaction out of you. You are so much your dad's kid."

Ellen shrugged. "I guess that means I'm cool!"

"Darn right you are." Jane picked up one of the poles. "Well, it looks like we already have one of our activities planned out for today."

"Going to the movies?"

Both ladies watched a half-asleep Jacob penguin walk out of the hallway. He wore blue shorts and a black shirt with a *Marvel* logo at its center.

"Not today—for the hundredth time in a row," Jane said.

"Nothing good out, anyway," Ellen said.

"The new *Thor* movie's out. I still haven't seen it."

"Oh, gee! *Love and Thunder*? The feminized one?"

"It looks good."

"It looks stupid."

Jacob stuck his tongue out at her as he grabbed the TV remote. He got on *Disney Plus* and selected *Falcon and the Winter Soldier*.

"Oh, God! Not that one."

"I think it's good," Jacob said. "I like the action and the effects."

"And preachiness."

"Then don't watch it."

Ellen stood up and grabbed her fishing gear. "For once, we can agree on something!" She turned to Jane. "Mind if I indulge?"

"Not at all." Jane looked over to Jacob. "Hey bud, after you eat, why don't you try fishing with Ellen?"

"Fishing's boring."

"No it's not."

"Then why do *you* always say no?"

Jane swallowed. "Well..." *No point in arguing.* "Two episodes, then I want you outside. Don't have to fish, but at least be out in the fresh air. Mom and Dad don't want you in front of the television all day. It's beautiful out. You'll have all winter to be cooped up in front of the television."

"Alright."

"It'll be fun. We can play games. Right, Ellen?"

"Sure!" Ellen's enthusiasm was partly genuine. Jacob was a little less annoying once the activity got rolling. Until then, she would leave him to his show, pretend *Endgame* was where the *MCU* officially ended, and catch some big ass fish.

CHAPTER 4

Royce sped through the small town of Lorenzo, MI, ignoring the landmarks he usually enjoyed during his morning route. There was Dayton Park, a nice little area with a playground and a little creek. He'd often wave to the kids who recognized him as he drove by. This time, they stared in fascination as he sped past them with his cherry flashing.

He passed the Army monument, which featured a Sherman tank and a WW2 artillery gun. His grandfather was a tank driver in Germany and would often tell stories about the armored vehicle. Royce couldn't help but feel sentimental whenever he passed it.

Then there was Barb's Bakery, where he'd sometimes stop for a donut or roll if he had a few minutes to spare. Instead of providing a pleasant second breakfast, all the bakery did was indicate he wasn't far from the incident he was responding to.

There was a masked activist standing on the corner holding a cardboard sign. *Tackle is ammo. Rods are rifles. Fishing is murder.*

"Could these people be a little more creative with their slogans?"

He took a left at the next intersection. A couple hundred feet down was Monty's Tackle Shop. There was a small but lively crowd in front of it. As he approached, he watched three potential customers return to their vehicle. A fourth one who, judging by the way he squared up with the leader of the group, did not take too kindly to being turned away.

Royce didn't need to get a good look at the leader's face to know he was Curt Lin. He was twenty-two years old, skinny as a rail, and wore the same black shirt which was two-sizes too big. It wasn't just the clothing that made it obvious, but the demeanor. Most of the protesters, no matter how obnoxious and ignorant they were, were usually bright enough to know when they were outmatched physically. Funnily enough, it was the one with the least intellect that they chose as their frontrunner.

Being a hundred and ten pounds soaking wet, Curt felt he could go toe-to-toe with a six-foot, muscled out, meat-eating man with a *Semper Fi* tattoo on his forearm. Most sensible people would call out such a fool for his stupidity. Then again, people as irrational as those in this group mistook stupidity for bravery.

Royce parked the vehicle and approached the crowd. Standing at the door was Monty Granger, a fifty-five year old Marine retiree. Often, fellow veterans would hang out at his shop, smoke cigars, buy some tackle, and clog their arteries with jerky. But right now, if Monty was to suffer a heart attack, it'd be due to the restraint he was showing at this moment. Royce knew the man well enough and saw the longing in his eyes to unleash on the idiots harassing his store.

His younger friend staring down at Curt probably would've already broken him in half had Royce not showed up. Royce rolled his eyes as several protesters filmed him with their smartphones. Not surprisingly, they often cried about the evils of capitalism—to their phones—which they bought. Well, somebody bought them. Royce suspected these protesters were not the type that held jobs.

"Little punk, you're playing with fire. Stop blocking my way," the customer said.

"No way! You think I'm gonna let you get more ammo so you can murder some more helpless fish?!" Curt said. He raised a finger to the customer's face.

Royce sensed the fuse nearly burnt down to its explosive base. *Better act now or it's gonna get uglier.*

"Ah-ah-ah! Break it up!" He put himself between them. The Marine reluctantly backed away. Now, instead of confronting him, Curt Lin decided it would be more suitable to confront the officer. "Dude, get your finger out of my face."

"You gonna shoot me?! Murderer."

Oh, Christ. It's too early for this shit.

"Want me to do it, Royce?" Monty said. Royce laughed. He needed to laugh. It was one of the few things that kept him level-headed while dealing with these types.

Curt turned to his followers. "You see?! These white men would *love* to shoot us if they could get away with it. Just like the deer in the woods and the fish in the lake! They've got no compassion. They're racist! Misogynistic! Fascist!"

"Jesus, Curt. You're really going for all the talking points today." The sight of red and blue flashers from up the road drew Royce's attention. *Finally.* Two vehicles approached and parked across the street. Royce tilted his head toward the female officer in the nearest vehicle. "Why don't you tell *her* how misogynistic she is."

Officer Pam Nettie stepped out of the Interceptor. Her black hair hung out the back of her police ball cap. A jiu-jitsu black belt, she had sleeve tattoos on both arms displaying martial art imagery. Though she wore Aviator sunglasses, Royce noticed the twitch in her cheek—a wink. She did that often.

Behind her was Chief Larry Elwood. Though by no means obese, he was in considerably less shape than Pam. Normally, Royce would point out his haircut. Usually, Larry had curly red hair which everyone at the station referred to as his redfro. But he must have taken a visit to the barber, who reduced it to his preferred buzzcut look.

Emboldened by the power of reinforcements, Royce tried his luck again with the crowd. "Can y'all please clear out?"

"You can't tell us to leave! This is public property!" one of the protesters shouted.

"Um, actually this building is owned by Monty here."

"Not the sidewalk!" Curt said.

"Dude, you're obstructing his door. It's practically the equivalent to someone being at your front door keeping your relatives from visiting."

"Dunno, Royce. Some people would see that as a good thing," Pam said.

Royce smiled. "True."

"Hey, jokers? Can we get something done here?" Monty said, pointing at the crowd.

"Yeah-yeah, bear with us," Larry said in his thick country boy accent. He clapped his hands. "Alright, y'all. You've made your statement. Time to move along."

"You can't make us do shit!" Curt shouted.

"Actually, I can, and I will. I'll get the state troopers out here if I have to. They'll eat the lot of you for breakfast."

Curt turned toward the crowd. "See that? They're threatening us." The crowd became increasingly unruly. More phones were held up.

Curt chanted. "You cast that line—"

"IT'S BLOOD ON YOUR HANDS!" the group chanted.

"You drink that milk—"

"YOU'RE GUILTY OF THEFT!"

"You eat those eggs—"

"YOU'RE MURDERING CHILDREN!"

Pam snorted then tapped Royce on the arm. "Eating eggs is murder, huh? Yet, when it comes to humans, why do I have a feeling these idiots are pro-abortion?"

Royce shook his head. "You're looking for consistency from those who function without reason."

"Or common sense." Larry lifted his radio. "I need all available units over here at Monty's Tackle. The group here is getting riled up and are refusing to move from the premises. Bring the bus and plenty of handcuffs."

"This is an abuse of power!" Curt shouted.

"Only in America can you break the law and then cry that you're being oppressed," Pam said.

Curt stepped up, putting his nose in her face. "Listen, you fat pig bitch—" He made the mistake of putting his finger to her chest. Aggressive contact. She grabbed his wrist, twisted his arm around his back, then put him on the pavement.

"I thought pigs were beautiful in your eyes," she said as she cuffed him.

Curt flailed. "OW! You're breaking my wrist! You're digging the metal in!"

"Oh, quit your crying," Royce said. He turned to the other protesters, who were busy calling the cops names and screaming about abuse of authority. "Alright…" he took out his cuffs and dangled them from his finger, "who's next?"

More police vehicles arrived. Finally, the crowd began to disperse.

"Sorry, Curt," one of them said.

"Wait! What are you doing?!"

"I don't want to get arrested," one of them said.

"What about the cause?!" Curt said, spitting soot from the pavement. They didn't bother with an answer. Some tried to save face by flipping the officers off as they left. 'Yeah, fascists! We'll get you next time—but not really, because we're a bunch of wussies.'

Royce exhaled sharply. "Glad that's over."

A police SUV pulled up. The department's tallest member, Holman, stepped out and approached. At six-eight, he towered over the rest of the group.

"Hey! Party's over already?"

"Yeah. You can thank Pam for ruining your fun," Royce said.

"You're a bunch of fascists!" Curt said.

Pam was grinning ear to ear. "We should start a drinking game. Every time he says the word 'fascist' we all take a shot."

"We'd all be blackout drunk by brunch," Larry said.

Holman looked down at him and laughed. "How much you weigh, kid? Eighty-pounds?" He knelt down and lifted Curt to his feet with one hand. "You need some meat on you."

"Fuck you!"

"Oh, boy! You said the sacrilegious word. *Meat*," Larry said.

"Whoops!"

The group laughed.

"Alright, *Goliath*, why don't you take the soy boy to the station and book him?" Larry said.

"With pleasure, sir."

"Hey, I'm gonna need a new set of cuffs," Pam said. Holman tossed her his set, then goaded Curt to the SUV.

"Is this how you treat prisoners?!" Curt said.

"You're not a prisoner, you're a detainee. There's a huge difference, though if you keep this crap up, you'll become an *inmate* at Jackson State Penitentiary." He pushed Curt into the backseat.

"You're all a bunch of—"

Holman closed the door, cutting him off. He smiled at his fellow officers. "This'll be a fun ride!"

"Don't goad him *too much*," Larry said. Holman gave a thumbs up then drove off.

Monty checked the outside of his store. "Thanks, boys and gals." He looked at Pam. "Especially you, ma'am. Gotta say, that was so satisfying to watch."

"Us Devil Dogs gotta look out for each other," she said. Monty and his customer saluted her, then entered the building.

Larry returned to his vehicle. "Well, that's enough fun for today. I'm heading back in. Pam, I'll take care of the report. Just do a quick supplement for me at some point today, will ya?"

"Gotcha, Chief." They waved as he left. She then looked over at Royce. "Wanna ride with me once you get your car to the garage?"

"Oh! I suppose so."

"You always act surprised when I ask you that."

"Well, I, uh—" Royce hated moments like this. Once upon a time, he was the stud of the century. Then he matured and became a single parent. Maybe it was the idea of introducing someone new to his daughter, or being afraid of taking time away from her. His mind was lost in a whirlwind of thoughts when it came to that issue, and it usually kept him from dating. "Just me being modest, I guess."

"Uh-huh." She winked at him. "See ya at the station."

Royce returned to his personal vehicle and started it back up. Before departing, he took a moment to watch her go to her car. She was a charming woman, well-shaped, and undoubtedly interested in him.

Of all the voices in his head right now, it was Ellen's. *"Dad, she really likes you. You should take her on a date."*

"God help me."

CHAPTER 5

Ellen watched the jitterbug splash down near the lily pads. She let it sink for a moment then started cranking.

Jane leaned back in the seat next to her. "Wow, you've got quite the cast."

"Had a good teacher," Ellen said. She leaned over the edge of the dock, gradually bringing the lure toward her.

Her babysitter was rocking back and forth. She wished her seat had an umbrella. Unfortunately, there was no shade on this dock. The only place that offered protection from that blazing hot sun was where the tree hung over the backyard. Jacob had no qualms about sitting there. He leaned back in his wicker chair, bending the back legs, despite his sister's warning for him not to do so.

"Hey, Jake, why don't you come out on the dock?"

"And burn to a crisp? No thank you." He tapped his feet on the ground, stir crazy. The need for his electronics was eating at him like a drug withdrawal.

"Stop leaning back. I already told you."

"I'm bored."

Jane pointed at the water. "Then try fishing. Learn something new for a change."

Jacob turned his chair away. "I'm good."

"Ugh." Jane shook her head, then wiped a towel over her face. "Whew!"

Ellen glanced at Jane. "You're sweating."

"I'm fine, kiddo."

"Your makeup's coming off."

"It is not. It's—" Jane looked at the tan stain on her towel. "Oh, hell!"

Jacob pointed and laughed. "Ha-ha!"

"Oh, shut up, you little shit!" Jane covered her mouth, then looked at Ellen. "Shoot. Sorry."

Ellen laughed. "My dad's a cop. We watched *Aliens* the other day. I'm no stranger to 'adult words' as Dad puts it."

"Still, you didn't hear me talk like that."

"I'll tell Mom," Jacob said.

"Joke's on you, kid. Mom doesn't give a shit." She covered her mouth again. "Oh, forget it. I'll be right back." Jane hurried back to the house, snapping her fingers at her brother as she passed him. "Jacob. Cast a line. Do *something* other than sulk."

Jacob groaned. At this point, doing something was less painful than listening to his sister nag him.

Ellen was making another cast as he approached. She gave him a quick glance, then turned her attention back to the lure.

Jacob sank into Jane's seat and watched. "How do you know when the fish bites?"

"You feel a sharp tug."

"Could mean you hooked a lily pad," he said.

"That's a snag. The fish will *pull* against your line as it runs. It's actually quite easy to tell the difference." She tipped forward as the line went tight, her rod threatening to fly out of her hands. "Like that!"

Jacob stood up. "Whoa!"

Ellen let the fish wear itself out, then slowly began to crank. The line angled sharply, then rose as the fish ascended. It leapt three feet into the air, twisting and flapping its tail before crashing down. Largemouth bass.

"Oh yeah!"

"Dang!" Jacob said. He noticed the smile on Ellen's face. It wasn't just because of the catch, but also his sudden interest in the sport.

After fighting the bass for a few more seconds, she lifted it over the dock.

"Sixteen-inches at least." The fish lashed about as it hung from the hook. She placed it on the dock, pried the hook loose, then held it at eye-level. "Hmmm, catch and release? Or lunch?"

"No! Eww!" Jacob said. "You're not seriously gonna gut it, are you?"

Ellen sighed. "Not if it's gonna get you woozy." She eyed the fish one last time. "Looks like it's your lucky day." She tossed it back into the water.

Jacob knelt by her tacklebox and examined the various lures inside. They came in all different designs. Some were shaped like crayfish, others like frogs, some like bugs, some like fish.

Ellen fixed her lure and was about to cast when she noticed him exploring. "What? You wanna try?"

"Well..." Jacob leaned away. "I don't know."

Ellen snickered. "I know that voice too well. 'Yes, but I'm too afraid to try, so I'm gonna say no'."

"That's not true!" Jacob returned to the chair. His eyes were still on the tacklebox and spare rod. He then noticed Ellen was still watching him inquisitively. "Alright, I guess I'll give it a shot."

"Alright then." The exasperation wasn't well hidden. Ellen would much rather be fishing herself than teaching him how to do it. Then again, if she did manage to get him genuinely interested, maybe he'd be a little less annoying to be around. At the very least, he wouldn't want to sit inside all day and watch television.

She picked up the spare rod. "What kind of lure you want to try?"

"Uhh…" He looked over the various options then pointed at a red grasshopper design. "That one."

Ellen attached it. Showing him how would come at a later time. First, she needed to make sure he knew how to throw a cast.

She stood up and placed it in his hand. "Press this button with your thumb. Hold it down. Bring the rod back over your shoulder, then let go of the button as you fling it toward the water." Jacob gave it a try. He released the button too late, flinging the lure straight down five feet in front of him. Ellen closed her eyes and reminded herself he was new at this. "Baby steps. Try again."

Jacob reeled in his line, tilted the rod to twelve o'clock, then cast again. Same result. He forgot to release, sending the spinnerbait down three feet in front of him.

"Here, let me show you." Ellen took the rod from him. "Watch." She cocked it over her shoulder then launched it far out into the lake, away from the lily pads. The lure struck down seventy-five feet out.

"Nice," Jacob said.

"Darn right it was." Ellen loved compliments, no matter who they came from. "Alright, with this kind of bait, you simply reel it in steadily. Don't go too fast, but not too slow either. Don't want it to sink too deep. Just let the fish think it's a real bug struggling to stay along the water—whoa!" The pole bent toward the water, nearly taking her with it. Ellen stumbled to the edge of the dock, finding her footing at the last second.

This was a big catch. The fish went deep, threatening to take her line with it. She held tight, gave it a few inches by lowering the rod to the water. Slowly, the tension eased. Ellen worked it closer.

"I think I see it," Jacob said.

"Me too!" Ellen raised the line, drawing the catch to the surface. It was fifty-feet out, but they could see its elongated body and crocodile-like jaw. A pike. It was at least thirty-six inches. "Oh, man! I wish Dad was here to see this! Jake, get my phone. I need to get a picture. Ohhhh man, he's gonna be so jealous."

"Where's your phone?"

"Over on the porch by the shade." She kept the exhausted fish along the surface. It splashed as it tried to run again, but was held in place by her line. "Yeah-yeah, nice try. You're not going anywhere."

It splashed again. All of a sudden, it was obscured by a rapid series of splashes. Ellen felt the line tug back and forth unnaturally. It was as though something was playing tug-of-war with her catch.

"What the heck?"

"What's happening?" Jacob asked, returning to the dock with her phone.

Ellen was too flabbergasted to answer. A five foot radius around the fish was alive with small, but rapid splashing, as though a blender was churning the water just below the surface. Residue emerged along the small waves. Then the line came free.

She reeled it back to her, noting the weightlessness. All that returned was little tooth-lined wedge that was the pike's lower jaw.

"Holy cow! It tugged so hard, it took its own jaw off!" Jacob said.

Ellen shook her head. "That's not possible." She looked back to the lake. The splashing had settled.

"What's not possible?" Jane asked.

Jacob smiled. "Ellen lost a fish!"

"I didn't lose it!"

He pointed at her lure. "Don't see it on your line!"

Ellen kept watching the spot where the splashing occurred. There were little bits of residue drifting about. Fins? It was hard to tell from here.

"Uh-huh, okay that's great!"

Ellen looked back at Jane. She was on her phone, her eyes glowing like someone who won the lottery.

"Yep! That's totally awesome! So you'll come here? Perfect! Yep, see you then! Bye!" Jane hung up and faced the kids. "You guys ever been on a pontoon boat before?"

"Yeah." Ellen tilted her head back. "Why?"

"Because we're going on one tomorrow!" Jane threw her arms up.

Ellen grinned. No way was Jane this excited solely for a boat. "*Whose* boat are we going on?"

"Ken Lewis'!"

Jacob winced. "Her high school crush." He stuck out his tongue.

"Aw! Well I think it's cute!" Ellen said.

"That's why I love having you here. High five, girlfriend!" Jane and Ellen slapped hands.

"Am I allowed to bring my fishing stuff?" Ellen asked.

"Absolutely!" Jane said. This time, it was Ellen who initiated the hand slapping.

Jacob groaned. "Do I have to go?"

"Listen, bud. You do this favor for me—and be a good sport about it—and *maybe* I'll consider taking you to see that *Thor* movie. Deal?"

Jacob thought of it, then extended his hand. "Deal."

Ellen's face turned to one of disgust. "Just arrange it on a non-Ellen day."

Jacob stuck his tongue out. "Your loss."

"Alright, kids, be nice to each other." Jane wiped her forehead again. "Alright, I give up. Makeup's coming off entirely."

Jacob put his hands over his face and gasped. "Oh, no! Don't reveal the beast!"

Jane turned to face him. "Those odds on seeing *Thor* just dropped, mister." He lowered his hands and smiled nervously. Pleased with the leverage she held over him, Jane returned to the house.

Ellen removed the pike's jaw from her lure and stared at it. There were several tears in the skin around it. It was as though the fish had gone through a food processor.

"Weird." She thought of what could've torn the fish up like this. There wasn't anything swimming around that could shred something to pieces in a matter of seconds. The only thing that made even a lick of sense was an otter. "Hey, Jake? You ever see otters swimming around out here?"

"No. I don't really pay attention to the water. Too boring."

Of course... She watched the residue drift apart in the distance. *Yeah. An otter. What else could it be? Probably caught the pike, wrestled it away while biting the heck out of it, then swam away.*

She looked at her tacklebox and debated throwing more casts.

Jane stepped back out. "It's almost lunch time! You guys hungry?"

The words seemed to trigger a rumbling in Ellen's stomach. "Yes, indeed I am!"

"Come on inside. Let's see what we're in the mood for."

Jacob sprang from his chair and went straight for the door. "Finally!"

CHAPTER 6

The remainder of the morning hours were fairly peaceful. Royce and Pam spent most of it patrolling the neighborhoods along the north side of town. There weren't that many radio calls so far. Most of the transmissions were simply other officers informing dispatch of their whereabouts and when they shifted between foot and mobile patrol.

It was around noon when Royce and Pam finally encountered some kind of 'action'. A white-collar worker, going home on his lunchbreak, was doing fifty in a twenty-five mph zone. Even that was tame, and Royce wasn't complaining. No matter how experienced one was in law enforcement, it was always a relief when a driver kept a good attitude when receiving a ticket.

"I'm a little disappointed," Pam said.

"What? You hoping he'd give a bunch of backtalk? Were you planning on putting his face in the pavement as well?"

Pam shrugged. "It'd be exciting."

Royce shook his head and turned the vehicle southwest to head toward the lake. On this street were mostly woods, with a few residential properties.

"Surprised you didn't stay in the Corps."

"Eh, it was time to leave," Pam said.

Royce had heard the stories before. Pam loved being in the USMC, but what the average civilian didn't know was that, when on deployment, there was a LOT of waiting around. What she didn't say outright, but Royce could sense, was that she was hoping to fall in love, get married, and have a family life. Hard to do that with a career in the military.

"What's for lunch?" she asked.

"Pot roast," Royce said.

"*Pot roast?!* In this heat?"

"You're complaining about the heat? I thought you'd been to Afghanistan. Doesn't the weather there make this place seem like a spa?"

"Actually, it's fairly comparable to here," Pam said. "The main difference is that here, you're not covered head to toe in gear."

"Oh! I didn't know that. Normies like me envision that place as like a hundred-fifty degrees."

"You'll feel as though you're living in a hundred-fifty degree weather if you eat a pot roast for lunch," Pam said. "It's ninety-two degrees out."

"That's what air conditioning is for." He looked over at her. "Why? What were you hoping for? An egg salad?"

"What's wrong with *that*?!"

"Thought you Marines ate meat for breakfast, lunch, dinner, and dessert."

"And midnight snack, thank you very much." She put her feet up on the dashboard and crossed her arms. "That said, sitting in this car all day, I don't mind eating something light. A pot roast would put me to sleep. Where would you get one, anyway?"

"Lorenzo Haven," Royce said.

"What's that?"

"It's the restaurant near the Green Valley Resort. How do you not know what it is? You've lived here for four years. It's not like this town is the size of Manhattan."

"I don't go to restaurants unless someone takes me," she said. "So, if you're offering…"

Royce felt his stomach tighten. He'd been around women long enough to read between the lines. All of a sudden, he was no longer in the mood for a filling meal such as pot roast. But now, he was backed into a corner. If he backtracked on his suggestion, it could be interpreted as if he didn't enjoy her company.

"Hey! Anyone in there?" Pam reached over and gently knocked her hand on his head.

"You trying to make me crash?"

Pam pointed ahead. "Trying to break you of that trance, because at this rate, you're about to do a good enough job of that on your own."

Snapping back to reality, Royce noticed the yellow dump truck parked on the road straight ahead.

"Oh, shit!" He swerved around the vehicle, then parked ahead of it.

Right away, Pam was laughing. "I wonder what was going on inside that head of yours to make you not notice that."

"I was going over the menu in my head," he said.

"Oh, the menu, huh?"

"Yes."

"Interesting. I thought you had it in your head you wanted pot roast. Isn't that why you even brought up the restaurant?" The butterflies in Royce's stomach were now the least of his problems. He could feel himself blushing, and there was nothing he could do to stop it. When Pam saw the redness, she burst into laughter. "What's the matter, Dashnaw?"

"Nothing." He looked over his shoulder at the dump truck. "Just wondering why the hell that thing is parked there."

"Oh, you're not getting away that easy. You promised me lunch at that restaurant. You go back on this now, I'll message Ellen on *Facebook* and make sure she gives you hell."

"Yeah, you would—wait? Ellen has a *Facebook*?"

Now it was Pam who was turning red. "Y—yes. Did...you not know that?"

"No. I didn't." His hands squeezed the steering wheel.

"Is she not allowed to have one?" Pam asked.

Royce slowly eased up. "I never explicitly told her not to. I'm just not a fan of kids being on social media. You're a cop. You understand the ugliness of the world around us. So many creeps out there targeting kids through these platforms."

"Well, for what it's worth, I think Ellen has pretty good judgement."

"She does, but she's still nine."

"A really damn bright nine-year old. I say she has pretty good judgement. Probably thanks to her dad... or her older lady friend." Pam patted herself on the shoulder.

"Oh, you're hilarious."

"Ah, come on. It's obvious you love her very much. I think the relationship you two have is very cute."

"Cute. What the hell do the two of you talk about on *Messenger*?"

Pam looked away. "Nothing much. Fishing and stuff."

"Uh-huh. 'Fishing and stuff'. Sounds to me like Ellen's trying to put some ideas in your head."

"I don't know what you're talking about."

"Riiiiight." Royce wasn't sure where to take the conversation from here. The only segue he could think of was that damn dump truck. "Why the hell *is* that thing parked there? The only construction in town that I know of is the new road being paved south of the lake."

"I don't know," Pam said. She stepped out. "Might as well check."

Royce put on the flashers, put the Interceptor in *park,* and walked over to the dump truck. The engine was off. Nobody was inside the cab. He pulled himself up to the window and shined his flashlight inside. Sometimes truck drivers liked to take a snooze in their vehicles.

Not in this case. This thing was empty.

"Looks like there's mud on the tires," Pam said. "Haven't been any rainstorms lately."

"No," Royce said. "It's been dry. Not sure where this thing could have picked up some mud." He glanced between the rear and front tires. "Hmm…"

"What?"

"Only the rear tires have mud on them."

"Interesting." Pam stepped up on the driver's side rear tire and pulled herself onto the side of the truck.

"What are you doing?"

"Looking inside the bed." Pam chuckled. "What? You're the only one allowed to play detective?"

"Alright 'Detective', what's in there?"

Pam peered into the bed. Her smile transformed into an expression that Royce could only describe as confused.

"Um, nothing. Just, uh… water."

"Water?"

"It's drying up. Just looks like the load was wet. I don't know."

Royce went to the other side, stood up on the twin axle, and looked for himself. Pam was right. The metal underside of the bed was wet and covered in what appeared to be drying weeds and soot. Aside from that, the bed was empty.

"Well, they're not hauling anything."

"At the moment," Pam said. "You think we should call it in?"

Royce thought about it for a moment, then shook his head. "Let's give them a chance to pick this thing up. Maybe one of the construction guys drove it up, parked it here figuring few people used this road, then met up with someone for lunch."

"Wouldn't they use their own car?"

"Yeah, probably. It's the only thing I can think of. Don't know why anyone would deliberately hide a dump truck.

Anyway, my thoughts on it are still the same. We'll check again before we head in for shift change."

Pam hopped down and returned to the Interceptor. "Fine by me!"

When Royce stepped down, he saw that Pam was headed for the driver's seat. "What exactly do you think you're doing?"

"Keeping us alive. Keep in mind, you almost plowed into that dump truck while thinking about…" She thought for a moment. "We never did discuss what you were thinking about."

"I told you. The menu."

"Right. Sure." She opened the door and got in. "Better hurry up. I'm so hungry now, I might leave without you."

"You'd feel bad," Royce said.

"Oh really? You think so, huh?"

"Damn right I do. You said yourself, you only go to restaurants if someone takes you. Leave me behind, then you're stuck with ramen noodles."

"Good. It's a date, then."

Royce was turning red again. "Wait? I never said—"

"Charlie-Zero-Three to Lorenzo PD Dispatch?"

Both officers turned their attention to the radio. The only time Animal Control contacted them directly was when they were dealing with a particularly vicious animal, or when they were encountering human interference. Considering the particular groups that had been lurking in Lorenzo, both Royce and Pam suspected the latter.

"Go ahead," the dispatcher replied.

"We're responding to a call over by William's Street, behind Olsen's Grocery Market. The store owner reported some raccoons and we're over here trying to wrangle them, but there's a small group here getting in our faces."

"Called it," Royce said.

"What exactly are they doing?"

"Acting aggressive. They seem to be animal rights type of people. They're keeping me and my partner from getting behind the store."

Royce looked at Pam. "That empty stomach able to hold off long enough for us to deal with more activists?"

"Damn right. Buckle up."

Before Royce could strap himself in, she floored the accelerator.

CHAPTER 7

When they arrived at Olsen's Grocery Market, there were nine activists on site. Either the animal control guy couldn't count, or more had shown up in the five minutes since the call.

The group had formed a line along the side of the building which led to the back. Two others blocked the main entrance. Already, three cars pulled out of the driveway and left. The store owner was visibly frustrated watching his customers leave. What could they do if they weren't able to get inside without potentially being assaulted?

"Good lord! When did this place become Chicago?" Pam said.

"Don't jinx us." Royce raised the radio mic to his mouth. "Car-Four to Dispatch, we're on the scene. Got nine activists blocking Animal Control and—" He squinted as a tenth activist stepped from around the front of the AC truck. This woman was in her early forties, had dark hair, was fairly fit though showing signs of aging—and probably would be considered pretty if not for that scowl. "Aw, hell!"

Right then, he realized he was still transmitting.

"What?"

"Sorry. Chief, if you're listening, we've got Alice Kirkman over here." Now, it was clear that the discrepancy in the number of activists was a result of more showing up. Alice was the frontrunner and likely the funder of this stupid group.

"Looks like I might get to put someone else into the pavement after all," Pam said.

"First, let's see if we can resolve this matter without doing that. Alice might be crazy, but she has a little more reach than minnows such as Curt Lin."

"Fiiiiiine, I'll restrain myself."

They stepped out of the Interceptor and approached the Animal Control truck. The workers met them halfway, cautiously watching the protesters.

"Thank God you're here," the tall one said. "I'm Gary. This is Sawyer." He pointed his thumb to the considerably shorter man. Standing side-by-side, the two men appeared as though they were about to step on stage for a comedy skit.

"They get violent?" Pam asked.

"No, but only because we backed down," Gary said.

Sawyer pointed at Alice. "That woman there, I don't think she's got all her ducks in a row. She seems unhinged to me."

Alice started to approach. "Excuse me?!"

Royce raised his palm. "Ah-ah! Stay back there. I'll talk to you when I'm good and ready."

"Yeah, Officer? I've seen you out on the lake, killing animals yourself. I'm pretty sure I know which side of the aisle you're on," Alice said. She crossed her arms, only to immediately uncross them. Probably because she didn't want to obscure the image on her T-shirt of broken bars, with the words *Until every cage is empty.*

Royce stood silent. The question he wanted to ask was: when the hell was she watching him go fishing? Needless to say, in Alice's mind, fishing was murder.

"Just step back. I'll talk with you in a minute." He turned to the Animal Control crew. "How'd this start? Were they here when you arrived?"

"No. I think they followed us here," Gary said. "Probably saw us as we were passing through town."

"That makes sense," Pam said. "Let me guess: they got here, then immediately formed a line. Oh! And started calling you names!"

"I see this isn't your first rodeo with these people," Sawyer said.

"That's correct," Royce said. "They saw your truck, then determined there was a helpless critter to rescue."

"Well, it's not something we want left running around," Gary said. "The store owner reported that these two raccoons are pretty aggressive. They might have to be tested."

"Gotcha." Royce sighed, mentally preparing himself to step up to the plate with Alice. "Give us a sec." He nodded at Pam, who accompanied him to the group.

Alice placed her hands on her hips, her scowl never fading. Royce imagined she was used to having people cater to her most of her life, from her parents when she was a child, all the way to the cast and crew of her various productions. He didn't follow celebrities on social media—hell, he didn't even know Alice Kirkman was a celebrity until one of his fellow officers mentioned it. She definitely had the demeanor of an entitled person seeking attention. The delusions of grandeur was off the charts, even for an out of work actress who was never really well-liked to begin with.

"Alice, I'm gonna say this *once*. The Chief, Mayor, the townspeople, and most importantly, *I,* have had it up to here with you people." He raised his hand to eye-level. "We're done playing nice. Call your people off."

"Now," Pam added.

Alice shook her head. Without professional makeup crews from Hollywood productions, her face was showing clear signs of withering. Stress caused by anger. Royce couldn't understand how someone could let themselves be so irrationally controlled by emotion.

"We're done playing nice too, Officer," she said. "These guys make a living torturing wild animals that are simply trying to survive. You call that justice?"

"I wouldn't call it justice to let these animals bite the employees of this store."

"If they have rabies, then it's not 'justice' to leave them out to roam freely," Pam said.

Alice raised a finger to Royce's face. There was a slight quiver in her voice, as though she was expecting him to flinch and was surprised when he didn't.

"I'm not gonna stand here and watch as you allow these animals to be abused by these men. We'll stand here all day. We'll go without food and water for as long as we have to, if that's what it takes."

Pam chuckled. "Really? You're *that* determined. If that's the case, why don't you collect the raccoons yourself and drive them to safety?"

"Because they don't want to be touched!"

"Or because y'all are a bunch of pussies who care more about getting attention and patting yourselves on the shoulder, than actually caring about the issues you bitch about." Pam took a step forward and removed her sunglasses, looking Alice dead in the eye. She was like a UFC fighter at the weigh-in, staring down her opponent. "Last chance. Move your posse, or we'll be calling a wagon to scoop y'all off the pavement."

Alice refused to budge, though she was beginning to shake. Adrenaline was surging. "You lay a finger on us, and I guarantee you'll be handing your badges in tomorrow morning."

"This isn't Los Angeles," Royce said. "The mayor here actually lets us enforce the law. Hence, people enjoy living here.

You can cry to all the news organizations in the world, it won't change anything. But you're on thin ice." He looked to the blockade of activists. "You have ten seconds to move your asses, or you'll end up like Curt Lin."

Alice now stepped back. "Curt? What'd you do to him?"

"We gave him a nice bunk and three warm meals a day until he goes to court," Royce said.

"Wanna join him?" Pam said. As she spoke, three more police vehicles appeared, led by Chief Elwood. Larry parked his SUV and marched to the scene. He was visibly frustrated.

"What's the verdict, Dashnaw?"

Royce pulled out his handcuffs. "Well, sir, they're not moving, so I guess they want to join their activist buddy. What's on the menu in the jail today?" Larry smiled. "I took the liberty of checking. Chicken tenderloins, mashed potatoes and gravy—made from chicken stock."

"You hear that, Alice? Ready to meet some yummy, innocent chickens?"

Alice shifted her stance. For a moment, she looked as if she were about to strike the officer. She lost the nerve almost immediately and stepped back."You all are filthy pieces of shit! I see when you're not shooting minorities, you take joy in assaulting protesters and harming animals."

Pam shook her head. "For the love of God, shut up with that shit. We're not dumb. None of you people even live here. Why you feel the need to come here of all places and harass the residents, I'll never understand. But we serve the *residents* of this town, not a bunch of outsiders who feel they need to force their beliefs onto everyone else."

"Alright, looks like you've made your choice," Larry said.

Finally, the activists began to separate. Alice watched her followers break under the will of the law. These cops weren't like the ones in the cities they visited. They were more than willing to use force to get their way. The fact that the Chief himself was here ready to get involved in the action was telling on its own. In Chicago, L.A., and New York, the police chiefs hid in their offices and made the occasional press conference, in which they spat the usual talking points. Not Larry Elwood. He already had a set of cuffs in one hand and his other resting on his taser.

Equally as intimidating was the goliath-sized Officer Holman. Towering over the Chief, he was built like a tank. He wouldn't even need his taser—he could take half of that crowd on his own with his bare hands.

The mere sight of him cracking his knuckles like an evil *James Bond* henchman was enough to make most of the group finally disperse. They got in their vehicles and sped off, not even bothering to save face by cursing the officers on their way out.

Her power was broken. She had a split-second to weigh her options. She didn't want to show weakness to these people she saw as fascist bullies. Unfortunately, they had the power. As much as she wanted to stand by her beliefs, going to jail in this town was clearly not going to accomplish anything. She'd do more by doing another *YouTube* podcast, ranting about the abusive Lorenzo PD.

She pointed at Royce as she backed away. "I hope you're happy."

"Actually, I am," Royce said. "So happy, I might celebrate by going fishing later on today. Nothing hits the spot like beer-battered bass fillets. Hell, when I'm on the water, I'll hold up my catch for you to see, since apparently you like to watch from afar."

Alice tensed. For a moment, Royce was certain he was going to be hit with a barrage of insults. Surprisingly, nothing was said. Alice's stance grew more relaxed. She even smiled—though it didn't convey friendship.

"Maybe I will. Go ahead. Go out on the water. Who knows? Maybe I'll walk the lake with my binoculars and see how you fare." She turned and walked to the last activist who remained on site with her. He was a fairly large individual—not nearly as large as Holman. He had a crew cut and a black mark on his face. A powder burn, by the looks of it. He was clearly the most loyal of the bunch, ready to follow Alice to hell and back. If she was going to jail for the cause, so would he. She waved him over to her blue Tesla Model S.

Pam chuckled as the activists departed. "Of course she's driving a hundred-thousand dollar car. I seem to recall seeing fifty tweets about wealth inequality from her."

"You expect consistency from these idiots?" Royce said. "We live in an age where *Twitter* likes are the dominant currency. It's like a drug. People are constantly seeking dopamine hits from social media. People like Alice *never* mean what they say."

Pam slapped his shoulder. "I don't know. She sounded like she meant it when she said she'd watch you fish."

The officers and Animal Control workers laughed.

"She makes a good point," Gary said. "Who knows? Maybe that chick secretly likes you."

Sawyer winked. "Probably hopes to do a little bit of 'fishing' of her own. In which case, she'd be the catch…"

Royce cringed. "No thanks. Besides, I'm not her type. After all, I don't have a movie role to give her."

"Whoa! Damn!" Gary said. He thought about that statement for a second, then turned to the other officers. "Wait… she's an actress?"

"*Was* an actress," Larry said. "Ever hear of an *HBO* show in the early 2000s called *Centurions*?" The two workers shook their heads. "No surprise. It only lasted a season."

Gary raised an eyebrow. "Was she any good in it?"

Larry snorted. "No, but the reason she got the role was obvious. Lots of, how should I say it? Let's just say there were days where she didn't have to spend a lot of time in wardrobe."

Officer Holman dug his phone out. "I'll *definitely* be checking this one out, now."

"Me too," Gary said.

"So, what's up with this chick now? She retired from acting?"

Larry chuckled as he tried to think of a delicate way to answer. "Let's just say, her career went into the toilet almost immediately after some allegations occurred."

"When was it never *out* of the toilet," Pam muttered.

"She's able to afford that car and travel all over the place, so she must've done something right," Sawyer said.

"Yeah, her producers certainly thought so," Larry said.

"Oh, shit!" Gary said. "Harvey Weinstein?"

"Not him, but essentially the same situation. Basically, she went 'above and beyond' in her auditions," Royce said.

The workers nodded. Now his remark of 'not having a movie role to give her' made much more sense.

"Well, at least she had the courage to out those guys for being jackasses," Sawyer said.

Larry broke out in laughter. "She didn't report jack shit! It was two other, less famous…and much younger… actresses who broke that news. In fact, the rumors are that Alice tried to help silence them."

"Yeah. She was more than happy to keep that gravy train rolling," Pam said.

Holman scrolled through his phone. "I'm checking her filmography. According to this, she's only done a few bit parts since 2017. Yeah, I think her career is all washed up."

"Now she's turned to podcasting and activism," Royce said.

"And eyeing while you're fishing," Larry said, sparking laughter from the other officers.

Royce looked at the sky. "Oh, here we go with that again."

"Hey now," Pam rubbed the top of his head, "who can blame her?"

Royce could feel himself blushing like a damn preteen. *Damn you, Pam!* Lucky for him, the store owner was watching the officers with increasing impatience. Royce cleared his throat. "Alright, you guys can go get your raccoon. Chief? You want me to write this report out?"

"Yeah, since you dealt with the bulk of this case," Larry said. "I'll get these reports to the mayor. Maybe we can run these idiots out of town, finally. Pam, don't forget about that supplement I asked for. No rush, though."

Pam marched to the Interceptor. "Good! Because Royce promised me lunch."

"Lunch!" Holman exaggerated a frown. "What about the rest of us?"

"He's not your type," Larry said.

Royce closed his eyes. *Great! Now HE'S in on this too?!* So much for the standards of employees in relationships. Then again, with Pam getting into the state police this upcoming fall, Larry probably didn't give a damn. Even if that wasn't the case, he probably wouldn't care too much. He was as laid back a chief as Royce ever saw.

Holman's eyes widened. "Ooooh…."

"No! No! Get your heads out of the gutter," Royce said. "It's just lunch. Doesn't mean anything like… *that*."

"Wow, Royce," Pam said. "Might as well put it on a billboard."

"*I'll* take you out, Pam," Holman said, loud and proud.

"Thank you. You know how to make a girl feel special!"

Royce was cornered. He knew Pam was just pulling his leg and wasn't genuinely offended, but he still felt like crap. He was trapped between not violating department policy, his concern of bringing a new woman into Ellen's life, and also…the part he struggled to admit even in the depths of his mind… blowing this opportunity.

The only thing to break the mental whirlwind was his thundering stomach. Even the butterflies he felt earlier couldn't hold back his appetite.

He opened the driver's side door. "Come on, Pam. I'll feed you. Holman, you can go and stare at Alice Kirkman's tits on your phone."

Holman smiled and tucked his phone away. "Noooo. I wouldn't do that!"

Larry facepalmed himself. "Just tell me you aren't doing that on the job."

CHAPTER 8

"Thank you very much for coming in. Have a good day!" Monty Granger waved the customers goodbye as they exited his tackle shop. They were a chatty bunch, full of fish stories which he called absolute bullshit on. He didn't mind, however. As far as he was concerned, as long as they were buying stuff, he'd listen to any bullshit they had to throw at him.

Still, this one took the cake. *A panfish that managed to bite through a metal ladder? Give me a break!*

He checked his watch. Three-o'clock. As soon as the minute hand landed on *twelve*, the door flung open. In came his twenty-one year old nephew, Tyler Bankowski. Monty was amazed how the young man turned out, considering his hippie sister and brother-in-law. The Granger genetics must have pulled through for Tyler because, despite living down in Toledo, Ohio, he preferred the country life up north. Maybe it was the rise in crime in the past decade. Hell, the last couple of years!

Tyler moved up to Lorenzo at the age of twenty, after wasting two years in college to regurgitate enough talking points back at the instructors to receive a two-year degree in business. It only took a month of working with his uncle to truly learn anything substantial. Monty had to be fair—there were a couple of helpful things the kid learned. One of his classes had the sense to teach about taxes and statistics. But not one got into the meat and potatoes of actually running a business. Stuff like overhead, stock, and customer interaction were simply glossed over. It was working at Monty's Tackle where Tyler got his true business education.

"Right on time, kid," Monty said.

Tyler took off his sunglasses and put his lunch in the fridge behind the check-out counter.

"You say that as if it's a bad thing."

"A real dedicated man usually shows up a half-hour early."

"Depends on the what it is I'm dedicated to." Tyler turned his head. Monty had to lean forward to finally see the hickey on his neck.

"Ooooh! In that case, you deserve a medal for even being on time. I'd be lying if I claimed I was never late to formation thanks to a little, uh, *visitation*."

"I hear you had some 'visitation' this morning," Tyler said. "Those activists?"

Monty's face wrinkled. Just the thought of those freaks made him want to punch somebody. If there wasn't such a thing as law and order, he would've wiped the pavement with those idiots.

"They use the word activist, but they're nothing more than attention seekers. These people will destroy your livelihood just to make themselves feel good. There are people who protest and try to make their point made, then there are people who use brute force. These activists are the latter. The cops better do something about them, because they're gonna get to the point where they'll start breaking windows and looting."

"That bad, huh?"

"Kid, trust me, I've seen these types. If they could get away with having people they disagree with hauled away to a gulag, they'd do it in a heartbeat." Monty collected the receipts from the morning and mid-afternoon. He knew that Tyler didn't bring up the protesters to make casual conversation. "You sure you're alright taking management duties tonight?"

Tyler was in the lure aisle with a cart full of new stock. "Yeah, I think I can manage."

"If you're worried, I can hang around."

"Nah, Uncle Monty. You go ahead and catch me an eighteen-inch bass."

"I'd *have* to catch it for you, considering you can't seem to catch anything bigger than a two-inch perch. But seriously, if you're worried about those jackasses coming here again…"

"I'll be fine. You have any instructions in the event they do show up?"

"Tell them once to leave. If they don't immediately vacate, call the cops and tell them to haul ass," Monty said. "That said, keep that Smith & Wesson of yours in plain sight. Just don't unholster it unless they give you no choice."

Tyler looked at the nine-millimeter pistol on his right hip. A lot of people open carried in this location. It was part of the culture. The only people who took any issues were city-dwellers who came to Lorenzo on vacation, particularly those from urban areas. The fact that there hadn't been a shooting in this town in over ten years made no difference.

"Understood, sir."

"You'd make a good Marine." Monty finished cataloging the day's finances, then collected his stuff. Ever since he took Tyler under his wing, Monty allowed himself to leave early on Fridays. He loved his business, but it required many long days. With Tyler in town to lighten the load, he was now able to spend time at home and on the lake. The thought of fried pike fillets for dinner sounded marvelous. "Alright, kid, you'll be here in the morning, right?

"That's the plan."

"Good. Definitely don't be late for that, we've got a truck coming. Call me if you need anything, alright? Besides, I'm gonna need you to tell me about what's-her-name." Monty pointed at the hickey on Tyler's neck.

"You got it."

"Don't party too hard when you get home. Eight-o'clock tomorrow. See you then."

Three-twenty-two—fifteen-hundred-twenty-two hours, as he would put it when in the Marines. Work was done. Time to fish!

****

An hour on the lake, and he hardly felt a tug on his line. Monty sat at the rear of his twelve-foot aluminum boat, watching the lily pads. He tossed another cast, landing it twelve inches from the line of vegetation. Usually, that was a hotspot for bass and some large bluegills.

Monty wasn't too concerned. In his experience, it was unusual not to get a single hit in this lake, but then again, patience was part of the sport. Sometimes, the fish weren't in the mood to bite. Plus, it was early yet. On plenty of occasions, he had spent two hours fishing without landing a single bite, only to move only a hundred feet and find a hotspot.

He lit his second cigar of the afternoon. With nothing biting his line, he decided to take in the scenery around him. A few hundred yards behind him, people were water skiing. There were a couple of pontoon boats further north. Most of these people were from out of town, using rentals from the resorts on the north end of the lake. The southern half of the three-mile long body of water was a little quieter. Most of the people who went out on this end were residents looking for peace and quiet, such as himself. The west side was lined with a few residential properties, while the east was, with the exception of a couple of scattered properties, made up entirely of tree lines and cattails.

Deciding he would have better luck over there, he hauled the anchor up and started the motor.

After crossing the width of Lake Carlson, he cruised south and settled on a small cove. The anchor set down at eight feet, perfect depth for largemouth and pike. Bored with crawler harnesses, he decided to have a go with his spinners.

He hooked a grasshopper-looking lure to his swivel, then set a cast a yard from the weeds. The cattails exploded as a large creature emerged.

Monty nearly fell back, the cigar falling from his teeth. "Jesus, Mary!" He calmed down, recognizing the lake's resident swan couple settling on the water. He looked down at his cigar, then groaned after seeing that it had landed in a small puddle near the transom. He picked it up and held it to the swans. "Bonnie! Clyde! You birds see what you did?"

The swans glided further south, honking at him as though in response. *Yeah? Whatcha gonna do about it?*

"Yeah, that's right. You go that way! Damn birds."

He reeled in the lure that apparently startled them and prepped for a new cast. The birds moved in unison. Mates for life, they were always moving along the lake, sometimes visiting the residents by stepping ashore on the lakefront properties. Despite feigning annoyance, Monty enjoyed their company. It was better than listening to someone complain about the burdens of daily life.

After drying his hand, he dug the last cigar from his shirt pocket. In his tacklebox was a small box of stick matches. He never used a lighter for his cigars, as the chemicals would taint the flavor. A soft stick-match flame preserves the flavor. The only drawback was that it sometimes required a little bit of patience.

Immediately, a soft breeze extinguished his match as soon as he lit it. He groaned, then waited for the breeze to die down. It was gentle, but still enough to lay waste to a tiny flame. Fed up with waiting, he knelt down to use the hull as a shield. He lit another match and held it to the cigar.

Finally! Now, as long as nothing keeps me from losing this one...

The flailing of wings and trashing of water made him jump again. "Holy—" Once again, the cigar flew from his mouth, and landed in the lake. On any other occasion, Monty would have gone on a tirade full of four-letter words. In this case, he didn't even notice the cigar floating in the water, as his eyes were locked on the abundance of feathers drifting around a fountain of blood.

Both swans danced along the water, their wings outstretched, their beaks agape. High-pitched trumpeting calls echoed into the sky—cries of agony. Their wings failed to lift them off the water. It was as if a suctioning power was keeping them connected to the lake. And under those lapping waves, something was tearing at their undersides.

Monty watched as the swans twisted in place, unable to escape this horrifying invisible force. All at once, the energy left their bodies, and they disappeared beneath the water. Not sinking—yanked. Large red swells moved toward the boat, carrying feathers and pieces of skin.

It took a lot to make Monty truly speechless. Having served in the USMC for twenty years, he had seen more than his fair share of crazy and disturbing things. He had seen legs separated above the knee. He had seen vehicles burst into flames after passing over an IED, and he had been on more clean-up missions than he cared to think about. But that was a warzone. This was Lake Carlson, his home and place of rest. Such dreaded violence didn't happen *here.*

Yet, he saw it with his own eyes. Worse, he didn't understand exactly what was causing it. The deadliest thing in this lake were pike—and no way would a pike take down two thirty-pound swans.

The water wasn't yet still. There was some kind of disturbance taking place where they went down, like a mini-earthquake isolated to ten square-feet. From the epicenter came a cloud of red and an increasing number of feathers. Those birds had been torn to shreds.

Monty wasn't going to sit here to find out what it was. Better to get home and call Animal Control.

He pulled his anchor up, pointed the boat west with his oars, then leaned over the back to start the motor. The first yank of the ripcord did nothing. He went for a second try, only to freeze and stare at the water.

Behind his reflection were two black eyes on opposite sides of a narrow face. Fins flapped to the side like wings, keeping the fish buoyant—and it was definitely a fish. A *panfish*, by the looks of it. Except, he had never seen one this big. It was the size of—oddly enough—a large frying pan. That wasn't even the most bizarre aspect of it: Never in his life had Monty seen a fish *stare* back at somebody with such focus. Usually, when fish kept such a strict gaze, it meant they were watching a potential meal.

He saw the surrounding weeds waving as more pan-shaped bodies swam underneath the boat.

The water erupted as they leapt all at once. Like mosquitos, they set on the fisherman. Monty fell backward, landing on the edge of his boat. His bodyweight and flailing motion rocked it to starboard, putting the gunwale below the waterline. Both man and boat sank.

His screams were lost under the lake. Once again, the water turned red, this time with *his* blood. Ribbons of clothes were torn from his body, followed by ribbons of flesh. Then muscle. Then organs.

Everything except bone.

CHAPTER 9

"Ending mileage is four-two-seven-eight-four."

Royce tapped the mic on his knee as he waited for Dispatch to copy his transmission. Here in Lorenzo PD, it was always customary for patrollers to report the mileage of their patrol vehicles at the end of the shift. Every five-thousand miles, the vehicles would undergo trips to the maintenance department. The Chief didn't settle for second best, either. If something was wrong with any of the vehicles or equipment, he made sure it got taken care of.

"Ready to go, chicken-salad man?"

He glared at his partner. "So I changed my mind."

"Right…immediately after I agreed to try out Lorenzo Haven. And you only ate about *half* of it."

"Yes. This is probably the third time you've brought it up."

"Just checking on you, Mr. Blush." She chuckled. "I remember chauffeuring my teenage nephew on his first date. Kid was so nervous, he could only take three bites of his meal."

"My God, you're subtle," Royce said. "First of all, that wasn't a date. Second of all, I'm not a rookie at dating."

"Just rusty."

Yeah, so maybe it's been a while. He nearly slipped up and said it out loud. Fact is, he hadn't been on a real date since Ellen's mother ran out on them. Nine years—all of his twenties without being with someone. The fear of having someone run out on Ellen was worse than the loneliness and sexual frustration. *Perhaps I joined the wrong career. Wonder if it's too late for me to become a priest.*

Speaking of Ellen…

Royce looked down at his buzzing phone. Ellen wouldn't bother calling him, especially at this time, unless she needed something.

"Hey, kid. What's going on?"

"Hi, Dad. I forgot to tell you I'm out of my pills

"You're out already?" It seemed every few weeks he'd stop by the pharmacy to pick up her thyroid medication. The swelling in her neck along with the fatigue she felt at the time was probably the biggest scare of his life. He had heard of kids younger than her getting cancer. By God's grace, it wasn't cancer, but hypothyroidism. All she needed was a pill a day to keep it functioning properly.

"They go fast, Dad. I thought it'd be best to let you know before you pick me up, since the pharmacy is right around the corner."

"How considerate of you. You could've just sent me a text, you know?'

"Come on, Dad! I know you. You probably wouldn't have checked your phone until dinnertime."

Royce shrugged. "Yeah, I guess that's a fair point. Alright, thanks for letting me know now. The refill should be in by now, so I'll run over there before I pick you up."

"Cool. Thanks."

"Yep. See ya in a little bit…"

Pam leaned over. "Hey, Ellen! How's it going?!"

"Pam! I'm good. I'm stuck over here at Jacob's house, but it's not too unbearable."

Royce cringed. *Please God, I hope Jacob wasn't close enough to hear that. Then again, the kid probably has his face buried in the television screen.*

"Put it on speaker," Pan said.

"What? Why?"

"What do you mean 'why'?! Don't interrupt two girls when they're talking. Put it on speaker, damn it."

"Excuse me, then. Not like you two don't have your own phones…" Royce hit the button, then leaned back in his seat and prayed the girl talk would be over quick. It was the end of the shift and he was ready to go home.

"Can you hear me now?"

"Yeah, that's much better. Had to twist your dad's arm. You know how he is."

"Yeah, he can be a killjoy."

"Thanks, honey. Keep it up, and I'll make us watch *Cocomelon* instead of *Predator* tonight."

"Ugh! You wouldn't do that. You'd crack before I would."

He smirked. "Probably."

"What's this? You're having a movie night? Did I hear the word *Predator*?"

"That's right, Pam!"

"Kid, you have great taste in movies! That's one of my favorites too!"

"You should come over and watch it with us! Dad's even ordering pizza!"

Royce perked up. "I never said anything about pizza."

"Doesn't matter now. You're on the spot, *Dad.*"

"Story of my life."

"Movie's at 6:30, Pam. We have a big couch! I think it'll be fun for all of us to watch it together."

Pam started to laugh. "That does sound like a really good time." She looked at Royce as she spoke. "But I can't make that call, girlfriend. That's completely up to your dad."

Oh, GREAT!

"Dad, pleeeease! Pam's fun!"

"I told you that kid is smart," Pam said.

"Yes—that she is."

"Tell you what. If you say yes, *I'll* bring the pizza. I'll even order a salad to settle the butterflies in that tummy of yours."

"What?" Royce's next attempt at a sentence was a complete stammer, much to Ellen's amusement. He closed his eyes and groaned. "I'm the man of the household. *I'll* order the pizza. And no salad… unless you all want it on the side."

"Sounds good to me!"

"Same here!"

"So cool! See you at six-thirty, Pam!"

"I'll be there, kid!"

"Glad you're all happy. Okay, Ellen, I gotta go. I'll grab your prescription and be over to pick you up shortly."

"'Kay! Bye! See ya later, Pam!"

Royce hung up and stared at his immensely amused partner. "I'll text you my address. Might be in the middle of the lake, who knows?"

"Oh, ha-ha. Too bad your new friend Alice will be disappointed, since I'm sure she was looking forward to watching you on the lake. Nope, you're stuck with me instead." She expected a witty remark or an eye roll from him. Instead, his face transformed to one of guilt, as though he were caught doing something he shouldn't be. Pam raised an eyebrow. "What? Is that a bad thing in your eyes? That why you act so shy around me?" He nodded, not in agreement, but in gesture of something behind her.

Rather some*one*.

Pam turned around and saw Chief Larry Elwood staring into her car window. She smiled and rolled it down. "Oh! Hey, Chief!"

"You called in your mileage, but never turned in the key. Was worried that maybe you ran off with it."

"Sorry, boss," Royce said. He removed the key from the ignition. "Got caught up in other things."

"Yeah? Date plans? *Predator?* Pizza? Yeah, I heard more than you think. If only you two *police officers* were more observant, you would've noticed. That's not the issue here. Fact is, there's a major violation that I'm worried about."

"Whoa!" Royce raised his hand in protest. "If you're worried about the Department's policy, we're just hanging out with my kid…"

Larry's eyes narrowed. "You think I'm stupid, Sergeant?"

"What? No!"

"I think you do. You know *exactly* what the violation is, Dashnaw. That look of shame gives it away. Frankly, I'm disappointed—that you would buy pizza for Pam and not your boss! What madness is this?!"

Royce was leaning back in his seat, his eyes seemingly locked on the ceiling. He knew Larry was a sarcastic son of a bitch who enjoyed pulling pranks on his officers, and yet he was still caught off guard.

"Well, for starters, didn't you say your wife was making you shed a few pounds?"

"Oh, I see how it is!" Larry said, patting his stomach. "Yeah, it comes with age. You eat less but still manage to get fatter. So I say to you kids, enjoy your youth while you have it. And don't let a good thing go to waste." He was looking Royce in the eye with that last statement. He pulled out his personal keys and turned away. "Behave yourselves. Don't be up too late. If I come in tomorrow and see either one or both of you called in sick, I'm not gonna believe you!"

"Okay, Chief," Pam said between laughs. She turned back to look at the embarrassed Royce.

"Is there some higher force at work here?"

"You should be grateful to be around so many people who care about you." She stepped out of the Interceptor. "So, six-thirty, right?"

"That's the decree."

"I'll be there. You start that movie without me and I'll beat your ass so hard, it'll be as red as your face."

"I'm sure you would. Gotta kick someone's ass, since you're so disappointed you didn't get to beat down more protestors."

"Ugh! Don't remind me." She walked inside to punch out. "See ya later! Don't be late!"

"Late? It's *my* house!" Royce leaned back and closed his eyes. "Lord help me—what did I get myself into?"

CHAPTER 10

Larry Elwood's daily routine involved an hour at the gym after work—something his wife requested. His job and homelife involved a fair amount of sitting, and at fifty-three years old, it didn't help the body's already slow metabolism. It didn't help that he still maintained the same appetite. He was at the age where he had to 'earn' any good-tasting meals, or else be stuck with a variety of health foods that made him want to put his head in a vice.

The summer heat and physical exertion left him drenched with sweat as he stepped out of the gym. Planting himself in the driver's seat, he first checked his phone. Amanda hadn't texted him at all since noon. Already retired from thirty years at the County Clerk's office, she got bored relatively easy and often missed him. Usually, she'd message him at least twice between noon and four. Today, nothing. Probably just busy. For Larry, it provided an excuse for him to mess with her. "What? You don't like me anymore?" would probably be today's go-to joke.

Right now, even more than to annoy his wife, Larry wanted a shower and a beer. This would be his routine for the next seven years. At the big six-oh, he'd retire with thirty-nine years of police service. Of course, the work wouldn't end there. Amanda wouldn't let him sit around at home. He'd probably have a series of home projects to work on. Once those were finished, he'd have to look into something else to do. Part time college instructing didn't sound too bad. He already had his Master's Degree.

There was seven years to figure all that out. Right now, beer was the priority.

It was a twelve minute drive from the gym to his house. When he was appointed as Chief of Police, the substantial pay increase allowed he and Amanda to finally fulfill their lifelong fantasy of owning a lakefront property. As with the majority of houses on the lake, their home was on the west shore. One thing he loved was the spacing between the houses. There was at least a hundred-twenty feet of lawn separating his neighbors from him. Not that he didn't enjoy company, but being in the police force, he discovered that neighbors had a tendency to notify him of the slightest ordeals. He'd be notified if they encountered someone speeding, or if they noticed a suspicious person, or any other grievance they had. One time, a neighbor felt the need to knock on his door and inform him that a traffic light had gone out.

"Yeah, uh-huh, I'll get right on that," he said before shutting the door. Luckily, these current neighbors minded their own business for the most part. They came over occasionally for cookouts or to watch football, but they knew well enough that Larry wasn't on the job twenty-four-seven.

When he arrived home, the sky was darkening. There was mist in the air, and a slight rumble in the distance. He parked next to his wife's car and checked the weather app on his phone.

"Typical Michigan," he said. At lunchtime, the forecast showed the weather to be mostly sunny with partial cloud cover. Now a full on thunderstorm was on its way. He had considered going out fishing after dinner. So much for that idea.

He entered his house. "Whoa!" It was dark inside. "Amanda? Is this our new lifestyle now? Living in the dark like cave people?" He laughed at his own joke and proceeded into the bedroom, intent on giving her a big hug and making her complain about him getting his sweat all over her. The bedroom was empty, the lights off.

"Sweetie?"

There was no response. He peeked out the back window to see if she was outside.

Not in the yard.

Larry proceeded to check the rest of the house, grabbing a beer out of the fridge along the way. Almost every light was left off. Had he not seen her car in the lot, he would've assumed she'd gone on an errand. The laundry was half-complete, with a load in the washer ready to be transferred to the drier. No way would Amanda leave the laundry only partially complete.

Thunder clapped over the lake. The wind started picking up. Leaves fell off the nearby trees and flew across the yard.

Where the hell is she? One possibility was that Amanda went for a walk. If she went out of the house for anything, she'd leave the lights off. No sense in wasting electricity. *Perhaps she went out there and didn't realize the storm was coming.* He stepped outside, jogged to the end of the driveway, and looked down the street in both directions. There wasn't anyone walking as far as he could see.

A raindrop splattered over his forehead. He could hear the sizzling sound of rain striking the lake. In the time it took Larry to jog back to the front door, it went from a drizzle to torrential downpour.

No Amanda, no texts since noon—something was off. He tried calling her phone. The ringtone echoed from their bedroom. He stepped in and found it on her dresser, plugged into the charger.

The second drawer was open. Amanda's day clothes, including her bra and underwear, was on the bed. Larry did the laundry enough to remember that Amanda kept her swimsuit in that second drawer. Swimming? That explained why the lights were out.

It *didn't* explain why he didn't see her when he looked—or why she was still out in the rain.

Larry looked again. Despite the torrential downpour, it was still light enough outside for him to see. The blue inflatable raft was on the shoreline. Nobody was swimming.

The raft looked odd. Amanda only purchased the kinds with armrests, and cupholders, and a headrest. Its shape, even behind the rain, should've been easily distinguishable. But it wasn't. It appeared to be flat.

Deflated.

Larry rushed outside. "Amanda?" He heard nothing but rain. Raising a hand to shield his eyes, he hurried to the shoreline. He stopped at the inflatable raft. It wasn't just deflated, but *shredded*. The entire left side looked as though it had been caught in a propellor.

In the cupholder was an empty wine glass.

He looked into the lake and called for his wife, his voice now lost in the thunder. He waded waist-deep, calling for her repeatedly. He thought of going to the neighbors to ask if they'd seen her, then remembered that one worked midnights and slept during the day, and the other didn't come home until six. Even so, with all the space between their yards, it'd be difficult to notice if something happened.

His heart was threatening to burst out through his throat. His stomach tightened, his legs shakier than after an hour of jogging on the treadmill. With the wind, rain, and mist in his face, it was now difficult to see anything further than three feet away, let alone under the water. He neared the dock and felt around the bottom. If something went wrong, she would've gone closer to the dock.

Nothing.

There was no choice now. He needed to get on the radio and call for emergency response. He turned around, took a step, then stumbled. His foot was lodged on something. It couldn't be the foot of the dock. No, he was at least a yard away. Besides, this felt more prickly, as if he stepped into a busted rabbit cage or broken live-basket.

The tips of hard, narrow objects scraped his calf as he lifted his leg. Whatever they were, they were attached to something larger. His fumbling attempts to free his foot caused him to trip.

Now on his right knee, and neck deep in the lake, he reached with his hands to pry himself loose from the thing. What he felt was rigid, solid, yet oddly wet—but not from being underwater. This was more of a slimy wetness, like from mucus, or rotting meat. He felt two components to the thing which were flexible, and attached by joints to the main body…where his foot was lodged.

Like shoulders to a torso…

The mental image was like a lightning bolt to Larry's psyche. He freed himself, then stared at the water, unable to see past the chaotic, rain-beaten surface. His efforts to convince himself it was probably nothing were useless. He NEEDED to know what this was.

Breathing shakily, he reached down, wincing as he felt the odd, grainy texture under the soft, slimy layer. It was pretty light, no more than twenty-five pounds. It only took a single tug to raise it out of the water.

Larry shrieked as the empty sockets of a human skull emerged through the water. Strands of hair particles clinging to thin remaining layers of flesh clung to the neckbone and shoulder. Thin bits of tattered flesh and residue obscured the whiteness of the bone. Below the neck was the battered ribcage that snagged his foot.

Miraculously, the wedding ring managed to remain on what remained of Amanda's left hand.

Shock and panic overwhelmed Larry. He shoved his wife's skeleton aside and tried to rush to the shore. He tripped again, this time over his own feet. He clawed at the soot as though climbing the side of a steep mountain, gradually hoisting himself to safety.

Then, from the abyss of the lake, came pain.

Larry jolted, feeling the sharp yanking of his skin near his ankle. He didn't think anything of it, until he felt another one in the same spot. Then a third. Before his brain fully registered that one, a fourth jerked his body. It was as though he was being grabbed by a series of tweezers, but lined with teeth. With each tug came a few inches of flesh off his body.

He threw his hand back, swatting away whatever it was, then felt around his ankle. There was no skin there—just tattered meat swaying from a rigid bone. Whatever had killed Amanda had now come for him.

The pain he felt around his ankle was now in his hand. Like hair clippers, tiny teeth ripped at his flesh. In moments, the pain engulfed his lower half. Larry writhed, his will to live withstanding, refusing to falter.

Fueled by adrenaline, Larry pulled himself toward the shoreline. The things circled around him, biting his face, his fingers, his arms, shoulders, and midsection. Still, he continued.

Finally, he broke the surface. With bony fingers, he pulled himself onto the rain-soaked sand. He looked behind him, staring with strange fascination at the skeletal structure that made up his waist, legs, and feet.

Then everything faded to black.

CHAPTER 11

A crack of thunder shook the ceiling, making Royce tense. He was looking at himself in the mirror, seeing the odd blending of excitement and apprehension staring back. He put on a red shirt and was looking at a pair of slacks.

"Uh-huh. Yeah, that's right. Don't skimp on the sauce..."

"Be nice, Ellen."

She entered his bedroom, phone tucked under her left cheek. "Well, Dad, if you remembered to call the pizza guy yourself, they'd get the nice treatment." She squinted as she saw the slacks spread on the bed. "What is *that*?"

"They're my pants." He looked down at himself, wearing only his shirt and some boxers. "By the way... you mind?" He shooed her away.

"Like I haven't seen you that way before." She redirected her attention to the phone as she turned away. "Yep... mushroom on one half, pepperoni on the other..."

"Mushrooms?"

Ellen ignored him as she finished making the order. "Alright, cool. Thanks, bye." She faced her dad. "Yes, Pam likes mushrooms on her pizza. I do too. So do a lot of people. I also imagine women like Pam like it when their dates remember to order the food they promised."

"Oh, wow. The sass is strong with you today." Royce yanked the pants off the bed. "First of all, it's not a date."

"Maybe not, since I'm intruding on it. I'll call it a pre-date. Next time you two can go out to eat, or something. And for the love of God, don't put those on."

Royce looked at the pants, then at her. "Why not?"

"It's pizza and *Predator* on the couch. You're not taking her to Spaghetti Warehouse. Good lord, you don't need to be so formal. Not this time, at least. Just put on some jeans."

Royce stared at his nine-year old daughter. "Okay, missy. When did you become so knowledgeable about the arts of dating—" he held up a finger, as though to silence any debate "—Not saying that this is a date."

"I'm a girl. I *occasionally* enjoy a good chick flick. Also, I'm a girl! It's in our genetic code."

He shook his head, then reached for his bottom drawer for some jeans. "You're killing me, smalls!"

"That's my job."

"It is, huh? One day, I hope you have a little girl just like you!" The statement backfired. Like any parent, Royce struggled with the fact that his little girl was growing up. The fact that she was so intelligent, articulate, and responsible only meant the little kid days were already over. She already thought of herself as too old to trick-or-treat during Halloween night, opting to pass out candy instead. She still liked dressing up though, so at least Royce could enjoy that.

He put on his pants, looked himself over in the mirror, and walked out into the living room. Ellen was wiping down the center table in front of the horseshoe-shaped couch. Another crack of thunder echoed overhead.

"Jeez. Glad I'm not the pizza guy. I wonder if this'll carry on into tomorrow. Maybe that little pontoon trip will be cancelled."

"Nah. Should start breaking apart in another hour or so, according to the satellite," Royce said. "You should pack your swimsuit if Jane is taking you on that trip."

Ellen shook her head. "I'd rather throw some casts."

"Fair enough." His tone was neutral. He trusted Jane to have good judgement. Still, this was going to be a boat ride with young men and young women aboard. He'd be surprised if alcohol wasn't going to be involved. Then again, Jane would have the good sense not to bring the kids if that was the case. "Hook anything today?"

"Yeah."

He waited for her to follow-up her answer. Must not have been anything noteworthy, or she'd be bragging about it.

"'Yeah'? So… what'd you catch?"

"I think I hooked a big pike, but I lost it."

"Aw. Well, that happens. Pike have sharp teeth. They often bite through the line."

"No, that's not what happened. Something took it."

"Beg your pardon? Something *took* your pike?"

"Yeah, it was the strangest thing I've ever seen. I was reeling it in, then all of a sudden the water around it went nuts. I felt the line tugging sharply, then next thing I know, I'm reeling in the pike's jaw."

"Is that so?"

"It's true! I don't know what took it. The only possibility that makes a little sense is an otter."

"I don't know. Sounds like a fish tale from someone who lost a pike."

"It is not. I've had fish get away before and I'm always a good sport about it."

"True—unless another kid shows you up. Maybe Jacob cast a line out and hooked something pretty big, and you got nothing?"

Ellen scoffed. "Oh, please! Jacob can't even bring himself to tough the worm, let alone throw a cast properly. He's definitely not gonna know how to set the hook. He's all about watching the *MCU* crash and burn. Of course, he doesn't see it that way."

"Let him have his opinion, Ellen. Just because we think it's crap, doesn't mean we need to force that opinion onto everyone else. Let people like what they like. And be patient with him. He might come around to fishing if you don't intimidate him."

"Yeah-yeah." The sound of a car door slamming shut drew their attention to the door. They heard running footsteps, followed by a knocking. Ellen noticed her dad taking a deep breath. "Speaking of intimidation…"

"Oh, hush."

"You gonna leave your date out in the rain?"

"First of all, she's not my *date*. Second…" *Oh, shit! She IS in the rain!* He ran to the door and opened it. The sight of Pam in jeans and a red crisscross cold-shoulder blouse was a knockout one. Ellen was right for him to keep the shirt and to do away with the slacks. "Hi. Get in out of the rain."

"You don't have to tell me twice." She rushed in past him, then fixed her hair. "Where the hell did this rain come from?"

"It's Michigan. You surprised?"

"No, but it fits the movie night mood." Pam looked at Ellen. "There she is! Give me a hug!"

"Hi, Pam." The two ladies squeezed each other tight. Afterwards, Pam looked at the empty kitchen counter in search of the food. "Pizza will be here shortly. Leave it to *me* to remember to make the call. Dad was too busy trying to decide what to wear. I think he was trying to impress you."

Royce's eyes widened as though he'd seen a ghost. He pointed a finger, *stop while you're ahead, you little twerp,* then retracted it and smiled as Pam turned to look at him.

She pinched his cheek. "Aw, that's very cute."

"Yeah, Ellen thought I should've gone with something much fancier, like slacks and a button shirt. I had to convince her it was better to go with something casual."

Ellen's jaw dropped. "That's a l—"

"What would you like to drink?"

Pam chuckled. "What do you have?"

Royce went into the kitchen. "Lemonade, *Coca-Cola*, *Sprite*…"

"I'll take a *Sprite*, please." Pam looked back at Ellen and lowered her voice to a whisper. "Don't worry, I know he's lying."

"What's that?!"

"Nothing. Just girl talk!"

"Uh-huh. Suuuure." He returned with the beverages. "Just so you know, I know when you're lying too."

Pam smiled and took the drink. "When are we starting the movie?"

Ellen plopped onto the couch, Blu-ray in hand, while mimicking an Austrian accent. "Come on! Do it! Do it now!"

CHAPTER 12

"I knew it! I totally called it! That son of a bitch!"

When Venessa Ryden pulled into her fiancé's driveway and saw that his car wasn't there, her realization was instant. She had her suspicions, but didn't want them to be true. She was a young woman on the brink of marriage. She was six months into her career. Most of her debts were already paid off due to working two jobs during college and living on rice and beans in the meantime. Her discipline and perseverance had paid off, and now it was time to reap the rewards. Life was good, or at least it was supposed to be.

Her worries started when she asked to borrow his phone a few weeks back. Her reasons were innocent. Her phone was on the charger and she wanted to look something up on Google, and simply was feeling too lazy to get off the couch and use the computer. The look of apprehension on Will's face was brief, but nonetheless noticeable. He played it off as a joke, which would've worked had he not took a few seconds to swipe his thump over the screen. It was facing away from her, so she couldn't see what it was. However, she saw the urgency in his movements. Since then, she couldn't help but suspect he was trying to delete something fast before handing the phone over.

Over the next week, he was acting weird. Almost depressed. She'd find him sitting on the couch staring at the window. It made her think of the memes she saw on the internet, with a couple lying in bed while the woman thought 'I bet he's thinking of another woman.' She used to find that cliché funny. Now she was living it.

Over the next two weeks, she tried to put it from her mind. She assumed she was overthinking things. Maybe he was miserable at work. He often complained about his job. Will settled on a career rather than pursued one. It was the easier choice which he admitted to regretting. He was the operator at a water treatment plant. He expressed hating the rotating shifts, the boring work, the constant smell of chemicals, and the sitting around. He preferred being active. It all made sense, until Venessa made a discovery that reignited her suspicions.

Though they didn't live together, she had pretty much made herself at home at his place. Spending much of her time there, it was easy to notice things. In one particular visit, she was tossing a paper plate in the trash when she noticed a piece of paper. A receipt. Most of the grocery stores and restaurants Will went to usually emailed his receipts to him, a perk of the current era of technology.

Curiosity got the better of her. The receipt was from Green Pastures Bar. A bar? Twelve miles out of town? Will wasn't much of a bar goer, and even if he were, there were at least ten bars that were much closer.

"Green Pastures, my ass."

If that didn't make his betrayal obvious enough, there was the visit she made after getting off shift one day. He was just about to hop into the shower after spending the last couple of hours 'at the gym'. But Venessa knew the smell of perfume. She got a brief whiff, but it was enough. That, and the fact that he declined her offer to join him. If anything was out of character, it was that, and the fact that he snuck his phone into the bathroom.

Despite this, she couldn't summon the nerve to confront him about it. She was still in denial at that point. After all, this wasn't her first engagement. *Two* failed engagements?! She couldn't live with the idea. But now, she had reached the point where she had to face reality.

Venessa stared at the empty driveway and accepted the truth. She assumed she'd burst into tears at this point. Instead, she simply felt angry. And, in a way, somewhat relieved. Probably because the weeks of inner torture and doubt were finally coming to an end.

She called his phone. The dial tone buzzed in her ear before going to voicemail. *"Hey. You reached Will. Leave a message at the beep."* Venessa considered leaving a scathing rant but instead hung up. She had prolonged this misery long enough. If she accused him, he'd just deny it. However, if she caught the prick in the act, that would eliminate any doubt right there.

With her smartphone, she googled Green Pastures Bar and found its address. 1635 Hoelzer Road Lorenzo, MI. Wherever he was meeting that bitch, it was at or near this town. Still, no matter how small the town, it would be like finding a needle in a haystack, especially in this rain.

In the following moments, she considered her options. Stay here and confront him when he gets home? Go inside, pack her things, and leave a note and engagement ring? *That would probably be the more sensible thing to do.* Yet, she didn't want to simply break up. She wanted *revenge*. Unfortunately, she couldn't slash his tires, since his vehicle wasn't here.

All sorts of ideas ran through her mind. She thought of smashing his computer or maybe even putting a virus on it, corrupting all of his data. The identity thieves and credit card hackers would have a ball. She thought of calling the energy company and having his account disabled. Venessa even went as far as to consider hooking up with some random guy for the night and sending some provocative photos to her now-ex.

That would get under his skin, but she couldn't bring herself to go through with it. She thought of her dad, who absolutely hated the thought of her allowing herself to be used by men.

Regardless of the course of action, she needed to collect her belongings. It would be awkward to collect them after the fact. She still had clothes, her fit-bit, some books, and her tablet…

Shit! The tablet!

She had left it in Will's car. A new idea took form. Using her iPhone, she used the Find My Tablet app. Even if the tablet was off, she would be able to find its location on the map.

"Bingo! Lakefront property, I see. Doing a little skinny dipping, are ya, Will?" Probably unlikely in the rain, but Venessa wasn't thinking that clearly. Now that she knew his location, all she wanted was to confront him on the spot… and maybe punch his new flame in the mouth.

She sped out of the driveway and swerved right, narrowly dodging an incoming car which ended up on the curb. By the time the driver started cursing at her, she was already a speck in the distance.

CHAPTER 13

"*What da hell ah you?*" Ellen said, leaning against a mountain of pillows, feet crossed, while munching the last slice of pizza. They watched the iconic sequence of Arnie escaping the titular creature's wrist gauntlet bomb, which resulted in a mushroom cloud visible for miles.

Royce got more relaxed as the film went on. He sat shoulder-to-shoulder with Pam on the center part of the couch, heels on the edge of the table.

"Such a powerful explosion. Apparently, all you need is a little hill, and you can easily survive it," Royce said. Pam and Ellen glared at him.

"Um, excuse me sir, you're not allowed to criticize this movie," Pam said. "Also, for your information, if you put enough soil between you and the blast zone, you can survive the shockwave and heat."

"Maybe if you're Arnie." He rewound the scene and watched it again. "You see that electrical discharge before it goes off? Maybe there's more to the bomb than a simple blast. Maybe it uses intense electrical impulse, like a massive bolt of lightning, to fry anything in sight."

"Wow…and I thought *I* watched this movie too many times," Ellen said.

"I thought talking about the lore was part of the fun."

"I have to agree with your dad on this one," Pam said. "Not sure I agree about the electricity thing. Electrons scatter off oxygen and nitrogen molecules, so an electrical blast would break apart in a short distance. It's not like water, which contains salts and metals. So, no, an electrical blast would not have worked unless Arnie was in a lake."

"Okay then, Professor Pam," Royce said.

"I think she'd make a good professor. She is smarter than you, Dad."

"Thanks for the vote of confidence," Royce replied. "I'm starting to think your next few dinners will consist of cabbage."

"Oh, God!" Ellen pinched her nose. "Eating it is bad enough. When *you* eat it, though…" She looked at Pam. "If you're gonna keep seeing him, don't say I didn't warn you about cabbage night."

"I could probably tolerate it if it was followed up with ice cream or something."

"Mmm. Ice cream sounds really good right *now*, actually."

Royce pointed at her plate. "Ice cream? How the heck do you have any room left at all after practically eating half the pizza?"

"Fills in the cracks," Ellen said.

"She makes a good point," Pam said. She leaned against Royce's shoulder and smiled. "I wouldn't mind a little rocky road right about now."

"Is that so?"

She looked at the window. "Storm's lightened up. Ever been to Central Dairy?"

"I have not."

"Look at that! Earlier you introduced me to a restaurant I haven't been to. Now I'm returning the favor."

"Ice cream shop doesn't count," Royce said.

"Oh, ha-ha." Ellen sat up. "I vote we go! It's hot and muggy anyway, even with the a/c."

Pam raised her hand. "Looks like the ladies have voted, Sergeant."

"I outrank you."

"Nice try. You taking us, or am I gonna have to kidnap your kid?"

"She's all yours," he said.

"Daaaad."

"Okay, okay. Gosh, first a movie, then pizza… next thing I know, you ladies will want donuts in the morning."

"I'm down for that!" Ellen said.

"Same here. Don't come to work without them. And don't act like I didn't offer to buy the pizza, Mister."

Royce chuckled as he stood up. "Yeah, you got me there." He found his keys and went for the door. "I'll drive."

Pam sprang to her feet. "I call shotgun."

"How far away is this place?"

"About fifteen, twenty minutes."

"*Twenty minutes*?! Jesus! Why don't we go to the Arctic Café?"

"Because I've had their ice cream. It's okay, but believe me, Central Dairy is SO MUCH better!"

Royce pretended to stab himself with the key. "Alright. This shit better be worth it."

"It will be. Pam's never wrong, Dad."

"You just say that because she's a girl."

"Girls *are* smarter than boys," Pam said.

"Oh jeez. Get your ass in the car."

CHAPTER 14

Had Venessa Ryden arrived at Lake Carlson under any other circumstance, she would have been lost in its beauty. Even in the rain, the sight of the large lake tended to spark an urge to dip her toes into the water, and make plans to visit the beach.

There were no peaceful thoughts passing through her mind in this moment. When the GPS brought her to a winding dirt driveway leading up to a lakefront property, only anger remained. So much anger, that Venessa had to hit the brakes.

A series of deep breaths followed. Being high on emotion during the entire drive, she hadn't rationally thought about how she'd handle the situation. All she knew was that she wanted to catch the asshole in the act. Now, she recognized her anger.

"Don't get violent."

It was easier said than done. The thought of beating his mistress was too pleasurable. Tempting. As for Will, he deserved the skank. It didn't matter if the woman knew he was engaged or not. To Venessa, she was, and would always be, a skank.

What if she did know, and took pleasure in being the other woman?

Venessa didn't have the mental fortitude to force that consideration from her mind. She was so angry, it was easy to accept it as fact. Just like with believing the woman to be a skank.

She entered the driveway.

Those emotions went into overdrive when she saw her about-to-be-ex fiancé's car parked in front of a two-story house. Through the back window, she could see the living room. The light was on.

Venessa turned off the headlights and remained in the vehicle, curious if she could glimpse any movement. Several minutes passed and nothing happened. She imagined Will spotting her car and retreating to the opposite end of the house. The idea of sparking such fear made her feel powerful. Unfortunately, it wasn't a strong possibility. It was still drizzling outside, the cloud cover making the evening black as night. Even if they spotted her vehicle, they likely couldn't see it well enough to recognize it.

After waiting another few moments, there was still no activity in the living room. With all the other lights off, Venessa concluded there was only one other place they could be—the bedroom. That thought put her rage into overdrive. She hesitated long enough to decide on a course of action. Go up to the door and knock? Let herself in if it was unlocked and catch them in bed? Improvise?

It became obvious that the last option was probably going to dominate, since she wasn't fully aware of what she was walking into.

"Let's do this."

She got out of her car and strutted to the door. As she approached, she looked to the side yard. There was a burnt out fireplace with a couple of chairs around it. Beside the pit was a box of matches, now soaking wet from rain exposure. There were beer cans in the grass. Either this resident was quite the slob, or something *more interesting* occurred to make them abandon all this stuff.

With a better view of the living room, Venessa could confirm it was empty. She twisted the knob. To her surprise, the door was unlocked. She slowly pushed it open and stepped inside, then listened for the sounds of pleasured moaning. The house was silent as the grave. Being three-thousand square feet, it was fair to assume she just needed to get closer to the action. Houses like this typically had its bedrooms upstairs.

The stairway was easy to locate. She carefully ascended the steps, fists clenched in case someone emerged from the darkness thinking she was a burglar. She maybe wasn't a thief, but she was an intruder, no matter the circumstance.

At the top of the steps she turned right. Still no sounds.

Maybe he's being gentle. Piece of shit prick.

She used her phone as a flashlight and aimed it into the hall. Two bedroom doors were on the right. Both were open. She went to the nearest one, listened, then peeked inside. It was empty, the bed perfectly made. There wasn't much in the way of belongings here, which led her to believe it was the guest bedroom.

The next one had to be it. She went to the door, and without hesitation, kicked it open. "Gotcha, you asshole!"

Her phone light found another empty bed. This one had been used more than the other, the shelves packed with more belongings. There were no mistaking the female garments in the hamper. This was definitely where the mistress slept, yet she and Will were nowhere to be seen.

Venessa checked the closet, the bathroom, then finally, the whole rest of the house. Nothing. Either they were the stealthiest couple ever, or they weren't in this house.

Now, Venessa was frustrated. She had committed to catching them in the act, even risking a physical altercation in the process. From the looks of it, it was all for nothing.

Back in the living room, she took a seat in the recliner. Sitting as though she were the owner of this house, she stared at the various belongings. On the east wall was a picture of a well-groomed man in a tuxedo, leading his bride down an aisle. It was an older quality photo, not taken in the world of digital devices. Probably the mistress' parents.

There was a computer desk in the corner. On it was an expensive-looking laptop and a tablet. On the edge of a nearby bookcase was a set of car keys. Venessa stood up and glanced at the empty room, feeling defeated. Considering going back home, she walked outside.

She stopped after taking a single step past the door. A flash of lightning briefly illuminated something on the beach. She leaned back inside the doorway, and found a set of light switches. She flicked a few of them, turning on a porchlight and another light near the dock.

Venessa immediately knew what the items were. Clothes, both men's and women's. She recognized the button shirt and jeans that was previously worn by Will.

Standing over the discarded clothing, she felt her rage return. She looked to the lake. Were they skinny dipping somewhere out there? In the middle of a storm? Perhaps that was what made Will cheat—the need to be adventurous.

"Hey! Come on out, you two!" No response. "Will, I know you and that bitch are screwing around. You think I'm stupid?!" All she heard in return was lapping water. She squinted, trying her damnedest to see their naked bodies moving about. But it was too dark. "Fine! Stay here for all I care. Knock her up while you're at it. You two deserve each other. We're done."

Venessa was unsatisfied. She wanted to get back at them, not just spout useless words. She wanted to make them as angry as she was.

She thought of the picture frame and electronic devises. Damn the consequences—this *is* the consequence. Of THEIR actions.

The vengeful woman marched back into the house, yanked the computer off the table, held it over her shoulder with one hand and scooped up the tablet in the other. She dropped off the items at the dock, then went back for some more. By now, she was on a roll. She grabbed a wallet full of debit cards and cash, some expensive-looking jewelry, and a pair of Christian Louboutin Kate high heels.

"Shit! How rich is this bitch?"

She took them too, and with the items tucked under her arm, she returned to the living room. She eyed the wedding photo on the wall.

Do I want to go that far? That's a little low... She snatched it off the wall and went to the dock. *Oh well. This is what these idiots get for creating a whore for a daughter.*

She brought the items to the end of the dock. "You guys gonna come out? No? Alright. Hey, Will, I hope your new girlfriend is watching. See this?" She held up the tablet. "Catch!" She tossed it into the water. The laptop followed, splashing down eight feet from the dock.

No reactions. Either they weren't out here, or the mistress was really good at hiding her emotions. Venessa tossed the car keys and the shoes, listening to them splash somewhere in the darkness.

****

First, the scout was lured by the echoes of water distortion. Vibration traveled far and wide in the water, luring the fish from the weed bed in which it hid. As it neared the source, it felt the tingling from mild electromagnetic surges. These surges were not significant enough to harm the fish, though they did pique its curiosity.

There was vibration coming from the artificial structure in the shallows. A vague scent of flesh drew it to the foot of the platform. It nuzzled between the bones of previous victims, searching for the few strands of bloated flesh still intact. Its metabolism required constant nourishment, and with the numbers in its pack rapidly increasing, sufficient food was becoming scarce.

More foreign items struck the water, drawing the fish to the surface. These things weren't edible, but the movement from above suggested prey was nearby. In the past thirty-six hours, the scout and its pack had observed these land-based creatures. Their flesh was as nutritious as anything that swam in the lake. It was just a matter of getting them into the water.

Like with any species, no matter the intelligence level, it was capable of learning through trial and error. To reach prey beyond its habitat, it would have to leave its habitat, if only for a moment. Its genetic makeup had gifted it with a caudal fin, capable of generating speeds up to thirty-miles per hour—more than enough to launch itself into the air.

The fish followed the creaking sounds of wooden planks, then used its dime-shaped eyes to spot its target. The walking creature was oblivious to its presence, carelessly tossing the inedible items into the water like waste. The scout wasn't concerned with the things falling around it. It wanted flesh, and like an ant to the colony, it needed to alert its pack. Ants used chemical signals to alert their brethren. The shredder used the blood of its prey.

It sank to the bottom to grant itself distance for momentum. Ready for launch, it fluttered its tail.

****

Venessa was disappointed with the lack of response. Maybe they weren't out in the lake after all. She gazed at the water, now filled with expensive items. She took a little pleasure in knowing they'd be found by the mistress. Still, it was disappointing knowing she wouldn't be there to see the reaction.

There was only one thing left.

She lifted the picture, smacked the glass against the edge of the dock, then threw it into the lake. The water made fast work of the paper photo, reducing it to a wrinkled tissue. The glow of the light post captured its deterioration perfectly. A few tears were already forming along the edges. In time, it would break apart.

Venessa stood at the edge of the dock and stared. Watching the smiling couple fade away, Venessa wondered if she went too far. Electronics were one thing. That photo was a precious memory. Now, it was lost.

If I did go too far, karma will probably let me know.

A gaping hole exploded in the center of the photo like an exploding bullet wound. In the brief second it was airborne, Venessa saw the light reflecting off the greenish scales of the projectile before it struck her jaw. The pain was instantaneous.

Razor sharp teeth pierced her skin and sank all the way down to the jawbone. Venessa shrieked, spinning in place while tugging at the wet body.

It was a fish! It was over a foot-and-a-half long and flat. She didn't notice its size as much as she did its rapid bites. It shook itself from her jaw and attacked her wrists. Like a rampant canine, it shook its head after grabbing a mouthful of flesh. Venessa screamed, blood spraying from quarter-sized gaps in her palm and wrist. Finally, the fish fell free.

Flopping on the dock, it wasn't ready to quit. A fling of its tail catapulted it off the wooden deck right toward her shin. Its teeth pierced her pantleg into her shin. Venessa staggered backward—right into the water. Now in its fresh environment, the fish attacked more freely. It tore at her thighs and knees, generating clouds of blood that could be smelled across the lake. The scout had done its job. The school had been alerted, and judging by the vibration of distant water displacement, they were moving in swiftly.

On her back, Venessa was lost in a mindless panic. Water rushed up her nose and down her throat. Her frantic movements did nothing to deter her attacker, who was peeling ribbons of skin from her thighs.

She kicked, but was unable to shake it off. She swatted it with her hand, but only gave the fish a new target. She yanked her hand back after its teeth found the tip of her index finger. There was a rip and a *pop*. She couldn't see, but she knew the tip of her finger was gone.

In excruciating pain and losing air rapidly, she threw her hands out, hoping to grab anything within reach. Her fingers found something hard, grimy, and rigid. A tree branch, maybe? She didn't care about the odd sensation—she just needed to hit the fish with something. She tried to swing, but the thing was caught on something larger. It had plenty of flexibility,

Another bite threw her panic into overdrive. Adrenaline gave her the strength of a spartan. With a huge tug, she broke the item free, then swung it like a baseball bat, striking the fish in the head. It darted backward and smacked into the pillar. Stunned, it spiraled down into the weeds, pumping water through its gills.

Venessa planted her feet to the ground and rose out of the water. After taking a deep breath, she glanced at the makeshift weapon in her hand. It was white, bent at the center—like an elbow. Seeing the thin boned fingers in the dock light, she realized she was holding the arm of a skeleton.

She screamed twice. The first time out of fright, the second out of pain. A universe of pain. The water around her erupted with life as the whole pack packed themselves into the shallows, eager to get a mouthful of human flesh.

The sensation of muscle tissue being pulled off the bone generated such agony that Venessa couldn't even scream. Her only focus was on the dock. She slipped her fingers between the planks and hauled herself out of the water. She rolled onto her back, then looked down, seeing two of the fish still gnawing on her knees. She smacked them with the arm, knocking them into the water.

She was completely seized by terror. All rational thought had fled from her mind as quickly as she tossed the arm into the water. Crying and babbling, she got onto her feet and hobbled to her car. She got in, started the engine, turned the car around, and floored the accelerator—not noticing the rapidly approaching headlights coming in from the north.

****

"Alright, Mr. Wise Guy," Pam said. "So it's a little out of the way. But you'll love this place."

"I better. Fifteen minutes out of my way, this place better have the best ice cream on God's green earth."

"Oh, quit being such a buzzkill, Dad."

Royce looked back at Ellen. "Speaking of buzzkill, how many times do I have to tell you to get your feet off the back of my seat?"

Ellen's feet quickly returned to the floor pad. She leaned forward and pointed, eyes wide. "Dad! Look out!"

"Royce!" Pam shouted.

He looked to the road and saw the car speeding out of a driveway on the right. "Oh, shit!" He veered to the right and hit the brakes, narrowly clearing the vehicle. It veered wide as well, still speeding, and went straight into a tree.

Royce looked through his window at the *Toyota*. Its engine was folded inward, spewing smoke. More alarming was the endlessly blaring horn.

"Shit." He took a breath and looked at Ellen. "You alright, kid?"

She had her arms tucked close to her chin, her body tense as a wire. "Y-yeah."

"You're okay. Stay here. Pam and I are gonna take a look."

His partner had already stepped out and was sprinting toward the vehicle. She peered through the broken window and looked back.

"Jesus! Royce, call the station. We need an ambulance, pronto."

He dug his phone out and began to dial. "How bad is it, exactly?"

"It's a female. Roughly late twenties." She reached inside and checked for a pulse. "She's still alive and breathing, but— Jesus, she's bleeding severely."

Royce raised the phone to his ear. "Yeah, this is Sergeant Royce Dashnaw with the Lorenzo Police Department, off duty. We need an ambulance at 3627 Springdale Road. Got a vehicular accident. One injured person—woman in late twenties. Possible trauma. Bleeding severely... yeah, I'll wait." He groaned as the on-hold music came on, then looked at Pam. "Told you we should've gone to Arctic Café."

CHAPTER 15

In six minutes, there were two police cars and an ambulance on site. The one advantage of evening runs was the decrease in traffic, allowing for first responders to floor it.

Royce stood next to his SUV, keeping Ellen company. She was relaxed now. In fact, she was quite fascinated by the response process. She had seen cops pulling people over for speeding, but this was the first time she ever witnessed a rescue effort.

"I could be a cop."

"So you keep telling me," Royce replied.

"Does this happen a lot?"

"Car crashes? Unfortunately, yes. Though they don't normally occur like this."

Pam stepped away from the crowd and joined them.

"Must say, I've never had a first date take a turn like that before."

"Who says it was a date?" Royce said. "That driver say anything?"

Pam shrugged. "Something about fish." Royce almost laughed. Of all the things he expected to hear, the woman was babbling about fish. Pam wasn't laughing. Her expression was as grim as he had ever seen it. "She's bleeding bad. Her legs are all torn up."

"Well, when you smash into a tree…"

"No! It's like a bunch of razor blades had slashed her."

"Glass, maybe?"

"Not that I could see." Pam looked through the driveway. "Interesting nobody's come out."

"Maybe nobody's home," Royce said. He groaned, then dug his flashlight out of the glove compartment. Before leaving, he glanced at his daughter. "Ellen, will you be okay waiting here for a few minutes?"

She nodded.

"You alright, hon?" Pam said.

"Yeah. Just scary. Happened so fa—"

A bloodcurdling scream made her shiver. The group looked to the paramedics as they loaded the injured woman onto a stretcher.

"She's lost at least two pints of blood," the captain said. "Call the hospital. Let them know she's gonna need a transfusion."

The woman kicked and writhed on the stretcher, forcing the paramedics to strap her down.

"Ma'am! You're safe!"

"THEY'RE IN THE WATER! THEY'RE IN THE WATER!"

They loaded the woman into the ambulance. The captain continued barking orders into the radio as he climbed aboard the firetruck. "She's gonna need to go straight to an OR."

Royce whistled to the uniformed officers and waved them over. Two approached, a chubby one named Belgram, and the nightshift Sergeant, Dressel.

"Sarge, it's your show, but I suggest we take a look-see at this property."

Dressel pointed at the driveway. "I didn't get a chance to hear the whole story yet. You're saying she sped out of *here*?"

"Correct."

"Damn. I figured she was all over the road, then swerved to miss you guys." He looked at the car, then back at the driveway. There was only twenty feet of distance. "For her to flatten that engine like that, she had to be freaking gunning it."

"She certainly was. Fact that I missed her was a miracle. Or rather, a testament to my quick instinct."

Dressel noticed Pam snickering. "Let me guess: he's full of shit?"

"Always," she replied.

"Yeah, laugh it up. You can even laugh as we investigate the property. Just keep in mind, *something* scared her enough to race out onto the road."

"Also, those injuries were *not* from glass," Pam said. "Might be a domestic situation."

"Great." Dressel ignited his flashlight and kept one hand near his Glock. "Let's see how nice the residents are."

They walked down the winding driveway and announced their presence after nearing the house. With no reply, they continued into the yard.

"Someone had a little party here," Pam said, bumping a beer can with her foot.

"That beer led to more fun," Royce said, shining his light on the discarded clothing on the beach. "We can assume one man and one girl went into the lake at some point."

"The victim was fully dressed," Dressel said.

"True." Royce stared at the clothing. "Maybe she went skinny dipping with a date, got caught in the storm, and they went straight to the house. Had a little fun, then got dressed."

Pam walked over and gazed at the tank top and jean shorts. "No. These belong to someone with a skinnier body type than the driver."

"Fascinating observation," Royce said. He looked over at Belgram. "Go check the house. The door's open. Announce yourself first…and be careful. Something or some*one* sliced that woman up."

"Alright." Belgram peeked through the doorway, hand on his gun. He announced himself twice, then went inside.

Pam was shaking her head. "This is weird. Those were not knife wounds. Some were rounded off, the flesh frayed around the edges."

"Bullet wounds?"

"Not exactly. They looked…well, like bites."

"Bites?"

"Yeah, but very small."

Dressel waved at them from the dock. "It fits with the weirdness factor." He aimed his light into the water. "Look at all of this shit." Royce and Pam joined him and gazed at the variety of items floating or submerged in the water.

"Shoes? A computer?" Royce almost wanted to laugh again. "A picture frame? Jesus, I'm suspecting there was some degree of rage involved here."

"Wonder what else we'll find," Dressel said.

"Don't know." Royce moved to the end of the dock. "Still fairly shallow. I can see the bottom wherever I aim my light… oh look! I think I see jewelry. I'm starting to think there was some kind of skirmish here. Maybe that lady caught a lover skinny dipping with someone else? Confronted them, and things got nasty."

"Interesting theory," Pam said. "Now if we can find the two skinny-dippers."

Dressel got on his radio. "Belgram? Find anything in that house?"

"Negative, Sarge. It's empty."

"I think it's safe to assume they're not in the house," Pam said.

Dressel looked toward the driveway. "There's two other vehicles here. I doubt they went far."

"No…" Royce crouched down, his grin vanishing completely. His face paled, his eyes unblinking as they stared into the water. "Didn't go far at all…"

Pam and Dressel knelt down. When they saw the barren skull staring back at them, strands of tissue and hair waving in the water, they both staggered back.

"Tell me that's a Halloween prop," Dressel said, holding back vomit.

"No." Royce finally looked away. "This night just got weirder."

****

"You think they know?"

Alice Kirkman ignored Billy's concerns as she watched from the south shoreline. The red and blue flashers were now all over the property. The way they were all gathering near the water made it clear that a victim had been found.

"No. Not a chance."

"What if they found a body?" Billy said.

"Then all the evidence is gone," Alice sighed. "Call the professor. Tell him to hold the shipment for another few hours. Can't dump it now, not with the cops all over the lake. We'll have to do it at dawn."

"As you wish. I must warn you, we risk being caught."

"We'll be caught if we do it tonight!" Alice lowered the binoculars and walked back to her car. Billy sat in the driver's seat and waited for her to sit. "After you speak with Bohl, call Smitty and the others. Tell them to assemble at the cove and await our arrival."

Always the reliable devotee, Billy nodded.

CHAPTER 16

The sound of brewing coffee served as Royce's alarm clock. He stretched in bed, amazed that Ellen was more of an early bird than he was. Simultaneously, he was disappointed. Looking at the empty right side of the bed, he strangely felt lonelier than usual. For the last several years, he hardly paid any mind to it beyond the luxury of having more space. Now, it just looked empty. It wasn't a need for sexual gratification, rather a desire for lifelong companionship. Only once in his life did he think he had a soulmate, and that blew up in his face with Nagasaki force.

He looked to the window, appreciating the early morning sunlight. The humidity wasn't going to be pleasant, thanks to that sudden storm. Because of that, the lake was going to be busy. With the air hot and sticky, residents and vacationers alike would want to take a dip to cool off. He didn't blame them. If he had the day off, he'd consider it himself. With the sun shining bright through the clear skies, it was better to spend the day in the water than inside in the air conditioning.

Then again, maybe not. It was a miracle that he didn't have nightmares about those two skeletons. Had there not been some residue clinging to the bones, he would've assumed at first sight that they were discarded Halloween decorations. He had seen enough dead bodies in his time as a police officer to know it would take a very long time for someone to decompose to that level.

If this is a murder case, than we're dealing with a very elaborate and creative psychopath.

The smell of eggs found his nose. For the first time, Royce winced at the thought of eating any kind of meat. Of course, Ellen wasn't affected—she didn't even know the skeletons existed. Royce and Pam made a point not to tell her about them. No sense in unnerving a nine-year old.

After getting geared up, he went into the kitchen where his little chef had prepped breakfast for him.

"Morning."

"Morning!" Ellen was setting up her fishing poles and tacklebox.

"Oh, right!" Royce said. He had forgotten that she was going on a pontoon boat today. "Make sure you have your lifejacket, please."

"Dad, I'm a better swimmer than the instructors at your work."

"True, but I'd appreciate you being careful. In fact…" He sat down and looked at the scrambled eggs. He didn't look at them as his ordinary breakfast, but as minced meat—like the flesh that used to be on those skeletons. "…Were you planning on swimming today?"

"Maybe. It's nice, but muggy out."

"That it is." He played with his food for a bit, favoring his coffee.

"Something wrong?"

"No… I don't know. Ellen, this might sound weird, but maybe it'll be better if you don't go into the water." His daughter looked at him, unsure of what to say. No words were necessary—her face did all the talking. "I don't know what the problem is, but there might be something in the water."

"'Something'? Like a shark?"

Royce laughed. "No, not a shark!" *Sharks wouldn't have left those bones so intact. Then again, the one was missing an arm…*

"Then what? An alligator?"

"No."

"Piranhas?"

"NO! That's enough 70s and 80s horror for you! You've got much more imagination than—" he stared into the distance, struck by an epiphany. "Piranhas…"

"Good movie," Ellen said.

"They strip their prey to the bone in minutes…"

"Yeah. Wanna watch it tonight? We can do a double-feature! The original and the remake…then again the remake has a lot of the porn stuff…"

On any other occasion, the thought of his nine-year old daughter even mentioning porn, in any context, would have sent Royce into a frenzy. At this moment, he was lost in thought.

Could it be? Is that possible? How would they get into the lake? Would they even survive in this climate? Piranhas are South American, right?

His eyes went to Ellen's fishing line. "Hey, kid? You said you lost a pike yesterday, right?"

She glared at him. "Yeah? What about it? Gonna poke fun at me some more?"

"Describe to me again what happened, please."

Ellen stared for a moment, unsure of whether she was being set up for a joke. She and her dad, like true fishermen, always poked fun at each other for their fishing mishaps. If that serious expression on his face was just an act, it was a damn good one.

"I caught the fish on a spinner rig. I was bringing it in, then all of a sudden..." she shook her hands to mimic thrashing water, "something was grabbing ahold of it and tearing it apart."

"Wait... the pike was *torn apart*?"

"Looks like it. I told you about the jaw. And I saw skin and fins floating on the water. Looked like the thing had been put through a blender."

He stood up. "Let's get a move-on. I wanna get to the office a little early."

"But Dad! Your breakfast! You didn't even take a bite!"

He looked back at his plate. The appetite still wasn't there, but he knew he would need the energy. He found two pieces of bread, scooped the eggs and bacon inside, then wrapped it in a paper towel.

"Alright, grab your stuff."

"What's the hurry? Eager to see Pam again?"

"Yes, but not for the reason you think."

****

When they arrived at Jane Fields' driveway, Royce kept the engine running as he walked Ellen to the door.

"Dad, you sure everything's alright? You've been acting strange since the accident last night."

"Just some police work I have to catch up on, kiddo." Royce knocked on the door. To his relief, Jane answered it right away. She was in the process of getting her makeup on and styling her hair.

"Oh, hi! You're a tad early."

"Yeah, sorry. I should've been more considerate and texted you. Anyway, I gotta run."

"It's all good. How'd your date go last night?"

"My date?" Royce glared at a smiling Ellen. "Of course she told you. Uh..." *Move it, dude. No time for chit-chat.* "It went nice."

"Good! So glad to hear that. From what Ellen tells me, you two are very cute together. Hope it continues."

"Me too," Ellen said.

"Oh, good Lord." Royce kissed her on the head and marched to his vehicle, stopping briefly to look back. "Tell you what, if I can figure out this situation I'm dealing with at work, I'll invite her over again."

"Deal!"

"What situation?" Jane asked.

Royce debated internally on how to answer that. Last thing he needed was to sound crazy right now.

"Not sure yet. There might be some problem with the water. Do me a favor, and be careful when you're out on the pontoon, will ya?"

"What kind of problem? Don't tell me it's them wires over by the Redfords' property. Those things look like they're ready to fall loose at any moment."

"No, not those. I can't really elaborate, just... I recommend not swimming."

Jane nodded, her skin turning red where it wasn't touched by the makeup. It was the closest thing to an answer she would get.

"Okay. I'll pass it on to the others. Bye!"

"Bye. Ellen, be careful. See you later." He got in his SUV and buckled in. "Hopefully."

****

If anything was going right this morning, it was the fact that Royce didn't see any protesters as he drove through Lorenzo. Despite his rush, he allowed himself the joy of seeing his usual landmarks. It served as therapy of sorts. He glanced at his phone, tempted to call Jane and simply tell her not to go on the lake at all. Finding a body literally stripped to the bone like that wasn't normal. Even if some psycho killer used a knife to scrape everything away, it would've left distinct marks on the bones.

He passed Barb's Bakery, and made a turn at the next intersection. Right at the corner, he saw Monty's Tackle. A young man was standing in front of it, looking around concerned. At first glance, Royce thought it was another protester. As he made the turn, he realized it was Tyler Bankowski, Monty's nephew. There was no mistaking the worried look on his face.

Royce pulled over and rolled his window down. "Hey, Tyler. Everything alright?"

"Hi, Officer Dashnaw. Just waiting on Uncle Monty." Tyler stuck his hands in his pockets and looked around. "I don't know where he is. We've got a supply truck arriving any second and he needs to sign the invoice."

Though Royce wasn't the most well acquainted with Monty, he knew that the guy was always in his shop by six. Being late was not part of his doctrine.

"I assume you've tried calling him?"

"Four times, and a dozen texts. He won't answer. This isn't like him. Definitely not today of all days."

"When did you last see him?"

"Yesterday afternoon."

"Did he mention if he was going home or what his evening plans were?"

"Just fishing," Tyler said. "Now that he has help around the shop, he's trying to spend more solitary time. For him, being on the water never gets old."

Royce closed his eyes. *That damn water.* Part of him regretted asking.

"Is everything alright?" Tyler asked.

The officer snapped back into reality. "Yeah. I hope so. Listen, I gotta go. If you don't hear from your uncle in the next couple of hours, call the station. Tell the dispatcher to let me know. I'll swing by his place and check on him."

"Will do. I appreciate it, man."

Royce continued his route to the station. "Jesus, Lord above. What is going on with that water?"

CHAPTER 17

Royce arrived at the station right as the midnight patrol crew were transmitting their ending milage for the vehicles. Nights was usually operated by a skeleton crew of four patrollers and one sergeant. With Lorenzo being a small town with little crime, the public didn't see a need for the streets to be endlessly patrolled as though in a war zone. It was a part of living here that Royce usually appreciated. Today, he felt different. He wished a dozen cops had been out to catch any bizarre occurrences, particularly near the lake.

"Hey, look who it is!"

He looked over his shoulder and saw Pam approaching the station. "Hi."

"So far, it's an improvement over yesterday. No big crowds of protesters, so far. Maybe we scared them all off."

"Pam, have you seen Larry?"

She laughed. "I literally just arrived. You're the first person I've laid eyes on all morning." She flashed her eyelashes. "Too bad I can't say that in a different context." Her next laugh ended abruptly as Royce spun on his heel and went for the door. "Sorry. Probably too soon for that kind of remark."

"Huh?" He glanced at her, hand clutching the door handle.

Pam stood silent, realizing he didn't hear a word she said. "Are you alright, Royce?"

"I'm fine. I need to speak with the Chief and visit the coroner's office."

"What's the matter? Those corpses freak you out?"

"Pam, I think there's something in the lake."

"Something? Like what?"

"I don't want to speculate until we know more."

"Relax, Royce. What's got your panties in a bunch? You weren't this on edge at the property yesterday." She stepped up to the door and swiped her badge along the card reader, unlocking it. "You think there's something in the lake. You didn't reach that conclusion last night, so I have a feeling there's something you're not telling me."

Royce stared at his reflection in the glass window before opening the door. Yeah, he looked as crazy as he felt.

"It might just be a coincidence, but I spoke with Tyler— Monty's nephew…"

"Monty from the tackle shop?"

"Yes. Tyler said he didn't show up this morning. Monty's never late. He said the last place he was aware his uncle was going was out on the water to fish."

"So what? Maybe he forgot to set his alarm…"

"And then there's Ellen's pike…"

"What about it?"

"She said something tore it up after she hooked it." He pulled the door open. "I need to talk to Larry. We might have to warn everyone to stay out of the lake until we figure out what's going on."

"Royce, all this could simply be nothing. There's other explanations for the bodies…"

"Yeah? What about that woman in the car wreck? Soaking wet. Weird injuries all over, which you yourself described as little bites. What do you make of that?"

Pam had no comeback for that one. She wasn't even entirely convinced of her own theories for the skeletal state of the corpses. Instead of arguing further, she followed him into the briefing room.

The midnight sergeant was reading off his debriefing to the few patrollers already inside. It was Sergeant Calloway, an average-sized man with a country boy accent so thick, everyone joked he should be hauling hay down in Texas.

"Two speeding tickets over at Lacross Street, both around oh-two-hundred. Report of a missing dog at oh-three-hundred…"

Royce stood by the door. "Missing dog? They're calling at three in the morning for a missing dog?"

Calloway shrugged. "Homeowner works nights at a factory location. This was his day off…night off…whatever. Anyway, he always hangs outside with his German Shepherd, tossing a tennis ball around."

"Near the lake?" Royce said.

Calloway stared at him. "Yes… How the hell did you know that?"

Royce ignored the question. "Anything else bizarre occur last night? Any run-ins with the animal rights activists led by Alice Kirkman?"

"Thankfully, no, though I saw a few of them hanging out on a cove on the southwest end of the lake." Calloway didn't appreciate Royce's inquisitive stare. "They weren't doing anything wrong. It was public property and there's no curfew on it."

"They were just hanging out?"

"Yes. People do that in the summer. Even activists."

"Especially activists," Holman said. He nodded at Pam and Royce as he closed the door behind them. "I heard through the grapevine you guys had a little off-duty action last night."

The group of cops laughed, their immature minds reworking the meaning behind that statement.

"Yes, we responded to the…" he glared at the officers, "accident on Springdale. Speaking of which, have there been any new updates on that investigation?"

Calloway flipped through his notepad. "The female victim from the car has been sedated. I visited the hospital around oh-one-hundred to speak with the ER doctors. They haven't gotten anything coherent out of her. She simply screamed about a…" he pauses and snickered, not in the way of finding something funny, but in the way someone did when they read something weird. "Uh, about a fish."

"And the bodies?"

"Sergeant Dressel called the coroner last night. Dr. Majewski arrived early this morning, roughly oh-five-hundred. No details have been passed along just yet, but we're comparing dental records to the homeowner's records, as well as the driver's license found in the clothing on the beach. That's all I've got."

"Has the Chief shown up yet?"

"No. He's running a little late. Lieutenant Preston is still on vacation in Florida. So, until Larry show's up, you're the big boss today, Dashnaw. You wanna play detective, go nuts."

The clock struck seven and the midnighters didn't waste a moment lining up to punch out. They exited the station, leaving Royce with four officers in addition to Pam and Holman.

He eyed his crew for the day. At the front desk was John Yuki; his appearance a perfect blend of Caucasian and Japanese—much like his name. Royce was happy to see him, not because of his race, but his work ethic and trust in judgement. Same with Stacie Roncamp, who sat in the next row down. With short hair and a stern face, she gave the impression of being an active-duty soldier. She wasn't a veteran, but the next best thing, having worked in Detroit PD for six years before moving to Lorenzo.

On the other side of the room was Ryan Robert, whose name often drew Saving Private Ryan references, especially after the other officers learned his middle name was Patrick. He was partnered with Steven Buck, a pasty-white twenty-nine year old who saw less sunshine than the midnight crew. While he tended to remain indoors or in his vehicle unless called upon, he was far from unreliable. He amazed Royce two years ago when they had to chase a suspect down on foot after catching him in a drug deal. Considering Buck was always sitting or standing whenever Royce saw him, it was hard to view him as spry. That day, he took off like a cheetah, and tackled the drug dealer to the ground, even managing to pinpoint the exact location the guy tossed the heroin.

As usual, Royce had a small crew, but he could've been stuck with a worse one.

"It's five after. Still no Chief," Ryan said.

Royce walked to the hallway entrance. At the other end was the dispatch office. "Hey, Annette?" He waited until the dispatch supervisor peeked out from the other end of the hallway. "Has Larry called in?"

"Not yet. He's not here?"

"No."

"Odd. I'll let you know if he calls."

"Appreciate it."

The gargantuan Holman leaned against the windowsill with his thumbs tucked under his duty belt. "What's the matter, Dashnaw? You're looking a little on edge."

"Everything alright?" Stacie asked.

Royce looked at Pam, whose expression now showed mild signs of concern. "I'm not sure." He realized they were waiting to see if he had any special instructions. "I'd like for you to focus your patrols near the lake area."

"All of us?" John asked.

"Yes. All of you. In fact, I want one unit to be on standby near the resort. Keep an eye on the people swimming."

"Anything we're supposed to be looking for?" John asked. "Like… 'illegal' stroking in the water?" Royce didn't find his remark funny. "Sorry. You're telling us to watch the swimmers? I'm simply asking what for? We're not lifeguards."

"Plus the resort owners don't particularly like it when we're standing over their shoulders," Stacie said.

"Just—" Royce paused to lower his tone. They weren't being insubordinate. In fact, they were actually asking good questions. He just knew the answers would make him sound crazy. "It's possible we might have an animal of some kind loose in the lake."

Everyone perked up.

"An animal?" Buck said.

"Like a crocodile?" Holman said.

"I don't think that specifically, but be on the lookout as if there *is* one."

"Does this have anything to do with those bodies?" John said.

"Maybe. Be on the lookout. And... advise people to stay out of the water."

"Ohhhhhh, boy..." Stacie said. "It's your call, Sergeant, but you're asking for a lot of trouble from the entire town if we suggest that."

"Especially on this muggy day," Robert said. "Hell, I'm trying to resist the urge to dip in myself."

"Just be on the lookout, alright?" Royce looked at Pam again. "I'm going to the coroner's office. You coming?"

Pam opened the door for him. "Let's go."

The other officers remained silent as they watched the pair exit the station. After a few moments, they looked to Holman. Size radiated authority, even though he didn't hold any rank over them. That didn't change the fact that they naturally looked to him when in doubt.

"You heard the man. Our focus today is on the lake." His voice didn't convey conviction of Royce's suspicions, but he also knew the Sergeant wasn't normally this anxious. How could he blame him? Human skeletons in shallow water weren't exactly a common occurrence anywhere, let alone Lake Carlson.

"You think something's in the lake?" Robert said.

"I don't know. But Royce thinks so. Until the Chief gets here and overrides his orders, I'm going with his gut."

CHAPTER 18

No matter how many times Royce stepped into the coroner's office, he never got used to the smell. Lorenzo was a small town, but numbers didn't erase the fact that where there were people, there were fatalities. Usually it were people who died in their homes or in car crashes. Occasionally, there'd be a drowning, usually in a pool rather than the lake. Four years ago, Royce assisted the state police in searching for a missing person in the woods. The victim had committed suicide with a shotgun under the chin. That was the worst, both visually and in smell.

Dr. Eric Majewski fit the stereotypical mold of a coroner, completely unfazed by the grisly work environment. He only wore a mask when performing a procedure, and that was only due to protocol. Having seen plenty of bodies in his twenty-five years of practice, he was rarely puzzled.

Rarely.

Royce was curious if these skeletons would be the exception. This morning, he got his answer. He and Pam arrived at the office to find a flabbergasted coroner. The bodies, if they could be called bodies, were both on the cadaver tables. Lights were positioned over both of them. X-ray scans were placed on the wall to detect fractures and other irregularities.

"This is one for Sherlock Holmes," he said, standing between the cadavers. "When I first started, I almost didn't know where to begin."

"First time with a skeleton?" Pam asked.

"Not one that's this fresh," he replied. "Those I've dealt with in the past were from deaths from deep in the woods. Highly decomposed, as you can imagine. Not the case here. It's like all the meat and organs have been scraped off the bone—without causing any fractures."

Royce pointed at the missing arm near the body on the right. "Uh, no broken bones?"

"Oh, that. I can't say for sure, but I believe that happened either during the recovery of these bodies, or some other unrelated incident. It was removed from the socket by pure force. Yanked. Bottom line, whatever did that is likely unrelated to the overall condition of these bodies."

"You said you know for a fact they're—fresh?" Pam said.

"Dental records didn't take long, considering that we knew what to compare them with." He grabbed his notebook. "The one on your left is Lea Talley, and the other one is William Roper. Both twenty-seven years old. According to texts recovered on site, they were last alive at eight-thirty p.m. Wednesday night."

"So, we know for a fact they were alive less than forty-eight hours ago," Pam said. "How in the hell did they get like *this* in such a short time?!"

"Well, my first thought was that someone might've given them an acid bath, but there's no scarring on the bones. And the bits of flesh that remain aren't showing any signs of chemical exposure. What I did find, however…" the doctor grabbed a magnifying glass and held it to the fingers, "…was this."

Royce leaned in to look. The bone was covered in tiny little notches, as though a tiny drill had been jabbed into the hand repeatedly. These little craters were barely visible to the naked eye, not perfectly round in shape. Upon closer inspection, Royce almost thought of them as millimeter-long incisions than craters. There were no consistent patterns in their placement.

"I don't know what I'm looking at, Doctor."

"Tooth marks," Dr. Majewski said.

"Tooth marks?" Pam wasn't sure what was stranger, the mention of near-microscopic tooth marks on a two-day old skeleton, or the look on Royce's face. It was as though he was expecting this answer all along. "You said you think there's something in the lake. What exactly do you suspect it is?"

"I'm no biologist," Royce said. "To my high-school level of understanding, the only thing that can strip an animal like this are… piranhas."

"Piranhas? There's never been piranhas in Lake Carlson. Hell, not ever in North America, except in zoos and aquariums."

"While that's technically true, there's no denying this other oddity I found that fits with Sergeant Dashnaw's theory." Dr. Majewski led them to one of the lab tables. On a metal tray was a shiny white triangle, nearly half-a-centimeter in length. Not a perfect triangle, only one end was truly pointy, while the others were somewhat rounded. With the use of the magnifying glass, Royce was able to see that the edges were serrated. The blunt end with the rounded corners was somewhat jagged, as though broken off from a base. The pointy end was as sharp as a needle.

"It looks like bone," Royce said. He passed the glass to Pam. "That's not a tooth, is it?"

"I believe it is," Majewski said. With a pair of tweezers, he lifted the tooth by the wide end and walked to one of the victims. With the magnifying glass hovering over the damaged fingers, he inserted the tip into one of the craters. "Fits perfectly. Something bit right down to the bone. Shredded the meat away. Also, since you guys mentioned piranhas…" He went to his computer and pulled an image on the screen. It was a piranha's mouth, lined with pointy teeth. "I thought the same thing when doing my inspections. So, just to rule it out, I did some research. Turns out the teeth are nearly identical."

"Nearly? What's the difference?" Royce asked.

"Not much, other than the serrated edges. Piranha have serrated teeth, but not to this extent. These teeth make regular piranha teeth look like knitting needles, and that's saying something."

"A different species, perhaps?" Royce said.

"Maybe."

"Why haven't there been any other reported attacks up till now?" Pam said.

"Because everyone who encountered them ended up like this." Royce tilted his head toward the skeletons. "That woman last night, she was screaming about fish biting her. Midnight shift reported that dog missing after playing near the water…" Royce exhaled slowly and wiped a few beads of perspiration from his forehead. "And Monty Granger hasn't shown up this morning, and confirmed to his nephew that he was going on the lake."

"It still doesn't answer the question of how they got here in the first place," Pam said. "If there's a school of piranha-things in our lake, they had to have gotten here recently. So, there's only one explanation I can think of. They were *brought* here— within the last few days…"

"…Which is not too long after the activists showed up," Royce said. "God only knows how many of them there are. Doc, how many piranha are usually in a school?"

"According to what I've researched, there are usually thousands," Majewski said.

"Jesus! If those assholes brought those things, they would've needed a fuel tanker to deliver them."

"Or a dump truck," Pam said. They looked at each other.

That dump truck from yesterday. The wet bed, the mud in the tire treads,… the report of activists waiting in the cove.

Royce got on his radio. "Dispatch?"

"Go ahead."

"Has the Chief arrived yet?"

"Negative. He still won't answer his phone."

Again, Pam and Royce looked at each other.

"That's not normal," she said.

"Come on, let's go over there."

****

They had been to Larry Elwood's home three times before. Once was during the Fourth of July two years ago. Even though Royce and Pam were on duty that day, the Chief told them to swing by for a hot dog and burger. It was the start of what became a tradition. Larry invited his fellow officers to stop by for a cookout if they were interested. The last two times, Royce brought Ellen along. Might as well go, since they didn't have family around here.

The last time was only three weeks ago. Ellen and some of the other visitors took advantage of Larry's large private beach. Before dipping into the water, she made sure it was okay to throw a few casts off the dock. Larry, being the sweetheart man he was, enthusiastically said yes.

All these memories flashed in Royce's mind when he pulled into the driveway. Both Larry's vehicle and Mrs. Elwood's was present. Royce parked the Interceptor and stepped out.

"Hey, Chief?" After getting no reply, he approached the door. It was already open. The lights were on inside. "Larry? It's Dashnaw? You home? Hello!"

"Oh, God! ROYCE! GET OUT HERE!"

Royce looked through the back window and spotted Pam near the shoreline. He dashed outside, then saw the pale white face of Larry Elder staring at the sky. The sand around him had turned red from absorbing his blood. He was on his back, jaw slack, legs in the water—specifically, the bones of his legs.

All the flesh below the thighs was stripped away, the feet nothing but white, clawed appendages.

CHAPTER 19

"Whoa!" The blast of air conditioning was a welcome one for Ellen as she stepped out of the muggy summer air into the house.

"Too hot?" Jane said. She was applying makeup to her face.

"Too sticky. There's no breeze," she said. She pointed at the pad in Jane's hand. "I wouldn't bother if I were you. You're gonna start sweating, and all that work will go to waste."

Jacob turned away from the television. "Don't tell her that! Let her embarrass herself in front of the jerk."

"Hey!" Jane tossed a couch pillow at him. "Ken is not a jerk. Be nice! He's letting us all aboard his pontoon boat today."

"Greeeeat," Jacob muttered.

"Bud, you can't waste the summer in front of the television. Today, we're going out. We'll have fun, and maybe get a little exercise in the process. It's a miracle you're not overweight."

"Same with you, considering how much you'll probably drink while we're on the boat."

"I'm gonna keep it reasonable," Jane said. "I'm still babysitting—"

"Ah-ah!" Ellen pointed a finger. "*Supervising*!"

"Sorry. I'm still 'supervising' Sergeant Dashnaw's daughter. Like in the police force, I have to keep a mostly level head."

"I think I know where your head's at," Jacob said.

"Jeez, Jake!" She slapped him on the shoulder. "Gosh, nine-year olds these days! Must be the over-exposure to the internet. I'll have to let Mom and Dad know when they get back in town."

"Let me stay home, and I won't tell them about you drinking beer. Don't forget, you're only nineteen and not legal yet."

"Yeah, punk? Don't forget that Mom and Dad were doing the exact same shit when they were only eighteen. And they *admit* it. They won't care as long as I don't get blackout drunk."

"Why is it so important that I go?" He nodded toward Ellen. "You have your outdoor partner right there. You can do all the boring fishing and swimming with her. She can impress you with all the fish she can lose."

Ellen marched into the living room. "Oh, is THAT how it is?"

Jacob pretended to laugh. "Yep." He turned away, sensing the blood rushing to his face. He wasn't the aggressive sort and already he regretted expanding his attack to the feisty Ellen Dashnaw.

"At least I've got a nice tan. Also, I'm not rotting my brain with watching the woke crowd ruin the MCU. Looks like you're watching the *Loki* show. Yeah, gotta love the BS they shoved into that. Who needs good storytelling, am I right?"

"I like it," Jacob said.

"Of course you do. I wasn't debating your lack of good taste. You like bad cinema, hence you're eager to see Thor: Love and Thunder."

"Whatever. Go lose another fish."

"I would, except they're not biting at all. They probably could hear the crap on the TV, realized what it was, and had to get as far away as possible."

"Alright, you two," Jane said. "It's almost ten. Ken's gonna get here any minute." She looked at her makeup in the mirror. "Damn it. Ellen, you're right as usual. Makeup wasn't a good idea for today. I'm gonna get it off, then get in my bathing suit."

"Someone as pretty as you doesn't need makeup anyway," Ellen said.

"Aww! You're so sweet! No wonder I love having you here!" Jane walked into the bathroom with a glowing smile on her face.

Meanwhile, Jacob remained on the couch, cross-armed. "Kiss-butt."

Ellen didn't take the bait, despite the temptation. She thought of her dad's words. *"Let him have his opinion, Ellen. Just because we think it's crap doesn't mean we need to force that opinion onto everyone else. Let people like what they like. And be patient with him. He might come around to fishing if you don't intimidate him."*

She replayed that statement in her mind repeatedly. If there was anyone on earth she respected, it was her father. The last thing she ever wanted to do was disappoint him. Never once did he waste a word of pity on himself in the nine-plus years he raised her. She was aware of the ambitions he gave up to spend more time with her and provide for a better life. She didn't understand the desire to become a detective—just as Jacob didn't understand her passion for the outdoors. That was the thing she needed to understand about people in general: they had different beliefs and desires.

"Listen, you're stuck on this trip whether you like it or not…"

"Yeah-yeah, rub it in," he said.

"No, that's not what I'm doing. Honest." She waited until he looked over at her. "I'm just saying you might as well make the best of it. You might even have fun if you get out of the mental rut you're in. You seriously like sitting inside all day watching TV?"

"And playing video games."

"Not much better."

"To each their own."

"Again, not what I meant. Stop being so defensive. I like movies and games too—maybe different ones, but as you said: to each their own. My point is, you might want to try different hobbies."

"Like fishing?"

Ellen nodded. "Like fishing."

"Forget it."

"Tell you what, Jacob. Since we're gonna be on the boat anyway, how 'bout I properly teach you how to throw a cast. Once you experience the thrill of hooking something and bringing it in, you might have a different outlook on fishing." She waited for a response. Jacob sat quietly, eyeing the television. His demeanor remained that of someone dreading an upcoming event. Ellen sighed. "What if we worked out a deal?"

"A deal?"

"Yes. A deal." She clenched, hating herself for what she was about to suggest. *Damn you, Dad. Sometimes I hate being a good person.* "You put an honest effort into fishing today, and I'll let you introduce me to one of the shows you watch. We'd have to start from the first episode, because I haven't been keeping up with that crap—with those shows—at all."

He took a moment to consider it. "You gonna complain the whole time? Make fun of it for all the stuff you think is in it?"

"As long as you don't do the same for fishing."

Jacob nodded then extended his hand. "Deal." Like business associates, they shook on it.

Three high-pitched beeps drew their attention to the backyard. A boat horn.

"Ah! He's here already!" Jane said. "Stall him. I gotta get this makeup off!"

Ellen and Jacob shared a laugh. If there was anything they saw eye-to-eye on, it was the amusement of Jane trying to impress this Ken fella.

"Come on. Let's go outside," Ellen said.

They turned off the television, collected Ellen's remaining gear, and walked out the back door. The pontoon boat was docked, waiting for the rest of the party to come aboard.

Ellen stopped in her tracks. "Whoa!"

When she heard pontoon boat, she was expecting a twenty-footer, maybe a twenty-four footer at most. Either Ken Lewis had a really good job or he had a wealthy inheritance, because this was a nice luxury boat. It had two decks, a main deck that stretched for twenty-four feet and a top deck roughly two-thirds the length of the main. On the rear was a slide that went from the end of the top deck to the portside. There were five people currently aboard: three college age guys and two women.

A dark haired fella waved at them from the helm. He wore black sunglasses and an open Hawaiian shirt, which showcased his abs. The way he smiled reminded Ellen of a celebrity posing for photos on the red carpet.

"Hey, kids! Come on aboard."

Ellen chuckled, then continued to the dock. "He seems friendly enough."

"I've met him a couple of times. He's not bad," Jacob said. "Maybe a little eccentric."

"Like Tony Stark?"

Jacob laughed. "He doesn't pull it off as well as Downey."

"Is that Iron Man talk I'm hearing?" Ken said.

"Sort of," Jacob said as he stepped aboard. "Hi, Ken. Good to see you again."

"No problem, bud!" Ken removed his sunglasses and looked at Ellen. "Who's this? You brought a girlfriend?! Well done, man!"

Jacob turned beet red. "Uh, no! Ew! She's not my girlfriend."

"No? Dang, bud. Rub it in her face, why don't you?"

"Ha! I'm not offended. It's a mutual feeling." She extended her hand. "I'm Ellen. Thanks for letting me fish on your boat."

Ken shook her hand. "No problem, little missy—Ellen! Just do me a favor and catch me a nice perch. Can't seem to catch one bigger than two inches in this lake."

"You fish?"

"Damn right! How can one live on a lake like this and not fish?"

Ellen nodded. "Good point. Gosh! I'm enjoying the heck out of this trip already. No wonder Jane likes you."

Jacob snorted as Ken perked up.

"Say again?"

"Uh…" Nothing was worse than the awkward silence from revealing information that wasn't hers to reveal. *Shit. I thought he knew. Wasn't he the one who personally invited her yesterday?* Ellen laughed nervously, the way people did when stalling. *Too late now. Might as well commit.* She kept her voice down to not be overheard by the four others aboard. "Yeah— she, like, *really* likes you."

A gorgeous blonde came down the steps and came up behind Ken. Both hands touched his shoulders. "Hey, babe…" She looked down at the kids. "Hi, Jacob!"

He waved. "Hi, Grace."

"Where's Jane?"

"She's… getting ready. Should be out any second." He looked at the main deck. "Hey, Ken, where would you prefer Ellen cast her lines? Probably the back deck?"

"Aft deck," Ellen corrected him.

"Whatever."

Ken laughed. "Yeah, that'll be best. Just watch out for the slide. As long as you keep to the starboard side, you should be good. Got plenty of water and sodas in the cooler. Basically anything not in a glass bottle is kid friendly."

"Awesome." Jacob tugged on Ellen's arm. "Let's get set up. If Jane takes too long, one of us can run back up and get her."

They walked the length of the boat, passing under the canopy provided by the top deck. At the aft section, Ellen finally leaned in towards Jacob.

"What was all that about?"

"Grace is Jane's best friend."

Ellen smirked. "Oh no." It was simultaneously amusing and awkward. "Maybe I'm mistaken. Wasn't Ken the one who called her yesterday?"

"That was Grace."

"Ohhhhhh! Dang!"

The back door opened up. Ellen came out, wearing nothing but a long shirt over her bikini. Pink sunglasses covered her face. They did not cover the shock of her witnessing Ken and Grace's brief make-out session. They broke apart after Jane arrived on the dock.

"There she is!" Ken said.

"Hey, girl!" Grace said. "What took you so long?"

"Uh… just had to…" she pointed at the two of them. "When did *this* happen?!"

"A few days ago!" Grace said. "We ran into each other at the bar. It turned into a thing, if you know what I mean. After that, we thought we'd keep seeing each other."

Jane smiled.

Jacob covered his mouth and turned away, trying not to laugh. It was the fakest smile he had ever seen. Ellen was caught somewhere between amusement and pity. Jane was trying too hard not to look disappointed. To everyone else aboard, it probably worked.

Except for Ken, thanks to her blunder. Ellen wasn't old enough yet to understand the joys of physical relationships and the excitement of having someone interested in them. She did know a giddy person when she saw one, and Ken all of a sudden looked like a man on top of the world.

Is it really that exciting to have two girls fawning over you?

She sighed. "I'll never understand this stuff."

Ken started the engine and backed the boat away from the dock. "Alright! Who's looking for a nice day in the sun?!"

"A breeze would be nice," someone up top said.

"Oh, hey kids. Not sure if you've been introduced to the rest of the gang…" Ken said. The remaining three friends peered down at them from the guard rail.

"Hey!" a dude with curly blonde hair said. "I'm Skip! Glad you're able to join us. Catch me a three-foot pike, and I'll pay you ten bucks."

Ellen's eyes lit up. "Deal! Add another ten on top of that, I'll fillet it for you. Including the Y-bones. My dad taught me how to get them out without losing too much meat."

"Kid, I'll make it fifteen if you can do that!" Skip said. "Love pike, but I can never get the damn bones out."

"Consider it done." She looked at the remaining guy and gal. They were shoulder-to-shoulder. Definitely a couple. The guy seemed less enthusiastic to see them aboard the boat. The girl seemed pretty nice. She was a brunette, tattoos lining her shoulders, arms, and sides, and one of a star on her neck. Either she was a tattoo addict or she was an artist.

"Hi, kids. I'm Bailey. This is Dustin." She put her arm around her boyfriend's neck, getting a hint of a grin from him.

"Hi."

It was forced enthusiasm if Ellen ever heard it. *Oh well. He'll probably stay up there during the entire ride anyway.*

Ken pointed the bow to the lake interior. "Alright, let's get that breeze you want so bad, Skip!" He gunned the throttle. Hair flapped in the wind as the boat sped across the lake.

The whole group, even Jake, started whooping. Everyone except Jane, who sat on one of the seats with a sullen look on her face. That glare turned toward Grace, then to the house.

Ellen watched Jacob strut past her, grab a soda from the cooler, and return to the aft deck. It was the most active she'd ever seen him and the least she'd ever seen Jane.

Dang! Talk about switching prospects. Now Jacob is eager to be on the boat while Jane would rather be anywhere but here.

Ellen felt bad, but still, she couldn't help but find it a little amusing. Too late now.

"You alright?" Ellen said.

Jane nodded. "Oh yeah. Just—a little tired. Too much excitement."

"Too much disappointment," Jacob whispered.

"Say again?" Jane said.

"Nothing."

"Those odds of seeing that *Thor* movie just went down further."

"Can't be worse than your odds of hooking up with Ken," Jacob replied under his breath.

"Be nice," Ellen said.

"Where should we head to?" Ken called out.

"How 'bout that cove on the west side?" Bailey said. "That's a good spot. Might wanna hurry before someone else takes up that spot."

"Okay. Any objections?!"

Jacob snickered again. "I'm sure Jane does, but not about the boat tour." Ellen elbowed him.

After the rest of the group endorsed the decision, Ken pointed the pontoon boat west. "Alright. West cove, here we come!"

CHAPTER 19

"My God."

Royce sat on the hood of his Interceptor when he heard Officer Holman. He was walking up from the shoreline with a hand on his stomach. He clearly felt the same way as Royce did in that moment.

Several yards behind him at the shoreline, an ambulance crew was zipping Larry in a black bag.

"You gonna be alright?"

Holman didn't answer right away, which answered the question in its own way. He wasn't easily squeamish, but everyone had their breaking point.

"I've seen bodies," he said. "Shit, I've seen really screwed-up bodies. Each time, I was able to go on my lunch break and eat a sandwich without thinking about it. But this—this—"

"It's different when it's someone you know," Royce said.

"Yes. Exactly."

The passenger door opened. Pam stepped out, looking as pale as Holman. What they described was exactly what she felt. She had been on numerous recovery missions when in the service. When she saw the remains of people she didn't know, it was disturbing, but she could shield her emotions. When it was someone she knew, that was when she knew she wanted out.

"I think I'm feeling a little extra confident to join the State Police," she said. Royce nodded. It was going to be hard coming to work every day after seeing Larry like this.

Two more cop cars pulled up, both coming to a screeching stop near the Interceptor. John Yuki and Stacie Roncamp stepped out of one, and Ryan Robert and Steven Buck hopped out of the other. All four looked at the ambulance before turning to their Sergeant.

John removed his cap. "Is he...?"

Royce nodded.

Stacie kicked the tire. "What are we going to do? I mean... how can this happen? I don't understand."

"There's something in this lake," Royce said.

"I don't get it," Ryan said. "How can something just appear out of nowhere?"

"They were dumped here," Royce said.

"What's 'they'? And who's the 'who'?" Steven said. He was already sitting back in the passenger seat. Even a tragic moment such as this didn't lessen the need for air conditioning.

Royce looked at Pam, quietly questioning whether to inform them of their suspicion. It was still technically unproven, though seeing the injuries to Larry's legs practically confirmed it. She nodded.

He stood up and faced the officers. "What I'm about to tell you may seem strange, but it fits the scenario at hand. We have reason to suspect there are carnivorous fish in this lake. Piranhas, or at least something similar to them."

"Piranhas?" Steven said, looking at Royce like a crazy man.

Holman raised a hand to silence him. "I find it hard to believe myself, but I saw what happened to Larry—and his wife!"

"Wait, his *wife's* dead too?!" Stacie said.

"Yes. They found her by the dock. At least, they're pretty sure it's her." Holman looked at Royce. "She's just like those bodies you found last night."

"Something's in this lake stripping people to the bone," Pam said. "The coroner found a tooth lodged in one of the bodies. He suspects the same thing we do."

"But how?" Stacie said.

"Doesn't matter right now," Royce said. "We need to clear the lake this very moment. Go to the resorts and demand they bring everybody in."

"We'll try, but it's a public lake," Ryan said. "We don't have the authority to arrest people for being in the water."

"Then tell them what's going on. I'm gonna speak to the mayor," Royce said.

"I agree with you, Royce, but I'm afraid the public won't believe us," Stacie said.

"She's got a point," Holman said. "We need to know how many are in here and where they all are. It's a big ass lake for us to police."

"How the hell can we figure that out?" Steven said. "Not like we have anyone we can beat the truth out of."

Royce looked at Pam. "Yes, actually there might be." She looked back at him, nodded after understanding what he was thinking, then got in the Interceptor. He got in and started it up.

"Get your asses to the resorts. That's where the most people will be. Do whatever you can to get everybody out of the water."

"Where are you headed?" Holman said.

"To the jail."

CHAPTER 20

"Alright! Here we are!" Ken Lewis brought the boat to a stop and secured the forward anchor. "Someone willing to get the aft anchor for me?"

"I got it," Ellen said. She picked up the rope tied to the piece of concrete and lifted. "Holy crap!" Even only falling from an inch of height, it hit the deck with a loud *thump*. "What's this made out of? A skyscraper?"

"What's the matter? Too weak?" Jacob said.

"Oh, ha-ha."

"Comes with being a girl, right?" Jacob said.

Ellen stepped back and waved a hand at him. "Alright, mister wannabe macho. *You* try lifting it."

"No problem." Jacob knelt down and grabbed the anchor by the stem. That overconfident grin turned into a pitiful grimace. He got the anchor up a few inches before dropping it.

"You guys putting a dent in my boat back there?" Ken said, sparking laughter from Grace.

"Wouldn't be an issue if you didn't have a fragment of a brown dwarf down here," Jacob said.

"Brown dwarf?" Ellen looked at the anchor and laughed. "Uh, is it a middle eastern dwarf? What part of him is here? And are they overweight?"

"First of all, that's racist as heck," Jacob said.

"Oh, please."

"Second of all, no, I'm not talking about a little person. I'm talking about a dead star that has compressed all its matter. Super compressed. Like a chunk this big would weigh a thousand pounds."

"First of all, you're referring to a fragment of a neutron star, not a brown dwarf," Ellen said.

"No…"

"Dude, a brown dwarf is like a gas planet. It doesn't even have the mass to fuse. A neutron star is the collapsed core of a supergiant."

Jacob threw his hands in the air and turned away. "My God! You're such a nerd!"

"Hey, at least I read and don't get my science from b-grade science fiction movies!"

"Don't knock sci-fi movies," Skip said. He came down the steps and grabbed the anchor for the kids. "Oh, LORD! You kids weren't lying. This thing does feel like super-compressed matter." He tossed it into the water, where it generated a huge splash.

"Damn, hope the concussion didn't kill anything down there," Ellen said.

"No kidding. I'm eager for you to catch me a pike," Skip said. "Twenty-five bucks is waiting with your name on it, kiddo."

"Hey! What if I catch it?" Jacob said.

Ellen burst into a fit of laughter. "We're more likely to find a brown dwarf that can fuse itself into compressed matter than see you catch a pike."

"She's a feisty one," Skip said. "To answer your question, Jacob, if you catch a big pike, you'll get the money."

"Just the ten bucks!" Ellen said. "He has to fillet it for the other fifteen, which he doesn't know how to do. I, on the other hand…"

Jacob's expression soured. Despite his belief that boys and girls were equal, it still felt embarrassing to have inferior skills at anything to a girl. He tried to fight the feeling, but it wouldn't go away.

There was only one thing to do: make the best of it. What better way was there than to continue their sniping session.

"Yeah, she might as well fillet my catch. She'll need something to clean, after all. If her fishing luck is anything like yesterday…"

"Oh, shut up."

The sound of laughter drew their attention to the top deck. Dustin was looking out at the water with a snide grin on his face.

"I like to 'fish' myself. Often get quite the catch on my rod…"

Bailey laughed and slapped his arm. "Stop."

"Jesus, dude!" Skip said, covering Ellen's ears. "There's KIDS on this boat, you creep."

"I don't get it," Jacob said.

"Good! Keep it that way." Skip uncovered Ellen's ears.

"Don't worry. It's nothing that'll harm my pretty little soul." She looked past him at Jane, who was still sulking in the shade. "Jane, have you met Skip?"

"Jane and Skip. That has a nice ring to it," he said.

She stood up and smiled. "Sorry, Skip. I forgot to say hi."

"Whatcha doing these days?"

"Waiting for college to start again, I guess." She glanced back at Ken, unable to see him, as Grace had her arms around his neck. New relationship excitement was a powerful drug. So powerful, they didn't care if there were other people or kids around.

Skip was wincing as well. "You know, they invented rooms for that stuff."

Grace finally broke her lips away from Ken's. "Whoops. Sorry, but not *that* sorry."

"Sure you're not," Jane muttered.

"What's the matter, sweetie?!" Grace said. "You almost look like you don't want to be here. When we talked yesterday, you seemed excited."

"I guess…" Jane tried to think of an excuse. "Maybe I woke up on the wrong side of the bed this morning."

"Oh, I'm sorry. Though, I'm glad to know you're not sick or anything."

"Yeah—that would've gotten me off this boat for sure…"

"Good thing! Because I'm really enjoying this!" Jacob called out.

"I would be too, if I was up there with you!" yelled somebody out in the water.

Skip moved over to the guardrail and saw two people kayaking past them to the north. A man and a woman whom they knew from high school.

"Mitch and Tory! What's up!"

"Nothing much," Mitch said. "Taking advantage of the day is all."

"Looks like you guys have the same idea!" Tory said.

Ken climbed to the top deck and waved at the high school friends. "Damn right we do! Wanna join us?"

"We have beer," Bailey said.

Mitch looked over his shoulder at his girlfriend. "What do you think, babe?"

"Let's finish off our little exercise routine. Then we'll circle back and join you, if it's not a bother."

"Not at all!" Ken said. "You heading back to Mitch's place?"

"Yep!" Mitch said.

"You ever going to get those cables fixed? Every time I see those things dangling over the water, I feel like I'm gonna get turned into Electro."

"I've called the cable company. They're sending someone over on Monday."

"Thank God."

"Hey, not my fault the cable's drooping lower than Dustin after a cold shower."

"Hey!"

Mitch laughed. "The assholes didn't align it right when they initially installed it," Mitch said. "I'll tell you more about it when we get back."

"Yeah. Let's finish our lap around the lake," Tory said. "This is my exercise for the day. I have to earn that beer in your cooler."

"Looking at them arms, I'd say you've earned them," Ken said. Tory looked at herself and smiled. A compliment from Ken Lewis was like a compliment from Brad Pitt.

"We'll be back in an hour or so."

"See ya." Ken turned and saw Grace glaring at him. "Oh, relax, hot stuff. I'm just bantering."

She crossed her arms. "You mean it?"

"Sure do!" He kissed her lips. "Come on! Let's have some fun!" He hopped onto the slide, started the pump to get water flowing over it, then zipped down into the water, disappearing under an enormous splash.

"Oh, THANKS!" Ellen said. "Scare away the fish, why don't you?"

Ken emerged, whooping as though he just won a gold medal. "This water feels GREAT, ya'll!"

"Fantastic. Might wanna come in, unless you want one of these kids to hook ya," Skip said.

Ken drifted for a few moments, then swam for the deck. "Fine. I'd rather eat first anyway. I know that goes against the rules of swimming, but screw it. I'm starving. Dustin, fire up that grill!" He pulled himself up onto the deck. "Who's up for some brunch?!"

A splattering of water behind him made Ken leap forward.

"Whoa!" Skip said. He only saw the tailfin and a brief glimpse of the fish's overall shape before it darted out of sight. Laughter swept the boat. "You see that?"

"Felt it on my shoe," Ken said. He caught his breath. "That totally didn't scare the shit out of me."

"Yeah, suuuure," Skip said. He continued watching the water, hoping to catch another glimpse of the fish. "Ellen, did you see it?"

"No."

"Darn. I don't know what kind of fish it was, exactly. Almost looked like a panfish, but damn, it was freaking big!" His eyes widened, as did his smile. "You catch that, and I'll pay you thirty bucks!"

"Deal!"

With the jitterbug hooked up, Ellen cast the line. It splashed down seventy feet out. As she reeled it in, she glanced at Jacob, who was staring at his rod with a bemused look on his face. After a sigh, she asked, "You need help?"

He nodded.

Ellen brought her lure in, then reached into the tacklebox. "Now, pay attention this time…"

****

"Thousand-one, thousand-two…" Mitch felt he had done five times as many strokes. According to his beloved girlfriend, from the dock at the house, across the lake, all the way around the south end of the lake would make a thousand paddles. "Why don't we just double-back and join the others?"

"Not until I've burned enough calories for the day."

"Oh, jeez. Like you won't burn calories swimming around that pontoon."

"It's about discipline, Mitch," she said. "I've set a goal for certain physical activities every day. Today, I've set a goal for ninety minutes of kayaking. Tomorrow, it'll be a treadmill walk."

"I can think of certain physical activities that'll help burn calories."

"I'm sure you can."

He glanced back at her and winked. To his surprise, she winked back. Now his head was completely in the gutter. Tory had sparked hope that another joyride could take place.

Being a twenty-year old male, Mitch hoped that particular joyride would come sooner rather than later.

Three-hundred strokes later, they were approaching his house. Of course, it wasn't *his* lake house, but his parents' who allowed him to use it whenever he pleased.

"You know... the rule is you have to get a certain amount of time in. You didn't say it had to be in one long sitting."

"What are you suggesting?" Tory asked in a tone indicating suspicion.

"Well, we could go inside. Get some 'rest', maybe?"

"Uh-huh. For my well-being, right?"

"Absolutely! I wouldn't consider such a thing for *any* other reason. Not at all!"

Tory laughed, then doubled her pace. She brought her kayak alongside his, then leaned over for a kiss. Taking the bait, Mitch leaned over to connect his lips with hers.

She allowed the makeout to continue for a few seconds before grabbing him by the shoulder and pulling him into the water.

"Hey!" Whatever Mitch was going to follow that up with was drowned out by the water. Tory laughed as she watched her boyfriend flounder. He surfaced, spat water, then glared at her. "I'm gonna remember this next time you expect me to join in on these little exercises!"

"Aw, what's the matter? Don't like getting wet?"

"Not the way I was planning." He swam over to her kayak.

Tory waved a finger. "Don't even think about tipping me over, mister!"

"Oh, so it's okay when YOU do it?"

"You're catching on."

"Yeah? Well, catch on to this: You owe me now." He clicked his tongue. "My feelings are hurt. My girl tossed me overboard. Only *one* way I can possibly feel better."

"One way, huh?"

"Yep."

"Man, if your feelings are hurt now, imagine how they'll be after I do THIS." Tory leaned over and pushed Mitch down with all her might. Playing along with the act, Mitch sank and thrashed his arms out as though drowning.

Tory laughed, watching him now reach up toward her, seemingly pleading to be rescued.

"Oh, gee. Quit being such a baby and swim back up, mister. I know you can swim."

Mitch thrashed erratically, now with both hands reaching toward her. She watched the fingers grasp at nothing before being obscured by some fog which seemed to accumulate under the water out of nowhere. At first, she thought it was soot being stirred up by his feet.

When the cloud reached the surface, she noticed its blood red color.

Tory plunged her hand into the water. "Mitch! Grab my—" She reared her head back and screamed.

Razor teeth sank into her flesh. She could feel her skin ripping at the palm, forearm, elbow, and all five fingers. Squealing, Tory yanked her arm from the water and looked at it. It was as if everything below the elbow had been put through a garbage disposal. Slabs of skin hung from the limb, blood free-flowing in large red rivers onto her lap.

A series of *thumps* struck her kayak, rocking her back and forth.

Tory looked down, seeing nothing but red water gradually dispersing. From that horrible red cloud came massive projectiles. In the split-second they were airborne, she saw triangular teeth and waving fins.

The fish landed in her lap and immediately began ripping into her thighs. Tory threw herself to the right, her scream cut short by the lake after her kayak tipped over. Sinking gradually, she spun like a top, throwing her arms without rhyme or reason.

A hundred bodies, the size of a frying pan, darted in at once. Mouths the size of silver dollars tore into her flesh. Jaws opened and shut at a speed equivalent to a hummingbird flapping its wings.

They left nothing untouched. Several of the attackers went for her face, biting at her ears, nose, and lips. Others pried their heads into the openings created in the body for a taste of the interior organs.

The school jampacked against the prey as it fell against the weeds, each determined to get a mouthful of flesh before all was stripped from the bones.

CHAPTER 21

It took Royce several infuriating minutes to convince the supervising Correctional Lieutenant to let him speak with Curt Lin. Over and over again, the buffoon repeated his need to speak with the Chief before authorizing an interrogation. When informed of Larry Elwood's death, the Lieutenant thought it was a bad joke until he confirmed it with dispatch. With the Patrol Lieutenant out of town and no Deputy Chief, Royce Dashnaw had operational authority that superseded the Lieutenant's rank.

Royce leaned against the wall, watching the door as he heard approaching footsteps. Pam was already cracking her knuckles.

"We're not going by the book on this one, right?"

"Hell no," he said. "We'll break his fingers, elbows, legs, collar bones, and anything in-between until he cracks. He and those psycho friends of his put something in the lake and it killed Larry. We don't have time for 'by the book'."

The door opened and Curt Lin stumbled inside, stopping briefly to sneer at the two officers. The correctional officer escorting him stood in the corner, as was standard for them to do in meetings involving inmates.

"You can wait outside," Pam said. The correctional officer looked at Royce, who nodded.

"Get a cup of coffee."

Uneasy, but also unable to do anything about it, the officer stepped out and closed the door behind him.

Curt crossed his arms. "Miss me already? Don't worry. We'll be seeing more of each other after the judge addresses the complaint I filed against you. Excessive force. I hear the courts look down on cops who use that—OW!" Pam twisted his arm and put his head against the table.

"How's *this* for a violation?"

"What are you doing?! This is a violation of my rights!"

"For the love of God, shut the hell up with that shit," Royce said. He grabbed Curt by the hair and pulled his head off the table.

"You're totally losing your badge over this!"

"Maybe. Maybe not. The difference is, I don't really give a shit at the moment," Royce said. "Especially after what I discovered in the lake."

"And what's that? Someone drop a tacklebox? Litter the water with lead?"

"That'd make you mad, wouldn't it?"

"Not you, though. Murderer," Curt said.

"Ah, yes. The white-knighting for all of God's creatures begins," Royce said. "Where'd you guys get the dump truck?"

"I don't know what you're talking about." Pam twisted his wrist, making him yelp. "I don't know anything about a dump truck." She twisted again. "Fuck the hell out of you! Freaking right wing nut jobs!"

"Actually, we're taking more of a Soviet style approach. Hence, we're completely disregarding your humanity and your rights," Pam said. "It's the kind of world you advocate for. Too bad you don't know a thing about it. Anyway, about the dump truck—" She twisted again, bending the joint to the verge of snapping.

"One of our people rented it from some construction company," he finally squeaked.

"'One of our people?' You obviously mean Alice Kirkman," Pam said.

"Fine. Whatever."

"We know she's been dumping something in the lake. What is it, exactly?"

"Don't know what you're talking about. We're using the truck to transport wreckage from a friend's old property near the woods at Bayville Street. We're getting together in a couple of weeks to start construction on a new two-story residence. We're a tight-knit group who help each other out."

Royce shook his head. "The problem with guys like you, Curt, is that you're *way* too emotional, and don't use any of your brain cells. First of all, why would you lie about a dump truck if you weren't doing something stupid and illegal with it? You expect me to believe some bullshit about tearing down and building a new property? Dude, you're so wiry, I doubt you could even lift a shovel. And I highly doubt you guys would dare ruin the rainforests by buying lumber to build a new house."

"Plus, your friends didn't seem so tight-knit yesterday at the grocery store. They abandoned Alice in a heartbeat when they realized they couldn't bully us into letting them disrupt society," Pam said.

"You're the fascists," Curt said through gritted teeth.

"Yeah, I know. Problem with this generation is that you've used those words so much, and so incorrectly, that they've lost all meaning," Royce said. "Now, let's quit with the antics and tell us what we want to know." He nodded at Pam, who pulled Curt from the table and pinned him against the wall.

"Whatever you put in the lake killed our police chief. It killed several more people. What the hell did you put in the water?"

"I'm not telling you shit."

"Alright." Royce pulled some pliers from his pocket. Curt's eyebrows rose to his hairline. "You think I was kidding? We don't have time to do things the 'right way'. I'm tired of this shit. So, I hear it's really painful when you rip the fingernails out like so." He clamped the pliers to Curt's forefinger.

"Okay! Stop! Stop!"

Royce grabbed him by the ear. "Then talk!"

Pam yanked the activist away from the wall and threw him into a chair. He teetered on the back legs a moment before settling. He looked up at the officers, seeing in their eyes that they weren't bluffing. Worse, nobody was coming inside to save him. He heard somewhere that when cops lost one of their own, they were prone to get more aggressive than inner city gangs. Today, he learned the extent they were willing to go. As far as the Sergeant was concerned, he already accepted any consequences of his actions, even if they'd land him in jail.

Nobody could save Curt Lin. It wasn't about recording a confession for the court records. It wasn't about boosting their careers by putting him in prison. This was personal. His group had messed with the wrong police department.

"Alice was using her wealth from her acting career and lawsuits to fund some geneticist in a small town about two hours away. I don't know the specifics. She just said it was biological research meant to help fish in the lake escape from captivity."

"Escape from captivity?" Royce said.

"She wanted them to be able to bite through fishhooks and nets. To be able to free themselves when caught." He paused and saw the way the cops were staring at him. "I know it sounds crazy, but it's the truth. Alice has a passion for wildlife. She hates hunters. She hates fishermen. Basically, everyone who eats meat."

"Yeah, we figured that part," Pam said.

"You're telling us she had a scientist genetically engineer FISH?!" Royce said.

"Yes."

"How? What species did she mix?"

"I don't know that much. She just said she was populating the lake with new fish that would save the rest of the ecosystem from humans. I don't see what's wrong with that. Murder is murder."

"Damn right it is." Royce grabbed him by the chin. "You guys *murdered* Larry and his wife. You murdered two people at a residence, nearly killed a third over there. Might've killed several other people by now."

Curt was quivering in his seat. "I—I wasn't planning to *kill* anyone. I thought—"

"Don't play innocent," Royce said. "You guys were probably going to skip town in the next day or two. I guarantee you'd read about the killings online and not bat an eye. You're only playing innocent because you're in this jail. Get used to it, because no amount of police brutality will wipe the blood off your hands."

"No! I'm serious!" Curt said. He forced Royce's hand away, then stood up, knocking the chair over as he backed against the wall. "The fish weren't supposed to *kill* anyone. We were just trying to stop people from fishing."

"Stop fishing? Are you guys out of your mind?"

"Alright, *I* thought it was a little overboard. But Alice is in charge! She's got the money to fund this stuff. How was I supposed to say no?"

"By saying no," Pam said. "Royce, we need to evacuate the lake."

"How many are there?" he asked Curt.

"I don't know. Seriously! I don't know. I don't understand all this science stuff. I don't understand how she bred the fish. Only Alice knows."

"Where's the research facility?"

"Some town called Redleaf," Curt said.

"Have you been there yourself?"

"I've gone with Alice a couple of times. Yes."

"So, the geneticist will know who you are. Correct?" After Curt nodded, Royce looked at Pam. "You interested in a helicopter ride?"

"Let's go. Gotta make this quick, though."

"Hence we're taking a chopper instead of a car. We need more information. Holman and the others will evacuate the lake. I'll call the mayor while we're on our way out," Royce said. He grabbed Curt by the shoulder and pulled him toward the door. "Hope you don't get airsick."

"I do, actually."

"That's a shame, because you're coming with us." They rushed out the door, nodding to the correctional officer as they passed him. "We're done."

"Wait? You're taking him?" the CO said.

"Yes. It's important," Pam said.

"You can't just take inmates out of the jail. It requires specific authorization."

"Too bad. This is a time-sensitive issue. Every minute counts." Royce pushed Curt forward. "Get moving."

The correctional officer stopped, accepting the fact that he couldn't stop them.

"Hope you got a good lawyer. I heard what went on in there, Sergeant. Judge is gonna have a field day with you. Might cost you your badge."

Royce glared at him. "If the court is more concerned about his bruised wrist than the God-knows-how-many people he helped get killed, then they can have it." He followed Pam out the front door and lifted his radio. "Dispatch, call in every officer you can, on the double. I'm getting on the line with the Mayor's Office. All units, pull everyone out of the lake, pronto."

"Damn it," Pam muttered. "For the first time, I'm regretting working in a town with such a huge lake as its main attraction."

"No shit," Royce said. "There's got to be a way to kill these things. We need to know more about them."

"Then let's get to that chopper. No way are we wasting four hours in a round-trip car ride." She looked at Royce as they arrived at the Interceptor. He was chuckling as he pushed Curt into the backseat. *He's laughing? At a time like this?* "What's so funny?"

"Sorry. Just thinking of Ellen. If she were with us, she'd be saying *'Get to the Choppa!'*"

Pam joined in on the laugh, only to stop abruptly. "Royce? Where is she at today?"

He paled. "Shit. They're on a pontoon boat. Shit! Shit! Shit!" He whipped his phone out. "It seemed like a simple enough matter at the time to simply advise them to stay out of the water.

But I don't even trust *boats* being out at this point." He dialed her number, then slammed his phone down as the call failed to go through. "That stupid cell phone of hers. No signal whenever we're on that lake."

Pam floored the accelerator. In the meantime, Royce tried Jane Fields' cell phone. It rang and rang, eventually going to voicemail. He tried twice more, then groaned.

"She left it on the damn kitchen counter." Back to the radio. "Holman?"

"Go ahead, Royce."

"Get boat units out. Look for a pontoon boat with a bunch of twenty-year olds. Should have a couple of younger kids with them. Make them come to shore. Don't care where. Bring everyone in, but keep a special watch for that boat."

"Ten-four."

CHAPTER 22

When Holman, Stacie Roncamp, and John Yuki arrived at Green Valley Resort, the lake was as busy as ever. People were out on rafts, canoes, kayaks, and twelve-foot boats. Jet skis and speedboats were zipping across the lake. For as far as they could see, there were people swimming near the shorelines. The whole north end of the lake was alive.

Pete Riegle, the resort owner, immediately saw them standing in his driveway from the office window. A skinny man of sixty-seven, he stepped outside. "Good morning, Officers!" It was hard to maintain the smile after the news swept the town that Larry Elwood was found dead at his home. "My condolences about your boss. I met him once. He seemed like a good man."

Holman hardly took notice of Pete's attempts at comfort. His eyes were glued on the vast activity in the lake. There were so many people swimming—people who paid good money to be here. Green Valley Resort was a little overpriced, but it managed to fill up every vacancy. From what he could see, there were at least a hundred people in the water from Green Valley alone. That wasn't counting the lakefront properties nearby, and the neighboring lakefront cottage resorts that lined the northeast end of the lake.

"There's gotta be two hundred people swimming out there," Stacie said. "Some of them are pretty far out."

"I can see that," Holman said.

"Well, Maple Shore Resort and myself have done pretty well for ourselves these past couple years," Pete said. "This summer, we're making an all new record. Most of my clients are six-to-twelve person families, most of which are bringing their wallets into my merchandise shop. Can't beat that."

Again, his words went unnoticed.

"Let's get the speakerphone out," Holman said. "We'll call them in and hope everyone's in a mood to cooperate."

Pete scoffed, his friendly demeanor vanishing like a raindrop in the ocean.

"Excuse me?"

Now, Holman was paying attention to the resort owner. "Pete, I'm sorry to do this, but we need everyone out of the water right this minute."

"Mind if I ask why?"

"We believe there's something dangerous swimming in it. This thing might have killed Larry and numerous other people."

Pete looked at John and Stacie, hoping to see a smirk on their faces. This had to be a joke, after all. When he didn't get such confirmation, he looked up at the incredibly tall Officer Holman.

"What's in the water?"

"We're trying to figure that out as we speak," Holman said.

"I've seen people swimming every day all summer. Including yesterday. I haven't seen anyone get attacked."

"Not up here," John said. "The attacks have been isolated to the south end of the island. That doesn't mean the danger couldn't come up in this direction. We need everyone to vacate the water until we can solve the problem."

"Pete, this thing, or *things*, have killed Larry. We're not playing around," Holman said.

"Have you seen this creature?"

"No, but—"

"I'm sorry, son. Really I am. Chief Elwood was a really nice man who deserved to live forty more years in my opinion. But what you're telling me sounds way too unbelievable. Many of these people are repeat customers. If I start telling them there's something in the lake killing people, most of them will never return. Worse, word of mouth will quickly get around. You realize how much I've spent to get this business afloat? How much debt I had to chip away at, the number of years it took to do it? I spent a lot of nights eating ninety-nine cent meals, Officer."

"Pete, these people are in danger," Holman said.

"From what? 'Something'? You can't even indicate what kind of animal we're talking about, Officer."

"Listen, dude. We've found bodies literally stripped to the bone. Something in the water is causing that."

"OR you have a crazed killer on the loose," Pete said. "Son, I used to work on a ranch in Texas. We lived right on the border. Our neighbors were miles apart in those days. We often went back and forth, trading equipment and other resources. Just helping each other out, you know? Anyhow, when I was thirty, I received a call from Howard, my neighbor. His son-in-law, an immigrant from Mexico, was nabbed by the Cartel. My understanding is that they had a run-in with him some years prior, and it wasn't pretty. So we crossed the border to go after him, not wasting time with law enforcement. We found him in a couple of hours—or rather, his bones. Sons of bitches poured acid on him—after torturing him, of course. I moved up north after that." He sighed. "You might wanna get the State Police involved, Officers. Sounds like you've got someone like them Cartel boys up here."

"It's not the same, Pete," Holman said.

"Sorry. Not calling them in."

"Fine." Stacie grabbed a bullhorn from the back of her vehicle and marched to the shore. "I'll do it."

"You have no right! I *own* this property. I have the paperwork—everything up to that platform belongs to *me*."

Stacie stopped, glaring at the diving platform a hundred feet out. A few feet behind it was a sign that protruded from the water which read *private property*. Beyond that, the lake was completely public.

"Shit."

Now the griping about debt hit home harder—Pete must've paid the township quite a pretty penny to purchase a section of the lake. Most areas wouldn't allow privatization of public land or water.

Their hands were tied. Moving these people would be a violation of private property rights.

The problem it presented wasn't isolated to the Green Valley property. Now, when trying to get people to come ashore from the other properties, disgruntled residents would see the Green Valley customers swimming and accuse the cops of picking and choosing.

Holman resisted the urge to strangle the business owner. His only method of getting these people out would be to convince him of the threat.

"Pete, if we could PROVE to you that something's in the lake, will you cooperate then?"

"Yes, as long as it's evidence of an actual animal. Dead bodies... sorry, sir... but that sounds like a maniac. Most animals I know of wouldn't strip a person down like that."

There was no point in arguing further, since Pete's stance was clear. Holman returned to his police vehicle and got on the radio.

"Royce? You there?"

"Yeah."

"You confirm the presence of anything in this lake?"

"More or less. We've got a line on a genetics lab in Redleaf. The detainee from yesterday's bait shop admitted to their group dumping fish in the lake."

"Did he say what it is?"

"Some sort of hybrid mix. We're taking the chopper to the lab to get more concrete information."

"Do it fast, because we have people in the water, and Pete won't let us bring them in unless we can prove there's something dangerous in here. Unfortunately, an activist admitting they've dumped fish won't be enough for him."

"Working as fast as I can."

CHAPTER 22

Royce clipped his speaker mic to his collar and wrestled his headset back over his ears. "Damn it."

Pam kept her eyes on the world in front of her. Every two weeks, she conducted a short routine flight to keep the engines in check. This trip to Redleaf was the first real flight she'd conducted in a long time.

There was a sense of freedom in being fifteen-hundred feet high, watching the world pass by underneath her. She would have gotten lost in the beauty of Michigan's thick woods, rolling hills, and open farmland had it not been for the situation at hand.

"Problem at home?"

"That damn Pete Riegle," Royce said. "He apparently thinks we're overreacting."

"He won't let Holman get his people out of the water?"

"That's correct. We need to get in that facility and get proof."

"You should place another call to the Mayor's Office."

"I will when we get out. Maybe he'll answer this time. Doesn't matter. I'd like to have something concrete to present before we talk."

"A dead Chief isn't enough? Skeletons of victims aren't enough?"

"Doesn't change the fact that we need to know more about what's causing it," Royce said. The sound of Curt heaving into a bag made him look to the back seat. "Speaking of which…"

Curt leaned back in the seat, eyes closed and mouth open. "Oh, God. Please tell me we're almost there."

"You can't survive a thirty-two minute flight?" Pam said. "You're a special kind of wuss, you know that?"

"Go to hell." He took a deep breath. "Fine! I get airsick very easily. What's it to you?"

"How big is this lab?" Royce asked.

"It's pretty big. Should look like a factory from up here."

"We should be almost there," Pam said. "I imagine the lot should be big enough for us to set down."

"How's the security there?"

"Round the clock, as you might expect. There're two officers guarding the front gate. All armed. Definitely won't take kindly to us showing up uninvited."

"That's why you're here. They need to see a familiar face," Royce said. "We'll walk you up to the front gate and you will demand to speak with Doctor what's-his-name."

"Dr. Samuel Bohl," Curt said. "Not a hard name to remember."

"Oh, really? You respect this guy? Did he rescue a cat out of a tree or something?" Pam said.

"I'm allowed to acknowledge when someone is friendly," Curt said.

"Yeah? I'll tell you who was friendly, Larry Elwood and his wife," Royce said. "Let me tell you, that man was worth a hundred of you whiny brats."

"I already told you, I didn't know anyone would get killed. I wasn't even aware the fish were carnivorous. All I heard was that they were modified bluegills. What harm could come from bluegills?"

"Bluegills?" Pam finally took her eyes off the windshield to look back at him. "She had the doctor engineer bluegills?"

"That's what I was told. Just with sharper teeth to free themselves from hooks and nets." Curt shrugged. "Hey, if you want answers, go that way." He pointed to a large black, gated structure to the north. "That's it right there."

The campus was a series of greyish-black buildings surrounded by concrete and a steel fence lined with razor wire. Security vehicles drove along the outer perimeter and maintenance crews moved about the inner parts of the grounds.

"Can't believe I've never heard of this place," Royce said.

"You study science as a hobby, Officer?" Curt said. The Sergeant shook his head. "That's why. Most people don't pay too much attention to the research that goes on here."

"I can't imagine Alice is wealthy enough to fund all of this."

"She's not. Just Dr. Bohl's project. They're working on all kinds of shit down there. Food production, soil alterations to plant trees and crops in the desert, cloning to revive endangered or extinct species."

"If they're taking money from people with ill-intent, God only knows how these other projects will be abused," Pam said. She brought the helicopter over the south parking lot, found an area open enough to set down, and began her descent.

Security vehicles swarmed the lot, backing off after failing to deter the aircraft. The staff on foot eased up after seeing the *Lorenzo Police Department* on the fuselage.

Pam landed the chopper and powered down the engines. Royce stepped out and greeted the staff. "Good morning."

"You're outside your jurisdiction, aren't you, Officer?" the Security Chief said. "This isn't public property. Can't just fly your helicopter here without permission."

"Well, sir, this is one of those days where permission flies out the window. I'm here looking for answers."

"What answers are those?"

"Answers that only Samuel Bohl can give." Royce pulled the fuselage door open. A lackluster Curt Lin stepped out.

"Hi, guys. I'm with Alice Kirkman, Dr. Bohl's sponsor for his project. I'm here to speak to him on an urgent matter."

The security officers glared at him in his jail jumpsuit, then looked at the officers.

"Is this a joke?"

"No joke. Whatever Dr. Bohl engineered is killing people in Lake Carlson. We need to understand what it is and how we can destroy it."

"It's true," Curt said. "Call the doctor. Tell him Curt Lin, Alice's assistant, needs to speak with him.

The Security Chief stood motionless, internally debating whether or not to force these people off the premises. Preferring to be safe than sorry, he unclipped his radio and switched to the *Genetics'* frequency.

"Yeah, this is Thirty-five-one. Is Samuel Bohl available?"

"He's in the lab. May I ask what this is about?"

"He's got a visitor. Apparently it's an assistant to Alice Kirkman. Claims it's urgent that he see the Doctor."

"Give me a sec. I'll let him know, then I'll let you know if he's available."

"Thanks." He lowered the radio and waited. It only took thirty seconds for the lab assistant to get back to him.

"He says bring him in."

"Copy that. Just a heads-up, he's got two other visitors with him. Law enforcement from a town called Lorenzo." He lowered the radio, then waved the visitors to the vehicle. "Come with us."

****

The Doctor stepped into his office. Whenever at work, he wore a simple button shirt under his lab coat. For visitors, he preferred to add a tie. Appearance meant a lot these days, especially when dealing with potential sponsors.

Or law enforcement.

He straightened his shirt collar and wrapped the tie around it. As he formed the knot, he looked at the various photos on his pegboard. Up on top was a paper cutout of three bold words: **Species Near Extinction.**

One photo showed a herbivore known as a scimitar oryx. Native to the Sahara's northern plains, their numbers dropped after the area turned to desert. Thanks to hunters, the species in the southern regions were reduced to extinction. The only ones to remain were preserved in captive breeding grounds in a few locations worldwide.

Another was the southern rockhopper penguin. Known for their hopping motions that defined their name, they were probably the least endangered species on the wall. Still, Bohl estimated that their days were numbered after discovering their population had decreased by thirty percent during the last three decades.

Others on the board were the amur leopard, with only a hundred surviving members, the snow leopard, the northern white rhino, with only two females still alive, and Tapanuli orangutan. However, it was a photo of a shelled retile with an enormous neck that often drew Dr. Bohl's gaze.

The Pinta Island tortoise. Originally from Ecuador, these creatures were almost gone. Having been dumped on Isabella Island by merchant ships, the only surviving members are believed to be hybrids, as the rest have died off.

Hybridization. It was probably the answer in at least somewhat preserving species on the brink of extinction. His colleagues believed cloning was the answer. Jumpstart the species by growing new members in artificial wombs, then release them into the wild.

There was a major mathematical issue surrounding this method. It would take years just to produce a dozen cloned members of a single species. The few numbers and the time it took to grow new ones meant that there would be little genetic diversity in the species.

Steven Bohl's method was different, and while it sacrificed the purity of the species, it prevented them from going fully extinct as well, while allowing more room for them to grow their numbers naturally. Hybridization would allow the new members to breed with their endangered counterparts, as well as the species whose genes it was spliced with. With the endangered species' DNA being dominant, it would allow them to repopulate and pull themselves back from the edge of the bottomless pit known as extinction.

"Why would law enforcement be interested in a genetics lab?" he said to himself.

He straightened his tie, fixed his collar, and went to the front administrative area.

****

Royce crossed his arms, looking at the portraits of researchers and explorers on the walls. He only recognized a couple of the faces, such as Jacquez Cousteau and Rachel Carson.

In front of them was a desk, where a few secretaries were seated. Despite the heavy security, they looked like any regular run-of-the-mill white-collar workers. Men were mowing the lawns outside, people in business casual outfits moved in and out with coffee and donuts in hand, and a painter was on a stepladder doing patch work near the ceiling. If anything illegal was going on here, the staff was doing a good job of hiding it.

Royce and Pam noticed a few glances, but nothing that indicated alarm. Each facial expression was the same: *What the hell are cops doing here with an inmate?*

"We probably should've gotten him something better to wear," Pam said.

"Maybe. Too late now," Royce said.

The double doors on the right side of the desk opened up. A middle-aged man with thick curly hair and beard stepped out.

"Hello, Officers. I'm Doctor Samuel Bohl." He looked at Curt Lin in his jumpsuit. "Not quite what I expected to see when I heard you were visiting."

"It's quite a story, Doctor," Curt said.

"I bet it is." He looked at Royce. "Considering the attire, I supposed it was you who insisted on this visit. No offense, but you don't look like detectives."

"No, we're not," Royce said. "Just your typical small town cops who believe their community is in grave danger."

"This fella is associated with your sponsor, Alice Kirkman. Is this correct?" Pam said, tapping Curt on the shoulder.

"It is. I suppose this one went wayward? Though, I don't imagine he's gone through any trial, considering I've seen him a few days ago. That means he's only recently been arrested."

"Doc…" Curt stepped forward. "We need your help. The… 'fish' that Alice transported out of here, I need to know the full details of what they are."

Dr. Bohl wrinkled his brow. "Doesn't Ms. Kirkman explain these things to you?"

"She just told us she was repopulating a lake," he said.

"Ah, yes. Her private lake over in Ottawa county," Bohl said.

Royce leaned forward. "Beg your pardon?"

The Doctor watched his body language, searching for any signs of sarcasm. From what he could see, the officer was as serious as a heart attack.

"That's what I was told. She got in touch with me, told me she wanted to contribute to my research, as long as I would splice the genes of two very distinct species. I saw it as a good way to practice the art of gene-splicing—and yes, it is an art. Hence, you don't see it all the time." Dr. Bohl gestured to the door. The cops and Curt followed the Doctor into the hallway. They crossed several yards of tile before they reached the entrance to Genetics. "In here is where you'll find my creations."

He scanned his badge and the doors opened electronically. His guests, following his hand gesture, stepped in first. Walking from the typical, boring hallway into this room was like jumping a hundred years into the future.

They entered a world of advanced technology, run in large by computers that looked as though they came from another planet. Equally as alien-looking were the numerous specimens being held in large stasis pods. Each pod consisted of a pyramid-shaped base with flickering lights and heart-monitors. The 'tip' of those pyramids consisted of a thick glass tube that stretched to the ceiling. Inside, twisted, ghastly nightmares stared back at the new visitors.

Royce locked eyes with one with a furry snout and pointed fangs. A lion's head. The simple sight of a lion wasn't what disturbed him, but the fact that the head was protruding from the creature's *shoulder*. Up where it should have been, another, larger head stared upward, jaw open, as though the beast was screaming for God to put an end to its misery.

There were others. Some small, some large. Each was a different species, or rather, an *attempt* to recreate a certain species. Many were fish, others were birds, and a couple mammals. Some birds had three wings, others had misplaced talons and beaks. Some of the fish had pectoral fins where their stomachs were supposed to be. The mammals were the worst. Some had their guts on the outside, as though born inside-out.

Curt turned around and dry-heaved.

"Hybridization," Dr. Bohl said. "It's a process involving a lot of trial and error, unfortunately."

"Why the hell are you keeping these things alive?" Pam said.

"None of them feel pain."

Royce looked at a stasis tube with some kind of near-extinct primate with its brain exposed through its skull. "You sure about that?"

Bohl nodded. "We're studying their cellular structure. They'll be put down in the near future. We need to understand the mistakes we've made so we can continue producing successful hybrids. Gene-splicing is an art, good sirs….and ma'am."

"And what species did Alice Kirkman have you splice?" Pam asked.

"Piranhas and North American bluegills."

Royce slapped both palms against his forehead. "God, I knew it. I thought I was crazy, but…"

"Mind telling me what's wrong?" the Doctor asked.

"Alice lied to you," Pam said. "She wasn't stocking a small private lake with an exotic species. She infested a large *public* lake with your little creations."

"What?" Dr. Bohl stumbled backward as though physically shoved. "What lake?"

"Lake Carlson, over in Lorenzo where we're from," Royce said.

Dr. Bohl ran a hand through his hair. Beads of sweat formed along his reddening brow. "You're serious?"

"Doc, I wouldn't fly my helicopter all the way over here, with one of our jail inmates in tow, just for a fun tour," Pam said.

"They're telling the truth," Curt said. "Alice lied to you. Lied to me too. I didn't think they were aggressive, but according to these cops, they've killed a number of people already."

Now, Dr. Bohl resembled a man on the verge of a heart attack. In the span of ten seconds, he went from being a casual scientist who seemed rather proud to show off his work, to having a severe nervous breakdown. He kept one hand on his sweaty forehead and held the other out as a blind man would.

"I gotta… oh, my…" Royce and Pam approached to catch him, but failed before he backed into one of the pyramid computers. He fell along the side of it, swinging his arm back to catch himself.

They heard the beeps of buttons being accidentally pressed, followed by something powering down.

Behind the Doctor was the primate hybrid-thing. In the blink of an eye, it went from being still as ice, to thrashing about with intense force. Meaty hands clawed at the glass. Air bubbles exploded from its tooth-lined jaw. The IV lines waved, threatening to come out of its neck.

The sound of chaos snapped Bohl out of his near mental breakdown. He spun around to face the machine, tapped a few keys and restarted the flow of sedatives.

Gradually, the monkey creature slowed its movements until it was once again in a sleep-like state.

Royce and Pam eased up, and lifted their hands from their weapons.

"Oooookay…" Royce took a deep breath. "Didn't expect *that.*"

"Must've had a bad dream," Pam said.

Bohl shook his head. "More accurately, I woke him up from a good dream. One where he's not in constant pain and agony."

"I'd say he resents you for it, Doctor," Royce said.

"Doesn't matter. He'd try to kill me anyway and devour my guts." He looked at them. Their wrinkled, half-smirked expressions hinted a desire for him to follow-up that remark with an explanation. "As you can see, these specimens came out flawed, to say the least."

"Practice makes perfect. Is that what it boils down to?" Pam asked.

"It does, actually," the Doctor said. "That's why I took Alice Kirkman up on her offer. She offered several million in funding and research on a specific combination."

"Bluegills and piranhas." Royce smirked. "Never thought I'd have to protect the world from panfish."

"It seemed like a simple assignment and a good way to study gene-splicing. Why not practice on readily available species? The whole idea was to splice the DNA of endangered species and enable them to breed with either side in order to rebuild their numbers."

"So, did it work?" Curt said.

"The splicing process worked. Over time, I didn't have horrid results like what you see here. Except…"

Royce leaned forward, not liking the way Bohl's voice trailed off. "Except what?"

"Except for two problems you really don't want to have—swelling in the brain, and intense hunger," Bohl said. "I warned Ms. Kirkman that these fish probably wouldn't last long because they need to eat four times their weight every twenty-four hours, or starve. Even for a millionaire like herself, producing enough food for these specimens would drain one's finances." He pointed his thumb at the specimen behind him. "These guys feel like they're starving all the time. That's why we need to keep them in stasis until we're ready to put them down."

"They need to eat that much?" Curt said.

"I warned Ms. Kirkman of this fact, but she insisted on filling her lake with two batches." He turned around and walked to the end of the lab. "Come. Follow me."

They passed through another set of mechanical doors into another lab. This one was as advanced as the last, the main difference being this lab resembled an aquarium. Largely because it was.

Most of the aquariums were empty, each one lined with bones at the bottom. They were of livestock, cartilage remains from sharks, and various other unlucky creatures that were served to the piranhas.

Bohl led them around the corner to a much smaller aquarium which was equivalent to a home set-up in terms of size. It held fifty-gallons and had a single fish inside of it.

The creature resembled a bluegill in terms of its basic shape, aside from the jaw—*that* was all piranha. A piranha on steroids.

Royce knelt to put his face up to the glass. "I looked those guys up online. They looked mean, but jeez, this fella looks like he'd strip a blue whale down to the bone in a day."

The fish turned and darted at the glass, bouncing off like a ping pong ball. Royce jumped back, nearly hitting Curt.

"Watch it, wuss."

Royce looked at him. "Pardon me?"

Curt cleared his throat then cocked his head toward the Doctor. "Um, dunno! He said it."

Royce turned his attention back to the fish. It was nearly two-feet long, its body narrow, but full of muscle. The dorsal fin was larger in comparison to its body than its normal bluegill counterparts.

"Do piranhas usually get this big?"

"No. I hate to admit it, but this is a byproduct of some GMOs we've placed in their food. Alice wanted to stock her lake this summer and threatened to pull funding if I didn't make it happen. So, I had to think fast."

"Explains the swelling in the brain," Pam said.

"How many did you make?"

Dr. Bohl was hesitant to answer. He felt like a man on trial, giving away the details of his wrongdoing after pleading not guilty. Only minutes ago, he learned that his project was responsible for numerous human deaths. How could he continue his work after this? What would happen with the higher-ups? Would the company be liable, or would Alice? He hoped the latter, or else, the company would certainly prioritize their own self-preservation and pin the tragedy on him. None of this changed the fact that lives were lost and many others were in danger.

"In total, five hundred, given to her in two separate batches. It was her responsibility to handle the transport. She must've been in a rush, because all she managed to get was a—"

"Dump truck," Pam said.

Dr. Bohl nodded. "Hard to believe she couldn't get something more efficient."

"Trust me, it was by design," Royce said. "She wanted something she could use to quickly and easily dump the fish into the lake. Something that wouldn't stand out too poorly."

"There's construction in town," Pam said. "If anyone saw a dump truck sitting around, it'd be easy to assume it belonged to one of the crews."

"I seriously didn't know," the Doctor said. "I've heard of Alice Kirkman prior to our business meetings. She expressed a similar desire to protecting endangered species."

"Yeah, but to her, 'endangered' doesn't mean 'threatened to become extinct'. She means IN-danger…of being eaten by evil fishermen."

"Huh?"

"She's an environmentalist gone extreme," Curt said. "Believe me, I can talk. I'm one of them. Frankly, I think all of you guys who kill animals for fun have something waiting for you in the afterlife." Royce and Pam turned around, their patience wearing thin. "BUT… though I stand by my previous methods, killing people is not going to change hearts. In fact, it's more likely to cause more of these animals to be put down."

"Wow! He actually rubbed a couple of brain cells together," Pam said.

"I hope you're being sincere, because we're gonna have to put down five hundred fish," Royce said.

"More," Bohl said.

"Wait, you said you gave her five hundred!" Royce said.

"Yes, but they reproduce so fast, rabbits only wish they could keep up. At least fifty of the females were loaded with eggs. Ordinary piranha eggs hatch three-to-five days after fertilization. These ones, however, only take one-to-two days."

"Oh, wonderful," Royce said. "Anything else you'd like to mention, Doctor? Did you sell Alice any freshwater sharks? Electric eels? Hell, at this point, I wouldn't be surprised if you told me you engineered a great white that can survive in saltwater and sold it to that crazy bitch."

"She did ask if that was possible…" Bohl thought out loud. A nervous laugh followed the statement.

"How do we kill them?" Pam said.

"Same way you kill any other fish. Impale them. Shoot them."

"Too freaking many, and I imagine they're hard to see," Royce said.

"Could we net them?" Curt asked.

"They'd bite right through the lines," Bohl said.

"Just as Alice intended," Curt muttered.

"Listen, there's a hard truth I must state," Bohl said. "If these things were put in a public lake, everything that was once swimming in there is dead. Those things strip and clean anything, and I mean ANYTHING, they come across. They can swim up to forty miles per hour. We've seen them leap out of the water to grab prey being lowered on a harness. They are vicious predators with no loyalty except to their school. Scouts branch out in search of prey. The scout takes the first bite and draws blood. That blood is like an air raid siren. The pack zeroes in on the target, reducing it to…" He pointed at the bones in the large aquarium. "The only way to kill them is to poison the water. At this point, the most effective thing to do is wait it out. They're loyal to their own species, but that loyalty only goes so far. Once starvation takes hold, it's every fish for itself. They'll turn on each other. Considering their size, numbers, and metabolism, in a couple of days, they'll wipe themselves out, and the victor will be left to starve. Then, Lake Carlson will truly be an empty lake."

Royce took one more look at the predator. It was facing him, its jaw open, ready to snap on his flesh. Triangular teeth glistened in the glow of computer monitors, its eyes black as his handgun.

He snapped a picture of it and sent it to Holman, then rushed for the door. "Come on. We need to clear that damn lake, ASAP!" As they ran through the facility, he dialed Ellen's number again. As he feared, she didn't pick up. "Damn it. Hope they got those kids off the lake."

They ran through the front doors, passing the secretary. She waited for the door to latch shut before picking up the phone and pulling out the business card her contact had given her.

"You see anyone investigating this, let me know," the woman had said before handing her fifty-thousand dollars in cash.

The secretary dialed the number on the card.

"Yes?"

"This is Ms. Bell. You've got a problem…"

CHAPTER 23

"Right. Thank you." Alice ended the call and placed her phone on her lap. "Damn it."

The dump truck's enormous tires sliced through the dirt as Billy Gile steered it into the back yard of their associate's private property. It was an area of thick woods twenty-minutes south of Lorenzo, outside of the town's jurisdiction. The neighboring area was equally as low-key, perfect for hiding the dump truck for safekeeping.

Billy stepped out of the dump truck, immediately noticing Alice's face contorted with anger and worry.

"What's the matter?"

"It's Curt."

"Bail get denied?"

"Hasn't been set yet. No way will I post it anyway. He went with the cops to Redleaf."

"What?"

"According to my contact, they arrived by chopper and met with Dr. Bohl. By the looks of it, they know everything."

"Shit!" He threw his glove and paced in a circle. So close, yet so far. With the task now complete, they were going to leave the country and lay low. There was no doubt that the news reports of bodies being found in the lake were connected to the school of fish they dumped into the water. They weren't supposed to be that aggressive, and they didn't think they'd have such an appetite for human flesh. But they did and already people were dead, and it was a short matter of time before the authorities investigated the matter. As long as they got out of town and removed all traces of their involvement, specifically the dump truck, there was nothing the cops would find to connect them with the presence of carnivorous hybrids.

"That damn cop!" Alice said.

"The one from the grocery store?"

"Him and the bitch that put Curt on the pavement. Not that I feel sorry for him anymore. The prick *willingly* told them about the lab and helped arrange a meeting with Dr. Bohl. Now they know about us."

"What should we do?" Billy said. "Even though it wasn't in their jurisdiction, since the Doctor willingly let them tour the lab and, in all likelihood, told them about us, they have probable cause to start an investigation. We'll have the state police after us. They're probably radioing all other departments right now."

"They need to file an official report first. They can't do that in the chopper. Besides, their first priority will be clearing the lake. We can prevent an investigation if we manage to prevent them from filing an official report—we need to *catch* them before they reach the station." Alice checked her watch, then looked up at Billy. "You up for a job?"

Billy placed his hands behind his back, like a soldier in a formal hearing.

"You know how committed I am."

"Good. Get with Conrad and Gerald. Tell them they'll get a special bonus from me. You'll need to act fast. My contact said they just left the building. They're probably lifting off as we speak. We know where the airfield is. Do what needs to be done and get out of there fast. And please don't leave a trace to your identity."

"You sure we want to take it this far?" Billy said.

"You interested in going to prison?" she replied. Billy shook his head. "Then this is the only way."

"What about the Doctor?"

"We'll take care of him later. Right now, we need to take care of those cops and Curt."

"Alright. I'll make the call." He let out an exasperated sigh as he dialed Conrad's number.

This wasn't a job he was enthusiastic about, but it beat going to prison.

CHAPTER 24

"This is a priority alert! Dispatch, I need you to call in any off-duty officers. Get every boat we can onto that lake and get everyone out of the water this minute. I have confirmation that there is a deadly species in the lake."

"Copy that."

Royce looked at the phone in his lap, cursing himself for allowing Jane to take Ellen on the pontoon.

"That's about three miles of water to cover. You think you have enough people to handle that?" Curt asked.

"No," Pam said. "We'll need help from the County and State."

"The Mayor's gonna have to make that call," Royce said. "This is an unusual situation, and they won't take it seriously unless ordered by a high-ranking official such as Larry or the Mayor. Larry's dead, so that leaves Mayor McNichols." He shifted in his seat and watched the landscape below. "Can this thing move any faster?"

"Relax, Royce. I'm pushing it to full speed. You don't want me to stall the engines, do ya?"

"Of course not."

"Then let me focus on the flying. You worry about being the leader."

"I can barely focus. I can't get ahold of Ellen or Jane."

"I'm sure they're fine," Pam said. "We'll be landing in under a half-hour. Just stay calm. I'm worried about her too, but I know how smart she is. She's like her dad in that regard."

The tiniest grin broke through Royce's grim appearance. "Flattery will get you nowhere."

"I guess I can't be too surprised. You've always kept a hard shell."

"Maybe."

"Check in on Robert and Steven. Maybe they've found her."

"Good point," Royce said, grabbing his mic. "Three-William-One, what's your status?"

"Uh, Sarge...something strange is going on."

Royce and Pam looked at each other.

"Elaborate, please."

****

Ryan Robert didn't know where to begin. How could he explain the ribbons of clothing clinging to the cattails and dock of the private residence? They had come across a trail of floating rubber and fabric and followed it to the Kaczynski property.

He had known Mr. Kaczynski. He had a wife and two kids, nineteen and seventeen. In previous boat patrols, he had seen them in the summer, playing in the water together. The boys didn't seem to suffer the usual attitude problems that most teenagers had. They openly loved their parents and weren't embarrassed to act as a family.

Ryan rubbed his forearm over his brow. Deflated rubber rafts bunched up on the shore. Mrs. Kaczynski's purple beach chair was overturned in the sand. Between it and the lake were deep, scraping footprints that kicked sand onto the towels nearby. These prints were not those made from casual walking, but from intense running motion. Worse, he saw no trace of a return trail.

There was no mistaking the types of clothing that had been shredded. Forming a squiggly line were the straps of a bikini top drifting away from the dock, the ends frayed. Pieces of what used to be a white t-shirt floated among the lily pads south of the dock.

Then there was the bloody handprint on the dock rail.

"You copy? I said elaborate, please."

Ryan looked at his partner.

Steven shrugged. "Just tell him."

"Sarge, something's happened at the Kaczynski property. I think—I think they were attacked in the water."

"Anyone in the house?"

"Not that we can see from here. Both vehicles are present. They were clearly hanging out in the water recently, but nobody is around. There's clothes that look like they've been put through a wood-chipper, and blood on the dock."

"Dispatch, get ahold of the County. Ask for Deputies to report to that address. All officers, GET EVERYONE OUT OF THE WATER NOW!"

"But Sarge, shouldn't we stay and preserve the crime scene?"

"Negative. Prioritize clearing the lake, or else you'll find more shorelines like that one."

"Copy." Ryan clipped his mic and looked to Steven. "Holy shit, man. I thought he was crazy when he said something was in this lake."

Steven throttled the boat further south. "They don't teach this shit in the academy, that's for damn sure."

CHAPTER 25

Ellen couldn't take it anymore. Five times in a row, she watched Jacob fumble his casts. Each time, he'd release the button too late, causing the lure to smack down a few feet away from the boat.

"I can't take any more of this."

"Look, girl, this might be easy for you. But the rest of us live normal lives," Jacob said.

"First, calling me girl is not an insult, especially since you're acting more feminine than anyone on this boat. Second, 'normal lives'?! Where do you think those fish sticks come from?"

"Fish farms."

"Yeah? Well... alright there might be a little truth to that. But have you ever tried beer battered fish?"

"No."

"It's delicious!" Skip shouted from the top deck.

"He's smart," Ellen said. "The point is, for a lot of us, if you wanna eat, you gotta catch the fish. First step to doing that is to get the lure in the water properly."

"Doesn't apply to me," Jacob said.

"Yeah? What about that money you wanna earn? Gotta catch the pike in order to win the bet."

Jacob looked away, not wanting to admit she had a point. "It doesn't matter. I don't understand how to make this work, anyway."

"I don't see why. I've shown you repeatedly."

"You stand there and make me look like a fool," Jacob said. "My mind checks out as soon as soon as that stupid, condescending tone comes out of ya. Then, you just throw a cast and claim you've taught me how to fish. You don't really *teach* me much."

Ellen opened her mouth to give a flaming hot response, but stopped at the last moment. Instead, she threw a few casts and reeled them back, using that time to consider his criticism of her.

"Alright. You have a point."

"Huh?"

"You've got a point. Don't make me repeat it again."

"You, Ellen Dashnaw, are admitting you're wrong?" Jacob sniffed then looked to the trail of smoke drifting from the top deck. "Am *I* the one smoking weed on this boat?"

"HEY!" Jane rose from her chair and climbed to the top. "Ken! I thought you said there wouldn't be any weed on this boat!"

"I never said that."

Jacob smirked as he listened to the commotion. "I might've started something."

"While they argue, let me give you a proper lesson." Ellen snatched the pole from him, reeled the lure up to the tip, leaving an inch of slack. "Watch. Raise the tip up at ten o'clock, bring it back to one o'clock, then forward to nine o'clock." She demonstrated, pointing the rod slightly up. She brought it back over her shoulder, then flicked it to nine o'clock, releasing the button in that same instant. The lure hit the water at fifty feet.

"Oh, okay," Jacob said. He took the pole back, reeled the lure in and raised it as shown. "Ten o'clock, one o'clock, and nine o'clock."

Plop!

Forty feet. Nothing impressive, but far better than what he accomplished prior. Jacob hopped on his toes.

"Woo-hoo! You see that?"

Ellen nodded and smiled. "Get the idea now?"

"Yeah, I think so… WHOA!" The line tightened, and in the blink of an eye, went slack. When Jacob reeled it in, he noticed a lack of weight on the other end. The lure was gone, leaving a coiled string.

"Dang." Ellen inspected the wire then looked back at the water. "You had a big hit."

"Do fish break lines like this?"

"Pike can." She reached into her tacklebox. "You need a steel leader."

"What are those for?"

"Steel leaders are meant for fish with teeth, such as pike. Keeps them from biting through the line." She tied his line to a twelve-inch leader then hooked a fresh lure to the end.

"Oh yeah. Sorry for losing your jitterbug, or whatever you call that thing," Jacob said.

"That's the nature of the game," Ellen said. She picked up her own rod and threw a cast. She landed it seventy feet out then started bringing it back. On the fourth crank she had a hit. "Whoa! We might've found a hotspot over here!"

The rod bent, the line jerking back and forth. Ellen gasped as the fish tugged with enough force to put her against the guardrail. Jacob grabbed her by the shoulders to keep her from falling over.

"Whoa! What's going on down there?" Skip said. He descended the stairway and stood by, ready to catch Ellen should she look as though she would fall over again. The rod was still bent, the line threatening to snap at any moment.

"She's got something big," Jacob said.

"It's no bass, that's for sure," Ellen said.

"I might have to fork up that money in a minute," Skip said. The line was still over sixty feet out. Ellen gave it a chance to tire itself out, then pulled back. It was like hauling a brick that was actively trying to get away. Skip put a hand over his eyes. "I think I see it."

"Me too," Jacob said. It was still under the water, but its scales were glistening in the sunlight. Its fins and tail flapped, the body shaped like a coin.

Ellen kept it there for several moments. Stunned by its shape, she forgot to continue cranking.

"Is that—a bluegill?"

"Can't be," Skip said.

"I suck at fishing, and even *I* know bluegills are nowhere near that big," Jacob said.

"Let me just reel this sucker in, and maybe I'll get a better idea." Ellen's plan was over before it started. By the time she started cranking, the line snapped. "You motherfu—uh, bad, dumb fish!" She brought in her line.

"Don't be shy, kid," Dustin called down. "You're in the right crowd."

"No, don't encourage her," Jane said.

"Why'd you bring her here, then?" Dustin said.

"To have fun. Didn't realize I'd be bringing her aboard a drug boat."

"Weed's legal in Michigan now."

"Doesn't mean you should be smoking it around her—oh, nevermind!"

"It's alright, Jane," Ellen said.

Jacob laughed. "I don't know who's worked up more? Ellen over losing her fish, or big sis for not being able to date Ken."

"What's that?" Skip asked, leaning down with a hand cupped to his ear.

"Oh, uh… nothing."

"Jacob!" Jane shouted.

"I didn't say anything!"

"The whole boat heard ya, kid," Dustin said. "Might wanna work on that whispering thing. You're louder than you think."

The kids and Skip looked at the forward deck. There, Ken Lewis was smiling ear-to-ear, while Grace stared at him in disgust. Their attention turned to Jane, who came down the steps then hid in the corner of the aft deck. Her face was beet red, her back turned to Ken.

"Damn it, Jacob," she whispered.

"See, kid! That's how you whisper. Couldn't make out a word she said. Though I can take a guess," Dustin said.

Bailey smacked his shoulder. "Will you stop?"

"Fine. Fine."

Jane was tucking her face into her hand. "Why me?"

"Hey, Ken?" Skip said.

"What?"

"Mitch and Tory should've been back by now."

"Yeah? So? They probably took a stop at his house for a little key-and-slot action."

"My God!" Jane muttered. "There's kids on this boat!"

Grace snorted. "Like she cares. Apparently she was looking to get a little 'key-and-slot' action herself."

Skip held up his hands and raised his voice. "The point is— let's head on over there. They'd probably prefer to leave their kayaks on his beach anyway."

"I'm actually up for that," Dustin said. "If they did make a little 'key-slot stop' it'd be fun for one of us to go on shore and give them a little surprise."

"Mitch would lose his shit," Ken said.

"Forget Mitch. Tory would go bonkers," Bailey said. She then chuckled. "I hate that I'm stooping down to your guys' level, but that does sound fun."

"Alright. Looks like the vote tally is in. We're intruding Mitch's place! While we go, let's come up with more key euphemisms."

Ellen leaned her rod against the rail as Skip pulled up the stern anchor. She walked to the portside and stood next to Jane.

"You alright?"

"Just a little embarrassed. I didn't expect this crowd to be full of jerks."

Ellen glanced over her shoulder. "Skip seems alright."

"Yeah. I guess."

"You do realize this 'going to Mitch's house' thing was meant to get the attention off of you, right?"

Jane watched the shoreline and the rippling water. "I guess I was too busy wallowing in my self-pity to make the connection."

"He's kinda cute," Ellen said. "Just say'n."

"Talking about me?" Jacob said.

"Hell no." Ellen stuck her tongue out.

Jane crossed her arms over the rail after fixing her shirt. The desire to show off her bikini body was long gone. "I have to tell myself the same spiel I told my brother. Just get through the trip and pretend I'm having fun."

"Just think, it gets better," Ellen said. "You promised Jacob to take him to see the next *Thor* movie should he behave himself."

Jane put her forehead on her arms. "Fuuuuuuuuuuuck!"

"Whoa! Talk about use of foul language!"

Jane ignored Dustin. She had passed the point of caring.

"Didn't realize you despised the current trend of Hollywood like I do," Ellen said.

"Don't really care about all that. These superhero movies just aren't my thing," Jane said.

"Don't think you're off the hook!" Jacob said.

"Yeees, Jake." The engine roared, the propellors spitting water. The pontoon inched forward, then sped to ten miles-per-hour. Ellen and Jane listened to the commotion overhead. "On the bright side, in fifteen minutes, Mitch and Tory are going to be more embarrassed than I. You're too young to understand, thank God."

"I understand better than you might think," Ellen said.

"Great."

"Not your fault. Dad and I watch R-rated movies, for goodness sake."

"Still not as bad as me bringing you aboard a boat filled with weed and vulgar innuendo. I guess I should've known better, considering the immature clowns in my friend circle."

Ellen smiled. "I've seen worse. My dad's a cop, remember?"

"True." Finally, Jane smiled and clutched Ellen's hand. "You're a sweet kid, you know that?"

"Darn right I do!"

"Like saying grass is green, right?" Jane turned around and leaned back against the rail, her color back to normal. She looked to the helm, where Dustin and Ken were planning their prank. "Luckily, Mitch and Tory take a joke pretty well. What's the worst that can happen?"

CHAPTER 26

When Sergeant Dressel received the phone call to come in, he wasn't expecting to be personally greeted by the Mayor at the station. There he was, Ol' Mayor Douglas McNichols, brown hair combed to the left as usual. He was straightening his tie and white shirt. The skin on his forehead was bright the way sweaty skin tended to be under light. It was obvious he had gotten the same call as Dressel.

"Hello, Sergeant."

"Mr. Mayor."

"You willing to take a ride with me to the coroner's office?"

"Sure." Dressel went inside and found a set of keys, then selected one of the vehicles. "You not know the way?"

"I know the way. I just don't wanna drive. I feel like I might be sick," McNichols said. "Larry and I have become good friends these last few years. His wife and mine go out to lunch every couple of weeks."

It made enough sense. Dressel opened the door for him like a chaperon, then got in the driver's seat.

"You speak with Royce?" he asked.

"Yes." McNichols dabbed his face with a handkerchief. "Fish? There's killer fish in the lake?"

"Did he text you the same photo he texted me?" Dressel asked. McNichols unclipped his smartphone and brought up the image of a two-foot panfish baring razor sharp teeth, as though it was about to lunge at the camera. "I guess so."

"Tell me this is photoshopped."

"I doubt Royce would play that kind of joke, especially with Larry dead." He started the engine and backed out of the space. As he shifted the lever, he noticed the Mayor dabbing his face once more. "You sure you're gonna be alright?"

"Yeah. I'll be fine. Let's get moving, shall we?"

****

Ten minutes later, he wasn't fine. All it took was a brief glance at Mr. and Mrs. Elwood's remains to put McNichols over the edge. He found the nearest trashcan and lost his breakfast.

After five minutes of additional heaving, he stumbled out of the building for some fresh air.

"Call me crazy," Dressel said, following him outside, "but I'd say those look like injuries that the fish in Royce's photo would cause."

"When I saw it, I just found it too hard to believe. That's why I had to see Larry for myself."

"It's just like those bodies we recovered last night," Dressel said. "And the same that bit that woman in that car crash. We didn't put two-and-two together right away, because she went head-on into a tree. Now in hindsight, it's obvious what happened. She somehow ended up in the water and got attacked. Before they could tear her up too much, she got out, and was in such a panic that she got in her car and floored it out of there, swerved to miss Royce and that's how she smacked into the tree."

"I don't get it. How the hell did they get in our lake?"

"Royce thinks he knows. We'll figure that out later. Right now, you need to get on the horn with the County and get some additional officers here."

"Doing it right now." McNichols grabbed his phone. Halfway through dialing, he noticed Dressel getting in the Interceptor. "Where you going?"

"Have one of your assistants pick you up. I need to get to work evacuating the lake."

McNichols nodded. "Yes! Go! Go!" He hit send and waited for the line to be answered. "Yes, this is Douglas McNichols, Mayor of Lorenzo Township. I need to speak to the Sheriff directly... I don't care what he's doing, get him on the line this very moment. This is an emergency."

****

"Unit Twelve responding."
"Unit Thirteen responding."
"Unit Fourteen responding."

In the time it took Dressel to drive to the police docks from the coroner's office, ten off-duty included their unit numbers, thus officially beginning their shift. There were now more cops than there were vehicles. Adding to the issues was the fact that there was no official briefing to bring them up to speed.

"All units, this is Sergeant Dressel. I need *everybody* to get to Lake Carlson and assist with the evacuations. Units Eight, Nine, Ten, and Eleven, go to the resorts on the north end of the lake and work your way down the west side. Units Twelve through Fourteen, drive down to the south coves and make sure nobody is in the lake. The rest of you, get to the docks and get on a boat. Use your personal vehicles if you have to."

The department had four boats in total. Boat Two was already in use. Dressel opted for Boat One. Good—the four other officers that he just ordered to the docks could divide into even numbers. It was better to have one officer at the helm and another to spot.

Boat One was fueled up and ready to go. Dressel untied the mooring and sped into the lake.

As midday arrived, the activity on the water increased. It was common this time of year for residents to take Fridays off and go out on their boats. Those who took half days were now arriving from work and getting ready to cool off from the post-thunderstorm mugginess.

Jet skis moved in tight circles like mosquitos. Dressel envied the joy they were experiencing, and resented the fact that he would have to bring an end to it. He debated whether it was necessary to intercept them. As far as he knew, all of the attacks occurred to swimmers.

He decided to hold off and move around the shore in search of swimmers. Dispatch had informed him that Ryan Robert and Steven Buck were patrolling south. It made sense to join them, as all of the known fatalities were down on that end of the lake. First, he would check the west side, where he was most likely to find residents swimming about.

It didn't take long. Once he got midway across the lake, he could see a group of friends gathered on one of the private beaches. Bare-chested college age men threw a football back and forth while women, presumably their girlfriends, either swam or floated on rafts.

Dressel switched on the sirens and lights, drawing their gazes. After arriving, he slowed his boat to stop, pointing the bow northward. The group of seven stared, bemused by his presence.

"Sorry to interrupt your fun, kids, but I need you guys to get out of the water right now."

"Uh, did we do something wrong?" one of the girls said.

"No. But there's—"

"What the hell is this?" one of the guys said. Considering his football player build and instant aggression, he was probably the alpha male of the group.

"For safety reasons, we're evacuating the lake."

"What about *them*?" the football player pointed at the jet skiers. "You don't take issue with them? Just us?"

"I'll get with them in a moment," Dressel said. "They're on vehicles—you're actually in the water."

"On *my* property."

"Listen, you little prick! You think I'm bothering you for my own enjoyment? Get your sorry asses out of the water *now*! There's something in the water."

"What?" One of the girls on a raft looked about frantically. "You mean a shark?"

"No. Piranhas, or something similar."

"Right, sure," the football player said.

"Dude, let's just get on the beach," one of the other guys said.

"Screw that, man," the football player said. "We've been in the water every day this week and we haven't seen anything."

"Guys, they've killed four people that we know of. Maybe more. One of our officers reported evidence of another attack on a beach a little south of here. *This morning!* They've been hanging on the south side of the lake, but they might be moving up this way and—"

The crowd gasped unanimously, even the football player. Dressel initially thought he did a standup job conveying the urgency of the situation. When he heard the crashing of waves behind him, he knew otherwise.

When he looked back, he saw one of the jet skis rolling repeatedly, the motor stalling, its owner nowhere to be seen.

"What the hell?" Seeing the other two jet skis closing in, their riders frantically calling out, it became clear they weren't simply goofing around. He throttled the boat and turned to starboard, glancing briefly at the group of college kids. "Get on shore now!"

Over the roar of the motor, he could hear the other two jet skiers calling for their missing companion. One of them waved at Dressel's boat after seeing him approach.

"Officer! Help us, please!"

Dressel stopped the boat a few yards from the overturned jet ski. The two friends were slowly moving in winding circles in search.

"What happened?" he called out. One of the jet skiers steered close to his boat.

"Marty's gone!" he said. "We were just skiing around, having fun. Marty went over this way, then all of a sudden he falls to the side."

"He 'fell'?"

"We were too far away to see what went wrong exactly. All we could make out was him suddenly falling over the side. He hasn't come up! He's probably drowning! Do something!"

Dressel was at a loss. How could he search for the missing person underwater in a timely fashion? Worse, how could he convince these people to vacate the lake?

"HEY!" the other skier called. He held a piece of fabric over his head. "I think this is part of Marty's shirt!"

"But…it can't be. He just fell off the boat."

Part of his shirt? Dressel's blood ran cold. *Could they have gotten him? He was on a jet ski…*

"Ouch! Son of a bitch!" The skier dropped the ribbon of clothing and yanked his right foot from the footwell. He gazed down at his missing big toe and the blood gushing into the water. "Wha—Holy Jesus! Something BIT me!"

Like miniature surface to air missiles, three fish jumped clear of the water. Each as big as a laptop, they struck their target and closed their jaws over his flesh.

With a fish dangling from his neck, right hand, and waist, the skier danced in place. A fourth one joined the fray, leaping from the water and colliding with his face. As though tackled by a defensive lineman, the skier fell off the jet ski.

The lake turned red. In the middle of that cloud was a series of thrashing limbs and fins.

"Oh my God!" the first jet skier turned to help him. Before he could complete the turn, he was struck by a ten-pound projectile with pointed teeth and jaws like scissors. He reared back and screamed, fish flopping from his nose. He grabbed at it, only to impale his palm with one of the spines on its back.

The fish twisted like a drill bit, then finally broke free. Blood jetted from the skier's face.

Dressel gasped. Seeing a man's face without a nose was simultaneously amazing and terrifying. All that remained was a gaping nasal cavity surrounded by tiny flaps of meat.

The Sergeant snapped out of his brief trance and reached over the gunwale. "Get aboard! Take my hand!"

His words went unheard. The skier was screaming at the top of his lungs, clawing as his bloodied, shockingly *flat* face.

From the red water came more tooth-grinned projectiles. One after another, they latched onto his body, the teeth sinking into his flesh like sewing needles through fabric. Scaly bodies dangled from his fingers and cheeks. Writhing on his seat, the skier made a Hail Mary attempt to jump to the safest place, which happened to be Dressel's boat. He wasn't following the Sergeant's commands. Just instinct.

Another fish bit his foot, hindering his attempt to jump. Instead, he simply plopped into the water.

Dressel could see the many bodies moving in under the surface. The skier was only a couple of feet from the boat. So close to safety.

He leaned over the side and reached into the water, immediately finding a fistful of the guy's shirt.

"Come on! Come on! AGH!" He reeled back into the boat. Clenching his forearm was a two-foot piranha. The jaws opened and shut with the speed of hair-clipper blades. He smacked his arm against the gunwale, shaking the fish off. It flopped on the deck, its jaws red with his blood.

Dressel kicked the thing, bouncing it like a softball to the transom. Already, it was flopping back toward him. Out of water, needing to circulate oxygen through its gills, the damned fish was *still* coming at him. Hunger dictated all actions, overrode all other needs.

He scampered away from it, his heels slipping on his blood. After bumping his head against the console, he finally stood up and grabbed his Glock.

In every refresher course, he always successfully drew his weapon and hit the target without fail. It was smooth as 'grab, draw, fire.' One-two-three. Simple and smooth. This time, when facing real danger, he could barely get the stupid gun out of the holster. He pulled, pulled, and pulled, the weapon seemingly refusing to detach itself from its safe-haven.

After the fourth try, his finger finally found the release lever on the holster. He pointed the gun and fired repeatedly at the bouncing fish. The first two shots splintered the deck. The next three found the piranha. Its body ruptured like a pinata, only instead of candy, guts and bones spilled out—along with one of the jet skier's fingers.

Adrenaline shook his hands, resulting in a sixth gunshot that struck the boat.

"Fuck!" He holstered the weapon and looked into the water. It was red for a two-hundred foot radius and in constant motion as though boiling over a giant stove. The jet skiers were dead, their remains actively being shredded.

"OH MY GOD!"

"GET OUT! GET OUT OF THE—AGH! THEY'RE ON MY LEG!"

Screams! From the shore. Those dumb kids never got out of the water. He could see the crazed motion from eight hundred feet out.

Pressing a piece of gauze to his arm, Dressel redirected the boat to shore and pushed the throttle to the max.

"All units. They're moving north. They're attacking. They're everywhere. Royce was right. They can fly out of the water like loons. Keep all—" His voice trailed off as he arrived at the shore. The beach was red. Entrails were washing up in the shallows, while the seven young people thrashed about. The water bubbled with the motion of a hundred fins.

One of the girls tried to balance herself on her raft, which deflated after the fish bit into it. As soon as she touched the water, the predators swarmed her. When she broke the surface, half of her face was missing, the jaw and tongue completely exposed—for the latter, it was temporary. She was driven down, her screams muffled, not by the water, but by the piranha that ripped her tongue from her throat. Even in the blood-filled water, Dressel could see the tongue trailing past the fish as it darted off, like a marathon runner carrying a flag.

The football player was attempting to race to shore. He was almost there, the water barely above his knees.

A dozen fish struck at once. Most went for his legs, pulling the skin and calf muscle from the bone. Three of them jumped and went for his shoulders and back. The buff alpha male wailed, arms outstretched. He spun in place and fell backward, his head mere inches from the shoreline.

Even in three inches of water, the fish weren't willing to let anything go to waste. They slithered in the sand like snakes, their backs completely exposed. Jaws snapped at the victim's cheeks and ears, ridding him of any identifiable features.

The player grabbed at one of the fish, ignoring the pricking from its spines, and pulled with all his might. The fish maintained a grip on his eyebrow. The football player squealed, his flesh peeling down his face like the skin of an onion.

Now, shock had taken its full effect on Sergeant Dressel. He stared unblinking at the carnage in front of him. Two of the bodies were reduced to skeletons, with bits of meat clinging to the bones. The others were not too far behind.

One of the bodies bumped against the port quarter. Dressel looked down, seeing the empty eye sockets staring back at him, the face void of flesh other than a flap of scalp. Bony fingers reached up, the body twitching as the shredders went to work on everything underneath.

The hands reached out, as though pleading for help.

Dressel shook his head. *No. He's dead. Or she—I can't tell.*

The jaw opened. With the lack of muscle and tendons, it extended twice as far as a human mouth normally could, providing a clear view of the back crowns, their centers black from fillings. A scream filled Dressel's ears.

This one was still alive.

That was the final straw for Dressel's mind. He stood there in a vegetative state, watching the fish uncover the ribcage and internal organs. His senses returned when he felt hundreds of teeth tear into his own body. Jumping from all sides of the boat, they latched onto him and dangled like Christmas ornaments.

Dressel fell on his back and squirmed. They tore through his uniform and into his abdomen. Like leeches, they pressed their heads into any cavity they created and proceeded to rip and tear.

Splashing followed, not of water, but of the pool of blood that flooded the deck.

They were so mad with hunger, so in need of flesh, that they abandoned the safety of their habitat to quell their insatiable needs. There was no planning ahead, no contemplation of suffocating. Even as suffocation took its toll, their focus was in attaining one last mouthful of flesh.

CHAPTER 27

"Dressel? Say again?... Sergeant? What the hell is going on?"

Holman was knee deep in the lake with a radio in one hand and a bullhorn in the other. Stacie Roncamp and John Yuki were a few yards to his left, dragging people out of the water.

"Come on, people! Out of the water!" the latter shouted.

"Holman, what's the update?" Stacie said.

"You're on the same frequency as me. Your guess is as good as mine."

"Dressel's not one to just ignore radio calls," John said.

"Let's just worry about getting these people out." Holman looked at Pete Riegle, who stood by the main building. After overhearing the previous radio transmissions and seeing the photo sent by Sergeant Dashnaw, he finally yielded to the demands of the police. Even with the knowledge at hand, he seemed more concerned with the lost revenue than the lives of his clients.

"You guys deaf? Out of the water!" John shouted.

Over a hundred people were still swimming. Over to the east, along Maple Shore Resort's property, another hundred were scattered over hundreds of feet. On top of that was another hundred on the western shore private residences. Additionally, there were half a dozen fishing boats, several kayaks, and a pontoon boat scattered past Green Valley's private property barrier.

Holman repeatedly watched the road. They were in desperate need of reinforcements.

"Where the hell are they?"

Multiple vacationers strolled from the water, some irate, others scared, all wanting to understand what was going on. Unfortunately, the answer only invited more questions.

"What the hell is this?" an angry father of four barked at Holman.

"Sir, the water is dangerous. An invasive species has infiltrated the lake."

"What invasive species?"

"Just… move along, please." Holman looked at the dozens of people scattered along the hundreds of feet of shoreline that belonged to Green Valley Resort. "Hey, Pete? You mind helping us out?"

Pete sighed and walked to the shore, only to get stopped by several of his customers. A barrage of questions invaded his eardrums all at once.

"I thought you owned this place?"

"What's happening?"

"Is it true that something's in this lake?"

"Wait! Something's in this lake?! And he let everyone go swimming anyway?!"

Curiosity and angst evolved into pure anger. Like angry villagers demanding justice, they crowded Pete Riegle.

Holman focused his attention on the people still in the water. Pete would have the mob on his own.

Sirens blared from down the road. They grew louder and louder then went silent as reinforcements arrived on the beach. Three cars parked along the side of the driveway. Five cops disembarked and ran to the water.

"Please tell me this is a big joke," one of them said.

Holman shook his head. "Unfortunately, it's not. Right now, this lake is probably one of the most dangerous places on Earth. Let's not waste time gabbing. I need some of you to go over to Maple Shore Resorts and get those people out of the water. I need the rest of you to go house-to-house on the west side and do the same."

"What about them?" another officer said, pointing at the pontoon boat several hundred feet out. People were sliding from the top deck into the water, completely oblivious to the threat at large.

"Shit." Holman squinted as he stared into the distance in hopes of seeing one of the police boats speeding into view. "Where the hell are the boat units?"

"The others are heading there right now. Maybe five minutes or so?"

"We don't have five minutes," Holman said. "Take the bullhorns out of your trunks and get their attention. Where's Calloway?"

"I don't think he answered his phone."

"Goddamnit. I hope they fire his ass. We'll take care of this ourselves. Now move it!"

Following his instructions, the group returned to their vehicles and went to the different areas of the lake.

Sirens echoed across the lake in hopes of gaining the attention of everyone on the water. Some of the fishermen reeled in their lures and brought their boats in, while others barely paid the officers a mere glance.

The officers on Maple Shore's beaches got out of their vehicles and raced down the shoreline yelling into their bullhorns.

"The Mayor of Lorenzo has declared an emergency! Everyone must get out of the water immediately. All water activities are suspended until further notice."

Holman could hear the distant commotion from Maple Shore's customers. Though he couldn't make out what was said, he knew the tone. The officers down there were getting hit with the usual questions.

Let them deal with that. Focus on getting the rest of these idiots out of the water.

"Let's go. I'm not gonna tell you again." He looked to the platform after hearing a splash. A group of teenagers were gathered on the floating deck, taking turns doing cannonballs. "HEY! Quit screwing around! Swim to shore now!"

"How 'bout you explain what's going on?" another vacationer said. From his age and tone, Holman assumed he was the parent of one of those kids.

How many times can I answer the same question?

"I'll explain later in full detail. First, help me get those —"

"HEY! HEY! HEY!"

Holman turned toward the commotion behind him. The mob was going beyond angry words to extract their revenge on Pete. One had him by the shirt and was wrestling him back against the wall.

"I want a refund, damn it!"

"Whoa!" Holman ran into the crowd, taser drawn. "Get off of him." Nobody moved. It was as though his police authority didn't exist. Pete, being the feisty guy he was, didn't back down.

"Not getting it. This is a temporary issue, I'm sure."

"The cops say people have died in this lake. I'm not staying at Slaughter Beach. Give me my money back."

"Mine too!" another shouted.

Holman pushed and shoved, directing some of the collective anger toward himself. All of a sudden, the peaceful town of Lorenzo was looking like one of the inner cities during the riots. Then again, many of these people often came from inner cities…

They pushed back, the mob mentality ridding these people of any common sense. Behind that barrier of people, a fight broke out between numerous angry vacationers and Pete.

The beach area was alive with chaos. Holman's faith in humanity was brought into question as he tried to wrestle his way through the group. Cell phones were held to his face, recording footage, as though this was some kind of police brutality scandal.

"What the hell's going on over there?!" Stacie shouted.

"Just keep getting those people out of the water," Holman said. To his relief, County and State vehicles sped onto the scene. Deputies and troopers saw the melee and didn't hesitate to break it up.

"This the big emergency?" one trooper asked.

"No. We need officers on the water to clear the lake."

"Our Sergeant said something about killer fish!" a deputy said. "Sounds like a big joke!"

"It's NOT a damn joke!" Holman's mind was now as chaotic as the mob. He grabbed the officer and stuffed his face against his iPhone. On the screen was an image of Larry Elwood's body on the beach, an image taken for documentation. "See this guy? That's our Chief! He was killed by those fish you think are a damn joke!"

"Dan!"

Holman pushed the officer away and looked to Stacie. "Don't lecture me! I'm done with these questions and people assuming the danger isn't real. In the last five minutes alone, I've dealt with a hundred—"

"No, Dan! LOOK!" She pointed to the boats. Holman heard the screams from one of the kayakers. A hundred yards from shore, the woman was rocking back and forth, the water sizzling all around her. Fish catapulted from the water, 'tackling' her off her kayak. The simmering motion intensified. In the center of the activity was a big red blotch.

Another scream echoed from a twelve-footer further west. The fisherman on board was on his feet, waving his arm back and forth. At first glance, it looked as though he was swinging some sort of paddle. The flapping motion of its flat body gave away the realization that it was a fish. A piranha. A shredder.

More of them circled the boat, their tiny dorsal fins cutting through the water as a sharks'. Some collided with the boat, rocking it back and forth. One of them made the jump, striking the fisherman's midsection and knocking him backward. He fell into the interior of his boat, smacking the back of his head against the seat. Only his legs were visible over the gunwale, twitching as the two fish ripped into him.

Red blotches materialized all over the lake, each one around a kayak or fishing boat. From each blotch came the sound of screams or thrashing water. The loudest came from the pontoon boat. The water came alive with the frantic motions of swimmers and the swarm of bloodthirsty predators.

The mob quieted down, stunned by the horror playing out in front of them.

More red splotches took form, this time in the shallows. The beach erupted into chaos, the stragglers now stampeding for the shore.

The teenagers on the platform watched the water, uncertain whether they should stay or flee. One took the chance and dove face-first. By the second stroke, he regretted his decision. The piranhas converged on him, their mouths creating little holes in his body. More bites made more holes. In ten seconds, only a third of his skin remained.

His companions wailed, helpless to do anything but watch. Unable to take it, one of them turned to the opposite side of the lake and covered his ears. Looking up at him from under the water was a narrow head with two black eyes and an open mouth layered with teeth.

The fish sprang with the speed of a mosquito, slapping him in the face and knocking him backward. His back struck one of his friends, creating a domino effect which concluded with all three tumbling into the water.

"Oh my God!" the disgruntled parent screamed. As quickly as people raced out of the water, several parents charged the beaches. The efforts by police officers to stop them resulted in fist fists and tasering.

The disgruntled parent who challenged Holman struck a deputy in the nose, preventing his effort to keep him out of the lake.

"Get back here!" Holman yelled. He reached out to grab him but missed. He chased the man into the water, only to stop at the edge.

The man continued, unconcerned for his own safety. "Darren! Swim to me!" There was no response and if there was, he wouldn't have heard it over the commotion. He saw the twisting motions of three teens, muscle tissue exposed and leaking blood. "No! NO!" He waded further.

Just a couple yards ahead, one fleeing swimmer fell forward, then rolled in agonizing motion. Blood enveloped his body, bits of minced fatty tissue bobbing at the surface.

Another person fell. Then another. The entire stretch of shoreline turned red and festered with the motions of people getting eaten alive. The thought of self-preservation came too late for the parent. He turned around, reached for Holman's hand, only to be seized by the legs and forced down.

Only five feet away, Holman succumbed to the urge to help. He took two big steps, attempted to grab the man, only to feel the piranhas bite into his shins and arms. He jumped back, cursing repeatedly. Even on the shore, one of the creatures continued to cling onto his pantleg like a teething puppy.

"SHIT! FUCK! GET IT OFF!"

He kicked repeatedly until the thing finally shook off. It flopped on the sand, sparking further panic. The spines along its back extended, its gills and mouth stretched to expose the pink anatomy inside. It moved like a creature conceived by pure evil and knew it. There was no grace in its movements, no beauty in its appearance—no forgiving factor whatsoever. It didn't even seem to feel the indifference that a normal predator would toward humans. Whether on land or in water, its only desire was to draw blood and shred flesh.

Holman drew his pistol and turned its face into a crater.

Screams erupted from both shorelines. As far as Holman could see, the lake had turned completely red. People pushed each other out of the way in an attempt to reach shore. Many of those who made it to safety continued running inland, while others attempted to rescue the many stragglers.

"Help me!" Stacie screamed. It wasn't directed at him in particular—just whoever was close enough to respond.

Holman sprinted toward her, the pain in his injured leg flaring with each step. He hit the water and grabbed an arm of the heavy-set victim she was attempting to haul onto shore.

"AH! Hurry up!" she screamed. Blood billowed around her legs. They were biting her. Together, they yanked with all their might and dragged the civilian onto the sand.

Stacie fell on her rear and swatted at the piranha attached to her ankle. Its thrashing came to an end after Holman plunged the blade of his pocketknife through its eye. He tried pulling it away, sparking a scream from Stacie. Even in death, the jaws were clamped tight. He pried them apart as if opening a bear trap, then kicked the lifeless body into the water.

He helped Stacie to her feet, then somberly gazed at the vacationer's corpse. They had succeeded in bringing him to shore, but not in saving his life. Everything was intact from the stomach up. Everything below the waist was reduced to bone. The stomach was deflated, intestines extending into the water, twitching like fishing lines as piranhas pulled at them from somewhere under the water.

"Get it off!"

When they spotted John Yuki in the crowd, he was dashing out of the water. His pants were torn, his uniform covered in blood, and his face ripped open by the wriggling piranha. It released its grip on his cheek, only to secure a fresh bite on his lower lip.

Holman ran to him and tried to grab at the thing. John, blinded by pain, spun out of reach. He tried again, only to miss. Blood free fell from John's face. All rational thought had left the man. He spun about, lost in full-blown panic.

"Hold still!" Holman grabbed him by the shoulders and threw him onto the ground. The fish twisted in place, twining John's lip. Holman drove his knife through the gills, the tip emerging on the other side. Pain meant nothing. The fish continued tearing at the officer.

Holman grabbed ahold of its tail and pulled. John hollered, his lip peeling down his chin like a window curtain, exposing gums and teeth. The lip flapped in the piranha's jaws as it attempted to wiggle free of Holman's grip. Pinning it to the ground with his boot, he repeatedly stabbed it until it ceased to move.

John Yuki moaned, his face resembling that of an undead fiend. He pressed his hands to his face and cried out, the slightest touch infuriating the nerves.

"I need an ambulance! Where's EMS?!" Holman's calls could not penetrate the collective panicking of hundreds of people across the two resort beaches. Every officer was busy with an injured victim. Some administered CPR, while others tried to cover wounds with anything they could find. The gauze in their first aid kits were quickly spent, forcing them to use blankets, bathing towels, and even their own uniform shirts to stop the bleeding.

People were laid out on the beach, their stomachs flayed open. Bones, mainly limbs, protruded from bloody flesh-skirts that dangled near the shoulder and hip joints.

Finally, ambulances arrived on the scene. Holman scooped his arms under John's shoulders and pulled him toward the lot. A team of three disembarked and hauled the stretcher out of the back. Seeing Holman coming toward them with an injured man in tow, they raced to action.

Suddenly, all three of them stopped at once.

"Hey! Come on," Holman shouted. The EMTs stood dumbfounded, then shuddered unanimously.

The sound of a roaring motor rose over the crowd. Mixing with that sound were that of intensified screams and gagging, and a swirling sound as though a giant blender was grinding something up in the water.

Holman regretted looking over his shoulder. The last thing he needed burned into his memory was the sight of the pontoon boat operator racing to shore with no regard for the human obstacles still in the water. People bounced off the hull with the weightlessness of ping pong balls. Jets of red showered the lake as the propellor cut through stragglers and piranhas.

The pontoon ran aground, with three feet of water between the deck and the beach. For the operator, it seemed inconsequential. For the predators lurking in the shallows, it was plenty sufficient.

Five of them jumped high and collided with their human target. Hit from five bowling-ball-sized objects, the pontoon driver stumbled off the deck and into the water. He sat up and howled. Two of the fish were tearing at his face. One broke away, taking his left eye with it.

Bleeding from the empty socket, the man reached for the shoreline, only for another fish to spring from out of nowhere and grab his thumb. The jaws clamped shut, cutting through flesh and bone with a single *crack*! Still reaching, he shivered as if in the middle of a seizure while the piranhas devoured every ounce of flesh from his legs and torso.

Holman helped the EMTs place John on the stretcher. His movements had slowed. He was going into shock.

"Stay awake, man."

More ambulances and firetrucks raced onto the scene. Chopper units, both police and news, flew overhead.

A black SUV came to a screeching stop on the side of the road. From its driver's seat came a middle-aged man, well groomed, in a grey suit and tie. On his suit jacket was a badge which read Midland County Sheriff.

The Sheriff watched the horrors unfolding on the lake, then looked to the tall officer standing near the stretcher.

"My God. It really is true."

"Unfortunately, yes."

"Is the entire lake…?"

"Completely infested, Sheriff. There's no choice. Those things kill *everything*. Our first shift sergeant has information. Based on what we know, Lake Carlson is officially a dead lake."

CHAPTER 28

"Holy crap! That's the third one we've seen in like two minutes," Bailey said. The helicopter rotors produced a deafening drone as it flew north over the lake, following the trajectory of the previous two.

"Looks like they're heading to Green Valley," Skip said.

"Something's wrong. That last one looked like a police helicopter," Ellen said.

Dustin belched after downing his third beer. "Hate to break it to you, kid, but it's not uncommon for them to do air patrols."

"No, I think she's right," Skip said. "One of the other helicopters belonged to a news agency."

Ellen pulled out her phone and sent a call to her dad. For several seconds, she watched those three annoying decimals on the screen, then the words *Call Failed.*

"Anyone bring their phone? I'd like to call my dad and make sure he's okay."

Jane cringed. "Darn it. I left mine on the kitchen counter."

"Same," Jacob said.

"Relax, kid. I'm sure your dad is fine," Ken Lewis said. "Hang on. We've reached our destination."

Dustin and Bailey joined him at the helm to go over their plan once again.

"Okay, get me to the dock. Just watch out for that stupid powerline." He pointed at the powerline stretching from the neighbor's yard to Mitch's. There was too much slack, causing the center to dangle down toward the dock. "I'll go up and see if the door's unlocked. If it is, Bailey will follow me in."

"I'll record it on my phone, that way the rest of you don't miss out on the fun," she said.

"Mind if I borrow that?" Ellen said.

"After this, kiddo," Bailey said.

"What if the door is locked?" Grace asked.

"They'll likely be doing their business in Mitch's room. We'll go up to the window and give them a little scare. Last I remember, he doesn't keep drapes over it."

"How would you guys know this?" Ken said. Dustin and Bailey shared a glance then giggled. "Oooooh… does Mitch know?"

"No. He asked us to check in one time because he thought he left the stove on," Bailey said. "Since we were there, we thought we might as well… well…" She winked.

"Wait, hang on a sec," Skip said.

"Oh, don't get holier than thou on us, Skip," Ken said. "It's just a quick prank."

Skip glared at him, then pointed at the dock. "Maybe if you paid better attention. The kayaks aren't there."

Ken looked at the empty dock. "Oh. Good point."

"Uh, guys?" Jacob pointed to a floating object a few hundred feet off the port bow. "Is that Mitch's kayak over there?"

Ken held a hand over his eyes to block the sun. "I'm not sure."

"What about that one?" Ellen said. "Over there to the south." That one was close enough for them to see the bright yellow hull. One floating kayak could've been a coincidence. Two was not. They were definitely Mitch and Tory's.

"It doesn't look like they're on them," Skip said.

Ken started chuckling. "I know what happened. They were so eager to get down to business, that they didn't even bother pulling the kayaks far enough onto the beach. Yeah, they're *definitely* inside."

"Hang on, before we do anything, why don't we go get their boats?" Bailey said.

"Oh, come on!" Dustin said. "They could be finished by the time we get back."

She cracked a smile. "Not everyone's as quick as you, Dustin." Her boyfriend ground his teeth while the group laughed. "In all seriousness, let's go grab the boats. The first one is already pretty far down the lake. Could be lost by the time we go get it."

"Just use one of your rafts and paddle after it."

"Ken!"

Ken slapped his hands against his legs. "Fine!" He turned the boat around and sped for the kayak that was floating north. They would grab it, then get the other one after circling back.

It took thirty seconds for them to reach the kayak. However, it was the flashing lights and blaring siren up ahead that now had everyone's attention. An eighteen-foot police boat was speeding toward them. Two officers were on board, both pointing and yelling in their direction.

"Oh, shit!" Ken began turning the boat around.

"Ken! What are you doing?" Jane said.

"We're smoking weed and drinking near minors. You can smell it from across the lake."

"It's not like you're providing it to them!"

"Don't even think about making a run for it, Ken," Skip said. He stood over the rich party-boy's shoulder. Ken wasn't used to seeing the mild-mannered Skip so intimidating. He nodded and switched the engine off.

The two officers slowed their boat to a stop. Ellen immediately recognized them from the station. "Ryan! Steve!"

"Oh, thank God we found you, Ellen," Steven said.

"Wait, you were looking for me?"

"Per your dad's request," Ryan said. "He couldn't get ahold of you, so he asked us—"

The radio radioed. *"We've got an overturned boat over by 3847 Reineck Drive!"*

"Call the Besteda and Metzger Township police departments and ask them to send any available officers to assist. Fire departments too. We need more ambulances."

Jane put her hand comfortingly on Ellen's shoulders. "Holy Jesus, that doesn't sound good."

"Is everything alright? We've been seeing helicopters heading off to the north," Skip said.

"No. We'll explain later, but right now, you need to get on shore right this minute. There are carnivorous fish in the water and they're killing everybody. Please, get on land now."

"Oh, come on," Ken said. "Fish? Really?"

"Dude, don't joke," Skip said. "Didn't you hear the radio? Something bad is going down."

"Give me a break," Dustin said. "We're on a boat. It's not like fish are going to get us while we're up here."

Ryan Robert shook his head. "This isn't a discussion. If you don't vacate the water, Steven and I will have no choice but to place you under—"

Like a miniature flying saucer, the little disc-shaped creature burst from the water. Its jaws clattered twice before reaching their target, eager to sink into soft meat.

It landed on the back of Ryan's neck, knocking him against the throttle. The boat went from zero to full speed, slamming into the port section of the pontoon boat.

An explosive impact rocked the pontoon to starboard. Dustin staggered down the slope, grabbing at the air in hopes of preventing his fall. His waist hit the guardrail, serving only as a fulcrum for him to tilt. Gravity and a forty-five degree slope sent him tumbling into the water.

He broke the surface and reached for the boat, only to see it rapidly getting closer. Still angling to starboard, the pontoon was being pushed by the full-throttle propulsion of the police boat.

"Oh…"

The hull swept over him, imploding his skull.

The police boat continued digging in, the propellors spraying a fountain of water behind it. Ryan swung his arms back, his head tilted back from the weight of the thing clinging to his skin.

"STEVE! GET IT OFF!"

Steven grabbed at the fish and yanked, freeing it—and a five inch ribbon of flesh—from Ryan's neck. The fish swung its head and bit at his palms. Snapping jaws created a dozen gaps in his flesh in the span of three seconds.

Steven Buck yelped and staggered back, dropping the fish between bites. It flopped on the deck, its mouth oozing blood. With each smack, it inched toward him.

Eyes wide like a man gone insane, he stomped on the fish repeatedly. There was the sound of cracking bones and scales scraping loose.

"Die! Die!"

Remarkably, the thing refused to die. Worse, it *retaliated.*

With a turn of its head, it sank its teeth into his boot. The jaws sank through the rubber like nails, finding his foot.

"Ah! Ah! Ah!" Steven danced on one foot, ultimately falling back against the transom. Leaning upright, he kicked the piranha with his free foot. He felt the skin near his big toe rip as the fish came free. Once again, it flopped against the deck.

He stood up, the adrenaline stirring him into a frenzy. Blood trickled from his hands and wrist, making the grip on his Glock a slippery one. He took aim at the piranha.

Ryan held out a hand. "No, wait!"

"I got it!" Steven said, following the flapping predator with his pistol. Had he not been so focused, he would have noticed its brethren circling the boat, biting the hull to test whether it was edible. The piranhas were not intelligent, but they knew how to track prey. If it required them to briefly leave the safety of the water, so be it.

One, seeing the land-dwelling creature standing on the structure, took the leap.

It struck his neck, driving him backward. The motion wavered his aim, but not his trigger finger. Multiple bullets escaped the muzzle, missing the fish and instead finding his partner.

Ryan shuttered with each hit, then looked down at the blood pouring through the five bullet holes in his chest.

Damn. I guess Holman was right about my vest... He slumped to his right, jaw slack.

More bullets flew through the air as Steven stumbled back. For the second time, he hit the transom. Except instead of falling against it, he fell *over* it—into the water. There, he came into contact with the only thing that could shred him faster than the piranhas.

The fountain of water behind the propellers turned dark red.

There was a combined sensation of flying backward and spinning. The pontoon was still propped on the police boat, whose bow was still lodged in the hull.

Screams filled the decks. Grace and Ken were shouting incoherently, the latter trying to steer the boat away from the police boat. Bailey was on the foredeck, screaming Dustin's name. Jane was clinging to one of the chairs, yelling for Jacob and Ellen to hold tight. The kids were on the aft deck, clinging to the guardrail.

Skip made his way to the helm and forced the panicked Ken away from the seat. "Move, dude! You're flooding the engine."

"How the hell can you even know that with all this happening?"

"I know boats. Now shut up."

Skip put the boat in reverse and turned the wheel to port.

"'Know boats' my ass," Ken said. "You're turning toward the freaking thing."

"What part of 'shut up' do you not understand?" Skip engaged the throttle. There was a scraping of hull as the pontoon pried loose of the police boat. With a crackling sound, the boats separated. The pontoon righted itself with enough force to throw its party across its deck.

The police boat shot forward, the change in direction sending it east. It struck the shoreline and shattered like glass against a brick wall.

The pontoon spiraled in place, settling three hundred yards from shore. Jane rushed over to the aft deck and hugged Jacob and Ellen.

"Are you two alright?"

"Yes," Jacob said.

"DUSTIN!" Bailey screamed.

"Oh my God. We're gonna die!" cried an equally hysterical Grace.

"We're not gonna die," Skip said.

"Where's Dustin?"

"He fell off," Jane said. She panned her eyes across the surrounding water. "I don't see where he landed—oh…" Thirty feet off the port bow was an area of red, simmering water. Drifting from that area was a tattered fedora hat.

Bailey grabbed her hair and screamed. Jane went up to the top deck and put her arms on her shoulders.

"I'm sorry, sweetie."

Down below, Grace was dry-heaving over the deck. Looking at the water only worsened the sick feeling. They were in thirty feet of water with almost a thousand feet of distance from the nearest land.

"Why aren't we driving to shore?"

Skip was trying to start the engine, to no avail. "Shit."

"What's shit? What's happening?" Grace said. Skip didn't answer. He peered over the side where the police boat had struck. As he feared, there was a large gash in the hull. Already, the waterline was climbing.

"We've got problems."

Ken stepped beside him and looked. "Oh, HELL NO! We're sinking!" Immediately, Grace and Bailey's panic went to a whole new level. Grace started bombarding them with rapid-fire questions while Bailey started to cry hysterically. The kids were silent, though their faces conveyed the intense fear swelling their guts. Jacob was sweating. Ellen was simply pale, only narrowly keeping herself from hyperventilating.

"I need to call Dad," was all she could manage to say.

Skip reached out to strangle Ken, only to retract at the last moment. "Was that necessary?" Ken took a deep breath, then pulled a joint from his shirt pocket. Skip held back on any remarks. If getting high would at least calm him down, then so be it. Any effort to stop him would be useless anyway.

Ken took repeated draws on the joint before Grace snatched it from him.

"Hey!" He reached for it, but already she was out of reach. "Fine." He took another one out and lit it, only for *it* to be snatched by Bailey, who descended the stairway in a single stride. Like Grace, she was looking for anything to calm her down.

Ken stared at his empty hand, which had two joints stolen. He glanced at Skip. "Should I offer *you* one?"

"No, thank you."

"Jane?"

"No."

"What about you ladies? Should I roll you up some extra? Wanna smoke my whole stash while you're at it?"

"Shut up, jerk," Grace said. She looked up at Jane, who was peering down from the top deck. "You can have him."

"No, thank you."

"Oh, I see how it is. When everything's nice and dandy, everyone wants to be with Ken Lewis. At the slightest hint of trouble, 'Oh, Ken Lewis is a jerk—even though we'll still leech off all his shit.'"

Again, Skip was tempted to strangle him. "Come on, dude. This isn't necessary."

Ken lit a fresh joint and took a long draw. "You're right. I know *what is* necessary: getting on land!" He sat at the controls and turned the ignition. The engine turned over once and died.

"Already tried that," Skip said. "It's dead."

Ken stood up and went to the aft deck. "We can start it manually. Out of the way, kids." He pushed Ellen and Jacob aside before they had a chance to move. A far cry from the charismatic, rockstar personality he exhibited at the start of the trip, he now cursed repeatedly while frantically reaching for the outboard. He found the ripcord and started pulling, clenching his marijuana joint between his teeth.

"Hold up, man," Skip said.

"I know what I'm doing," Ken said.

"Clearly *not*! Look!"

"Now's not the time for dick measuring."

"No, dude! LOOK!" Skip grabbed him by the shoulder and made him look at the translucent layer of fluid expanding from the engine. "It's leaking fuel."

Ken stared at it for a moment. A series of curses coursed through his lips, muffled by the marijuana cigarette.

Just because it's leaking doesn't mean I can't get the engine to work.

He pulled on the ripcord again.

"Stop, dude," Skip said.

Ken stopped, only to shove him back, then continued his fruitless endeavor. All he needed was for the engine to work long enough to get them to shore. He searched for the pump, which was dangling near the waterline. He slipped under the guardrail and reached for it.

"Wait, Ken! Don't!" Jane said.

"You wanna sink? No? Shut up."

"No! KEN! Get away from the water!"

Had it not been for the marijuana-induced haziness, Ken would likely have noticed the piranhas swimming up to the waterline before they bit his fingers. Two hundred teeth sank into his hand, lighting up nerves throughout his body.

Ken screamed, the cigarette falling from his lips and onto the gas line. Fire rose from the outboard like an enraged demon, consuming its operator.

Stuck under the guardrail, Ken writhed from the agony of fire consuming his face and piranhas consuming his hand and arm.

"Kids! Move!" Skip rushed for Jacob and Ellen, but it was too late. The fuel tank ruptured like a bomb, shaking the boat and throwing him backward. When he looked up, he saw Ken, still aflame, hurtling over the guardrail. Two other splashes echoed from the other side of the boat.

Skip stumbled back to the aft deck and pulled Jacob away from the guardrail. The poor boy, miraculously, was mostly unharmed other than a few burns on his arm and neck.

"Ellen?"

He listened to the sound of splashing straight ahead. Both Bailey and Ellen were in the water. Jane saw them and screamed. The explosion had pushed the pontoon north, putting both of them several feet behind it.

"Oh, no. NO! NO! NO!" Skip couldn't stand to see anyone else get killed. Especially a kid. "Ellen! Bailey! Swim to me! Follow my voice!" He heard Jane crying above him. She was watching the feeding frenzy taking place where Ken had gone down.

Grace saw it too. She muttered something incoherent, staggered backward, then sank onto one of the sofas where she passed out.

"Skip!" Jane shouted. "What are we going to do? What can we do? We need to help them."

"We will! I promise." The part he left out was 'I don't know how'.

The sight of blood and thrashing water made Skip face a horrible truth. Those girls were *not* going to make it to the boat. They needed to get out of the water, and they only had seconds left before the fish got to them. Had it not been for the burning fuel on the water, they'd probably be torn apart already. It was a luxury that would not last.

Think! Think! Think!

His foot hit the stack of inflatable rafts lodged under the seats. He lifted two of them and returned to the guardrail.

"Bailey! Ellen! Get on these!"

To his relief, his throws were accurate. The rafts were just heavy enough to make the distance, both landing right beside the girls.

Ellen grabbed hers by the handles and lifted herself out of the water. The first attempt resulted in her flipping over. Learning from the mistake in her technique, she quickly righted the raft and tried again.

"Oh, thank God!" Jane shouted after seeing the girl she was entrusted with lift herself onto the raft.

Bailey, whose senses were dulled by alcohol, weed, and adrenaline, floundered next to her raft.

"Climb on!" Jacob shouted.

"I can't!" she yelled. A mouthful of water went down her throat, causing her to gag. Her hands found one of the handles and she pulled. The raft teetered, then flipped over her body. There was no focus in her movements. Only a disjointed mess of flailing from someone who struggled to simply keep her head above water, let alone *lift* herself out of it.

"Get on!" Ellen said.

Bailey righted the raft and grabbed both handles. Once again, she failed to pull herself free of the water.

She yelped, jolting as though stung by a bee. She yelped a second time. Then a third. The sight of her own blood clouding around her induced a new wave of panic.

Bailey grabbed the raft handles and tried again. This time, she was managing to do it right. In two seconds, she was halfway out of the water, bleeding from her hips and legs.

A loud *pop* followed by a rush of air caused the raft to fold inward. Bailey slipped back into the water, her screams lost in the bloody void.

All everyone else could see was the expanding blood cloud and the intensity of the ripples.

On the pontoon boat, Skip turned Jacob around to keep him from witnessing the slaughter. Jane was once again crying, especially after seeing the little 'dots' converging on Ellen's raft.

The girl propped herself on her hands and knees, clearly aware of the danger.

She looked up at Skip, now over thirty feet away as the pontoon continued to drift north.

"Help! Please!"

Now it was Skip who was on the verge of full-blown panic. How that kid wasn't crying up a storm was beyond him.

"We'll get you out, sweetie," Jane said. "Oh, Skip, please do something. I can't tell her father that I let his daughter—" She couldn't bring herself to say the rest.

Thirty feet became forty. Even through that distance, they heard the *pop* from teeth piercing the raft.

Ellen clung to the handles, adjusting her balance as the air fled the center. Her eyes were wide, watching the fish swirl underneath her. They were converging on the raft, tearing pieces of rubber out from under her.

"Help!"

All Skip could think of was to throw her another raft. Once again, his aim was true. It landed just a few feet away from Ellen, the momentum taking it the rest of the way. She grabbed it by the handle and rolled over right as the other raft completely deflated.

Once again, she was propped on her hands and knees. The fish continued tearing at the inedible rubber, taking a moment to realize there was nothing of substance on it. It only took a few seconds for them to move in on the new floating object.

Ellen flattened herself against the raft. A moment later, one of the fish jumped overhead, its jaws snapping where her hip had been a moment earlier.

"Smart kid," Skip said. She had seen the piranha coming and predicted its action after witnessing what they did to the late cops. It was a tactic that only bought her a few extra seconds of life. The fish were starting to work at the corners of the raft. With no others to toss her way, Skip was at a loss.

Jacob, despite the adult's intent, couldn't help but watch. Not out of fascination or curiosity, but of a desire to help his friend. She was still over thirty feet away.

"We need to get her over here," he said.

"I—" Skip could only stammer. "We don't have anything long enough to reach her with."

Seeing Skip defeated broke Jacob. He turned around, closed his eyes, and covered his ears, refusing to bear witness to Ellen's brutal death. As he turned, his foot bumped something on the floor. He opened his eyes and saw the handle of Ellen's fishing rod.

"Yes we do!"

He picked it up and faced the guardrail. The fire had died down, allowing him to lean forward.

How did she describe it? Nine o'clock. One o'clock. Ten o'clock.

He tilted the rod back, then flung it forward and released the button. The lure stretched over fifty feet, falling over Ellen.

She grabbed it and wrapped it over her wrist to keep it secure.

"Holy shit! Good thinking, kid," Skip said. Together, they pulled Ellen closer to the pontoon.

Their problems weren't over. They had to pull gradually or else risk snapping the line, and the damn pontoon boat was already forty-percent deflated. She was still doomed to end up in the water before they closed the distance.

"Skip! The kayak! Over to your right!" Jane shouted.

There it was. They must have drifted right past it after the explosion. The kayak was roughly fifteen feet north of Ellen and maybe ten to the right.

Skip took the pole and went to the port corner. Reaching out as far as humanly possible, he swung Ellen to the raft.

With every passing second the raft shrank.

Ellen, seeing the kayak nearing, reached her arm out. She closed the distance and grabbed the rim of the seat.

Water surged over her knees. The raft folded into a V-shape, the center plunging below the surface. Ellen flung herself onto the kayak, rolling onto her back.

She righted herself, nearly capsizing in the process.

"YES!" Jane shouted.

Skip clapped his hands. "Nice work, kid!"

Ellen gave a thumbs up. "Thank you! Thank you! Thank you! Thank—" She cringed as one of the piranhas collided with the hull.

"Hang on, kiddo. We'll toss a new cast and pull you onto the boat."

Ellen nodded, ducking again after a second impact. She looked at the shore, then at the pontoon. There were two breaches, one in the portside, another small one where the outboard had been. It was only a matter of time before that boat was underwater.

"No, wait!" she said.

"You can't stay down there, Ellen," Jane said.

"Nor can *you*," she replied. She yanked the paddle from its holster and turned the kayak west. "I can get to shore and call for help."

The piranhas went after the paddle the instant it dipped into the water. Despite their tugging, Ellen managed to gradually inch the boat in the right direction.

"Ellen! It's too dangerous," Jane said.

"We don't have a choice. All the phones are gone and it's only a matter of time before we'd all go under."

"She's right," Skip said. "This is our only chance to get out of this mess."

Jane watched several of the little shapes crowding around the pontoon. Common sense took hold. She finally grasped the reality that the pontoon was doomed to fall to the bottom of Lake Carlson.

"Ellen, please be careful."

"She will," Jacob said. "She *has* to."

The pressure was on. Ellen freed the paddle from the jaws of a few stalking piranhas and continued brushing it along the water, maintaining a low position to avoid any jumpers. It was a painstakingly gradual process that required lots of patience, as normally a trip of this distance could be achieved in a few minutes. Each stroke, unfortunately, was a battle in itself, as the fish relentlessly dug their teeth into the plastic, forcing her to wrestle it free each time. But it was a process that worked.

Slowly but truly, she paddled to shore.

CHAPTER 29

Billy Gile adjusted the vent so the a/c blew right at his face. It wasn't just the heat and humidity that drew the sweat from his pores. His hands trembled as they rested on the steering wheel. The smell of oil and steel in the passenger seat made him feel the gravity of the situation.

He had done many unconventional jobs for Alice, almost all of which were in the name of environmentalism. Many of these jobs left him with sore knuckles. The first job was three years ago, when she paid him to jump a couple of deer hunters.

Murderers. Flesh eaters. Fiends. *That's* what they really were.

He beat both men to a pulp, making sure to knock every one of their teeth out with the butt of their own guns. His mask and gloves prevented his identity from being revealed. Billy had learned from the poor judgement of others who conducted similar operations. They always left a fingerprint or some other bread crumb for the police to follow, leading to arrest. Thanks to their mistakes, he was always careful to keep his identity hidden during these raids.

Alice had paid him to rough up fishermen in Ohio and Indiana, hoping to stir a sense of fear in the community. Who would want to fish when a mysterious masked man was attacking people? Except, slayers of innocent animals were persistent. Many with concealed carry permits brought handguns with them, something that almost led to Billy's demise.

After stalking a pair of men, he finally made his move, immediately bashing one over the head with a tree branch. When he turned to the other, he saw the muzzle of a .38 Smith & Wesson aiming up at him. This wasn't like the time when he ambushed the hunters. In that case, he knew they had weapons and knew how to plan accordingly and get the drop on them. Here, he made the mistake of assuming they were unarmed. It was only thanks to the grace of the fisherman's poor aim that he got away.

Billy remained mostly undeterred, though he convinced Alice to concentrate their efforts on chicken farms in northern Michigan. They let loose steer and horses from captivity, mostly in regions with long highways for easy getaway. Not many people wanted to take part in these missions, with many referring to them as illicit.

As Alice once put it, "What use is lawful protest when it gets you nowhere?" It took a little convincing at the start, but now Billy saw things the same way. If the law protects murderers, then someone would have to go *beyond* the law to do what was right. Billy and Alice were protecting lives. Lives that they believed were as equally precious as any human's.

Hunters were criminals. Butchers were sick psychopaths. Fishermen were bullies, incapable of picking a fight against someone their own size. Farms were prisons. Meat shops were haunted houses, possessed by the souls of the slain.

Every operation, even the ones that didn't pan out, usually consisted of careful planning. Keeping out of prison was a priority almost as imperative as the objective itself. After all, being behind bars did nothing for the cause. He couldn't even make a martyr out of himself. Every time an environmentalist got sentenced, it only hurt the cause, as it deterred others from taking part and doing their due diligence. Hence the need for precautions.

Today, there were no precautions. There wasn't time. There were no masks, barely an escape route, and only a small window of opportunity to achieve their goal.

Doing this carried a heavy risk of prison. Not doing this, however, meant *guaranteed* prison. Billy reminded himself of this whenever the anxiety threatened to get the better of him.

The mission was the precaution. If they didn't intercept those cops—and Curt—then a nationwide search warrant would be placed on Alice, which would also lead to him.

He could see the helicopter high in the sky, like a tiny mosquito closing in on a target. The police chopper pad was only a block away. It made sense that the cops were planning to return Curt to the jail. To get there, they'd have to pass through this intersection.

Billy parked the SUV in the lot of a diner. He had the engine off in order to not draw any attention.

"Time to turn it back on," Conrad said.

Billy looked to the contractor in the passenger seat. Conrad Mendelson was a man with a stone-cold gaze. Never once had Billy seen him smile. Conrad was not a military guy, but his complete lack of emotion made him think of the discipline of

British Royal Guard soldiers in YouTube videos he had watched.

This was the second time he had hired Conrad's services. The last was six months ago, when Billy learned that one of their group was going to report them to the police. Apparently, the traitor had a change of heart, and viewed the 'law' as more important than the lives they helped preserve. Keeping the person quiet was going to be an impossible task.

As with every case, Alice and Billy reminded themselves that prison was not an option. So, they got in touch with Conrad and Gerald, who swiftly took care of the problem. They were good with short notice calls, as long as the money was right.

Gerald Yale sat in the rear passenger seat. Though not the most talkative, he displayed more personality than his partner. Physically, he looked different too. His long, shaggy hair would've helped him blend into any activist crowd Alice organized. It was a sharp contrast from Conrad's bald head and dark skin tone.

He finished counting the money inside the tan envelope. They were as thorough regarding their finances as they were their executions.

"Hundred-fifty, all here," he said. "You guys really are desperate."

"You better pull this off," Billy said.

"I'm not the one who's sweating," Gerald said.

"Stow it," Conrad said. His tone was as emotionless as his glare. "They've landed. In about sixty seconds, they'll be coming out that gate. They'll come through this intersection and take a right in the turn lane. When they do, get in the straight lane and line us up with them. Honk your horn on your way out and make them think we need help, otherwise they'll make the turn before we line up."

Billy nodded. "That's when you'll—?" He mimicked a gunshot with his finger.

"Obviously," Gerald said. He engaged a lever on his weapon. It was an assault rifle of sorts. Billy wasn't good with weapons, but one didn't have to be to know that was a mean looking gun.

"We have an advantage," Conrad said. "Most of the cops, including the County, have converged at the lake. It should be an easy getaway. After we confirm the kills, you'll turn left and take us straight out of town. If no other police pursue, we'll meet our pickup and burn this vehicle. Understood?"

"Understood," Billy said.He sat quietly for the next thirty seconds. He could see the killer grip his shotgun and pump it. Hopefully, in thirty more seconds, this would be over.

Conrad leaned forward to look down the street. "Here they come."

Billy could see the Interceptor moving in. As it neared, he recognized the faces of the two cops that had interfered with their protest at the grocery store. As the Interceptor passed by, he could see Curt in the back seat.

He started the engine.

Piece of shit. You all deserve what's coming to you.

The Interceptor slowed to a stop. The time was now. Billy steered the vehicle out of the lot and made a left, angling for the turn lane.

****

The radio was alive with calls from all over the lake. With every passing minute came a report of additional casualties, some being uniformed officers.

Royce and Pam felt helpless listening to the traffic while still being a couple of miles away.

"Car Twelve to Lorenzo, we've located Boat One and your missing Sergeant at a private beach about half a click south of the resorts. I regret to report you have an officer down."

Royce put his head on the steering wheel as he slowed to a stop. Dressel was a good officer. More than that, he was a good man who'd give you the shirt off his back.

"Another one," Pam said. "Another cop killed by Alice."

"They're all over the damn lake," Royce said. He grabbed the speaker mic. "I copy."

"There's several other bodies here. Swimmers. Hard to know how many, given the state of the water right now."

"Is there any word on Boat Two?" Royce said.

This time, it was Holman's voice. *"Negative. They're not responding to any of our calls."*

Royce threw the mic against the dashboard. "Damn it!"

Pam put a hand on his shoulder. "I'm sure Ellen's alright."

Royce brought the vehicle near the stop sign, then started turning the wheel to the right. "She'd better be, for Alice's sake."

"Trust me, I'll testify against her," Curt said.

Royce turned to look at him, intent on giving him a bitter reply. Of course he'd testify. It was the best way to reduce his own sentence.

The look in Curt's eyes made him reconsider. Royce knew a liar when he saw one, and Curt SUCKED at lying to begin with. No, he was looking at a young man genuinely shocked at the aftermath of what he had gotten involved with. Maybe that could be faked, but what sold Royce on the genuineness was the look of betrayal in Curt's demeanor. He was far more downtrodden since they left the lab. He was told by Alice they were doing something to help wildlife, not cause a mass murder. Not only was it a major setback for the cause, but it was simply wrong.

Royce's gaze softened. Maybe he had misjudged Curt. He was a flawed individual, but not irredeemable. He simply needed a better strategy to convey his beliefs.

The honking of a horn drew his attention to a silver SUV pulling up beside them. Royce could see the man in the driver's seat. He had a blond crewcut and a weird black mark on his face. A *powder* burn.

Right then, it dawned on him—this was the activist who was with Alice Kirkman at the grocery store. Royce knew trouble when he saw it.

How does this guy know we're here? Better yet, why is he pulling up next to us?

Instinctively, his hand went to his Glock.

It was a good instinct. Royce saw the two men with the activist. More importantly, he saw the muzzle of a high-powered rifle emerging through the back passenger window.

Fifteen years of training came to fruition. Royce drew his Glock and fired through his window. The shaggy haired gunman's head whipped back, his forehead carved open by three hollow point rounds.

Royce turned his aim to the passenger in the front seat, who raised a shotgun.

Both men fired. Both men missed. Not due to faulty aim, but the speeding of the SUV. The activist driver had panicked and was speeding off. They didn't get far beyond the intersection before he started doing a U-turn.

****

178

"The hell are you doing?" Conrad said, his voice stern, but miraculously emotionless. "Turn us around. They've seen our faces. We're committed now."

Heart racing, Billy hit the brakes, then turned the wheel left as far as possible. He could see Gerald's face—what *used* to be Gerald's face—in his rearview mirror. The body slumped to the left, out of view. He was grateful, as it would've continued to be a distraction.

As Conrad stated, they were committed now. If nothing else, *he* would pursue the cops himself and finish the job. At this point, it wasn't a matter of honor, but self-preservation. If he would have to blow Billy's head off and take the wheel to do it, he would. The money was already counted anyway.

Billy swung the vehicle around. Conrad thrust the shotgun through the window and fired, peppering the side of the Interceptor. The cop driver was already gunning the accelerator, making a right turn while firing one-handed. Bullets skidded off the window frame, cracking the glass. Billy slowed, then slammed his foot on the pedal again, continuing pursuit.

"Keep on them," Conrad said. He reached into the back and took Gerald's assault rifle. His partner's open skull had no impact on him. It was as if Gerald had always looked like that.

Conrad checked the magazine, then raised the weapon out the passenger window. A series of deafening *cracks* followed, concurrent with the seemingly spontaneous appearance of holes in the trunk of the police car up ahead.

****

"My God! Holy Jesus! What's happening?" Shards of glass grazed Curt's neck, furthering his panic.

"Get down as far as you can," Royce said. He made a left turn down a small business area, the screeching tires leaving black marks on the road. The SUV followed, grazing the side of a parked vehicle as its driver attempted to straighten its path.

The gunman was now using a rifle. Bullets continued to pelt the trunk and back glass. After a few hits, it shattered, leaving nothing but empty air between them and their attackers.

For Pam, it was rather helpful. Shooting back out of the window was a strenuous position anyway. It was simpler to aim straight back through the back glass.

She planted a few gunshots through the enemy windshield, hoping to kill the driver. Initially, she thought she succeeded after the vehicle backed off. After a brief moment, it picked up speed again. More bullets flew their way.

"Hold it steady," Pam said.

Royce swerved to dodge a pedestrian. "Kinda hard to do that."

"We're gonna die!" Curt shouted.

"It'd help if you shut up," Pam said. "Then maybe we can keep that from happening."

Royce made another right turn and pushed the vehicle to its limit, only to hit the brakes immediately. There was a red light up ahead, and both lanes were taken up by parked cars. On top of that, the opposite lanes were taken up with oncoming traffic turning from the intersecting road, all of which stopped after seeing the flashing lights. Inadvertently, they boxed them in.

Seeing the SUV come around the corner, Royce brought the Interceptor onto the sidewalk, crashing through the table of a coffee shop.

The owner jumped through his front door, shaking his fist at them. "You son of a bitch! I'll have a word with the—HOLY SHIT!" He managed to jump back inside and narrowly avoid being run down by the SUV.

"Sorry," Royce mouthed.

Pam slammed a fresh magazine home and resumed firing. "Who the hell are these guys?"

"The driver works with Alice," Royce said. "They've obviously got word of our little visit. Someone at the office probably made a phone call."

"Dr. Bohl? He sold us out?" Curt said, hands cupping his ears.

"Maybe not him, but it makes sense that Alice would bribe someone else at the lab to keep an eye out for police procedurals that could tie any consequences of her genetic tampering back to her." He made another turn, nicking an oncoming car in the opposite lane. It was nothing compared to the hit it took from the SUV, which knocked the car back a few feet. The SUV remained functional, its gunman once again emerging through the window.

"Yeah—that bitch knew those fish were killers. Probably hoped to skip town before anyone made a connection," Pam said.

She and the gunman fired at once. Blood splattered the dashboard. Pam yelped and spun back, hand clutching her right shoulder.

"Shit, Pam! You alright?!" Royce tried to look for himself, but had to refocus his attention on the road to avoid hitting another car. It was mid-day. Everyone with a typical nine-to-five job was leaving early.

Pam adjusted herself in her seat. "Yeah, it's not bad."

"You sure?"

"I promise. Just keep driving."

They both ducked as more gunshots struck the vehicle. Pieces of seat fabric and stuffing rained down on Royce's lap like confetti. He looked at the hole in the corner of his seat. The bullet had flown right by his arm, even managing to tear his sleeve without touching his skin.

Next time, he wouldn't be so lucky.

An explosion of rubber shook the vehicle. Right away, it began pulling to the right, forcing Royce to fight the wheel to keep it straight. In the mirror, he saw pieces of the passenger rear tire flaking all over the road. The gunman shot again, hitting the driver's side rear tire. More rubber covered the road.

Sparks spat from both sides, as though welding torches were being pressed into the car. They were literally riding on metal.

Fighting to keep control of the vehicle, he passed the tackle shop and the bakery, thus missing his opportunity to make a sharp turn.

"Shit!"

Even with the pedal floored, they were losing speed. The SUV was closing in, the gunman lining up for a better shot.

Think, damn it. Think!

There was nowhere to turn. Nowhere to hide. No time to stop and make a stand. They'd be gunned down before they'd get out of the vehicle. All there was were businesses on the right and the World War Two memorial on the left.

The glistening of puddles on the hill caught his eye. The mud was still wet from last night's rainstorm. Slippery. Beyond that was the tank and the artillery gun.

The memory of his first year on the job flashed in his mind.

Royce turned left and sped off the road, carefully maneuvering to keep the trajectory right of the M4 Sherman.

****

"What the—" Billy watched as the cops drove down the hill.

Conrad reached over and turned the wheel. "They're just desperate. Keep going." He brought his foot over and pressed it over Billy's, flooring the pedal. The SUV shot onto the grass. Mud kicked out from under the tires.

"Whoa!" Billy tried turning the wheel, but the vehicle only managed to turn a few inches. The mud was practically ice. With the initial speed, they were flying forward with no control.

Up ahead, the barrel of the huge artillery rapidly got closer.

"Turn. Turn…" Emotion finally wrinkled Conrad's face. He propped up on his hands, eyes and mouth wide as they closed in on the huge gun. "TURN!"

The SUV plowed into the gun. The muzzle pierced the windshield. And Billy.

He sat upright in his seat, essentially just a head, arms, and legs protruding from different sides of the huge artillery barrel.

****

"Heads down," Royce said. The Interceptor fishtailed in the mud, finally coming to a stop after its rear bumper collided with the M4's tread. At the same time, they heard the crash of the SUV hitting the artillery field gun.

Royce and Pam rushed outside, guns drawn, and ducked behind the engine. After a few moments, the gunman stumbled out of the passenger seat. He fell to his knees, gun in hand.

"Drop it!" Royce shouted.

The man straightened his posture. He was disoriented, but not willing to give up the fight. He began to raise the muzzle.

It didn't get further than knee height before Royce and Pam hit him with over a dozen rounds. The assailant danced in place, blood splattering from his chest. He fell to the ground, jaw slack, arms to the side.

The two officers reloaded then moved in to secure the weapons. Both winced after seeing what became of the driver with the powder burn.

They looked to the car as Curt stumbled out. He fell on his knees and vomited.

After several moments, his eyes met theirs. "Yeah, I'm definitely testifying against that bitch."

CHAPTER 30

The thudding of the kayak created the sensation of being in a large drum. The fish attacked relentlessly, scraping the plastic exterior. Occasionally one leapt, only to splash down on the other side.

Every stroke was taken with caution. The paddle was frayed, with only half of the plastic intact.

"Keep going, Ellen! You're so close!"

Skip's voice was a distant echo, indicating she had gained significant distance. It was her only indicator, for she kept her head down the entire journey to avoid any piranhas that tried to jump at her.

Her back was aching from folding over. That, combined with curiosity of how the others were holding up, made it tempting to sit up. The pontoon boat had to have taken on significant water by now. At best, they had a half hour left before the deck was completely flooded.

She needed to pick up the pace. To do that, she needed to know exactly how far she had left to travel.

Another stroke. Another tug-of-war match with the piranhas. She yanked it free, paddled a couple of times on the left side, then peeked.

To her amazement, she only had thirty feet to go. Skip was right, she was close!

"Go on, sweetie!" Jane shouted. "Be careful!"

The urgency in her voice didn't help the mental image of their predicament. Ellen took that opportunity to glance back.

The pontoon was on a slant, the bow just a couple of inches from dipping under the lake. She could see the burnt section of metal where the outboard motor had exploded. The breach on that side was thankfully minimal, despite the size of the blast. Otherwise, they'd certainly be underwater by now.

Her thoughts on the matter ceased after noticing a swarm of panfish gathering behind her. Within a split-second, she watched those shapes ascend with rapid speed.

She screamed and ducked her head down. Water peppered her back as the fish made another desperate attempt. The force to launch themselves out of the water worked against them, for all it did was send them clear over the little boat.

Another one made an attempt and failed. Then another.

It was as if they knew their window of opportunity was decreasing. One made a leap and bounced off the edge of the cockpit. Before she could breathe a sigh of relief, another jumped from further back and landed on the deck lines. It flopped in place, turning its head toward her. The jaws extended and snapped shut.

Ellen swung the paddle like a baseball bat, smacking the fish off the deck. Two splashes ruptured the lake simultaneously: one from the piranha crashing down, the second from another piranha leaping at her from behind. It struck her right shoulder, biting on impact.

She screamed and flailed in place. Not here! Not now! Not after getting so close to safety.

Ellen raised the paddle over her shoulder and smacked down. The frayed end hit the fish, knocking it clear of her flesh. It hit the deck and bounced into the water.

Ducking down, she checked her shoulder. A little blood, not much worse than if a big hamster had bitten her. Still, it was a sobering reminder of the dangers swimming beneath her.

"Ellen! What's wrong? You okay?" Jane yelled.

"I'm fine!" she yelled back. She resumed stroking, repeating to herself, "I'm fine."

She heard footsteps up ahead.

"Hey, honey? You okay?"

Ellen peeked. To her left was Mitch's neighbor, standing on the edge of his dock. He wore business casual clothes and had his car keys in hand. The guy had literally just arrived home from work and probably heard her screams. She looked at the dock. Below it was at least three feet of water.

Ellen waved her arms. "Get away from the water!"

"What?" He looked down, then back at her. "Little girl, do you need help? I heard you scream…" He looked past her and gasped. "Oh my God! Did you come from that pontoon? They look like they're in trouble."

"They are! Please call for help. But get away from the water first." The man unclipped his phone and began to dial. "Sir! Get off the dock! There's piranhas in the water!"

"Hon, I've been at this lake my entire adult life. There's no—"

Two piranhas catapulted themselves into the man, knocking him and his phone into the lake. The man flapped his arms like wings, as if attempting to fly out of the lake while the pack closed in on him. He squealed and gagged, the pain stripping him of any coordination.

Ellen tucked her face down. She didn't need to watch this. Listening to the sound of grunting and splashing water was bad enough. Oddly, the *ceasing* of that sound was more disturbing. It was a reminder of the fate her friends were doomed to suffer if she didn't get help.

Only twenty-five feet to go by the looks of it. Ellen sat up and drove the paddle into the lake. She brushed with long motions, tripling her speed. To her amazement, the fish weren't attacking. The relief turned to bittersweet awareness. They weren't attacking because they were busy with the friendly neighbor.

The thought of taking advantage of his death made her feel vile. Despite this, common sense still prevailed. The guy was dead. Not taking advantage of the window of opportunity would result in her suffering the same fate. So would Jane, Jacob, Skip, and Grace.

She torpedoed her kayak to the shore. As soon as the bow touched the sandbank, she leapt from the cockpit and ran across the deck onto the sweet shore. After allowing a moment to catch her breath, she ran into Mitch's house. The backdoor was unlocked. Mitch and Tory clearly didn't think they'd be out long enough to justify locking their doors.

The place was dark and quiet, confirming the residents' fates. If only they hadn't gone to get the kayak first. By the time they realized Mitch and Tory weren't home, the cops would've spotted them. No crash. No dead engine, thus, they wouldn't be stranded out in the water. Dustin, Bailey, and Ken would still be alive. The latter may have been a jerk, but he didn't deserve being torn to shreds.

Amazing how such an innocent gesture led to all this chaos. It made Ellen consider how all small things can lead up to something far more significant, whether it be good or disastrous.

Unfortunately, things were still looking disastrous. There was no landline. The one iPhone she found had a code lock.

She ran to the neighbor's house in hopes that maybe a family member was nearby. The doors were locked, and the only car in the driveway was the man on the dock. With his phone in the lake, there was no hope of making a call. She ran to the next neighbor's house. Nobody was home and the doors were locked there as well.

"Damn it!"

Ellen returned to Mitch's house and rummaged through again. There had to be another phone somewhere.

"In this age of digital devices and social media, how could there be only two phones?!"

Social media…

Ellen ran into the living room. In the corner was a desktop computer. A personalized screensaver of home photos scrolled across the screen. She shook the mouse, bringing the computer to its home screen.

No login was necessary. *Thank God Almighty.* She got online and logged onto *Facebook.* After several excruciating moments of loading, she was finally able to get onto *Messenger.*

Pam's name was at the top of the list. She clicked on the tab and immediately started typing.

Pam! We're in trouble! Pontoon is sinking.

Piranhas have killed six people. PLEASE HELP!

Not a prank. PLEASE HELP NOW!!!!!

CHAPTER 31

"Be careful with her," Royce said to the paramedic. Pam sat in the back of the ambulance, smirking at her partner as he supervised her care.

"It's cute how much you care."

"That's not funny. You could've been killed."

"Relax, hubs. I'm still kicking. I'm sure these guys know what they're doing—OW! Motherfucker! Didn't you hear him?! Be careful!"

"Sorry," the medic said.

One of the state troopers on site approached the ambulance. His face was pale from inspecting the remains of the SUV driver, identified as William 'Billy' Gile. He was still skewered on the artillery gun. With much of the fire departments' resources and personnel focused on the disaster at Lake Carlson, it would be a while before they could properly remove the dead suspect from the weapon.

"Is the injury serious?" he asked.

The paramedic finished pulling her sleeve apart to reveal the wound. "You're lucky, ma'am. It's just a flesh wound. Considering the kind of rounds being shot at ya, six inches to the right, you'd have a hole the size of an apple blown through you."

"Ya think I don't already know that?" She winced during the bandage procedure. "Damn. Takes me right back to freaking Baghlan."

Royce perked up. "I didn't know you were shot in Afghanistan."

"Eh, not exactly. We were testing a field gun. I sat down to take a breather, ended up dosing off. The pricks decided to fire the thing off to give me a friendly wakeup for their own amusement. Woke me up alright. I practically flew off the ground, right into the edge of the tailgate. Every time I hear a loud explosion—takes me right back!"

He chuckled. "Sounds awful." He looked to the road as more flashing lights appeared. He expected it to be another state vehicle, only to be surprised when it turned out to be a cherry light on a personal vehicle. "Sergeant Calloway?"

Pam snorted. "Look at that. He finally answered his phone."

The midnight shift supervisor pulled over near the state Interceptor, then hobbled down to the scene.

"Hot damn!" he said in his thick Texan accent. "Can't lie, Royce. When you expressed concern about the lake, I thought you were being a wannabe detective looking for a raise or a promotion. Didn't think you were actually onto something."

"What the hell took you so long to answer the call?" Royce said, not taking the bait of Calloway's 'nice work, dude' routine.

"Uh, don't know if you know this—but I *work* nights. I go to bed as soon as I get home. I know this might seem like a foreign concept."

"Plenty of your staff arrived with no issues," Pam said.

"I'm a heavy sleeper," Calloway said. He put his hands up. "Listen, I responded as soon as I saw the message. I got to the station, grabbed a radio, and was headed to the lake when I heard your last transmission." He drew a long breath. "So... you guys alright?"

Royce nodded toward the SUV. "Better than those pricks."

"I can see that. Have you identified them?"

"I saw the driver with Alice Kirkman yesterday. My guess is that she sent him. The other two, I'm not sure. The one who did most of the shooting doesn't strike me as an activist type. He definitely knew his guns."

"Not well enough, clearly," Calloway said. "How the hell did you manage to see them coming?"

"Attention to detail. He's good like that," Pam said. "Hence, he was the first person to say piranhas were in the lake when even I was saying that sounded ridiculous."

"I can see he made us all look like fools," Calloway said. He looked at Curt, who was seated in the backseat of the State Interceptor. "What about him?"

"I think they were trying to kill him and keep him from testifying," Royce said.

"Damn, these people really stepped in it," Calloway said. He took another deep breath. "So, is it true about Larry?" Royce looked down and nodded. "God! Son of a bitch."

Pam looked down to her left. "Who the hell is blowing up my phone?"

"I'd rather you held still," the paramedic said.

"OR, you could pause for half a second while I grab my phone so I can see what's so important."

The medic took the hint and leaned back. Pam unclipped her phone. A big red number *3* hovered above her *Messenger* app. She opened it, finding three unread messages from Ellen Dashnaw.

"Royce?!"

"What's the matter?" he asked. Pam hopped off the ambulance and showed him the messages.

Pam! We're in trouble! Pontoon is sinking.

Piranhas have killed six people. PLEASE HELP!

Not a prank. PLEASE HELP NOW!!!!!

It would seem that this day was determined to give Royce Dashnaw a heart attack. First Larry, then learning that Lake Carlson had ten thousand piranhas, to nearly getting gunned down. Now this.

"Holy shit. Where is she?"

Pam took the phone back and started typing.

Where are you?

The three-decimal typing icon appeared. *2144 Dreher Road. I'm on shore, but everyone else is on boat. Sinking fast.*

"Ask if there's a number we can call her at," Royce said. Pam sent the message and waited.

No phone. Lost during crash.

...

Two policemen met us. Fish killed them.

"Oh no. Royce…"

"We gotta go."

"What's the matter?" Calloway said.

"There's a pontoon on the south end of the lake in trouble. My daughter's friends are on it. We have to go."

Pam was already sprinting up the hill. "Come on."

"What are you going to do for a vehicle?" Calloway said, pointing at the wrecked Interceptor.

Royce turned to the state trooper on site. "Trooper, I'm gonna need to borrow your vehicle."

To his surprise, the man didn't argue. The trooper tossed his keys then gave a casual two-finger salute. "I have to stay on scene anyway. Technically, you're supposed to too, but considering the circumstances—" He shrugged, then pointed at the wreck. "Just don't bring it back looking like that."

"You've got a deal. Thanks."

"What about Curt?" Pam said.

"I'll take him back to the jail," Calloway said. "You guys get going. Hurry up! If there's a pontoon sinking, every second counts."

"Thanks, man." Royce followed Pam up to the state Interceptor and opened the back door.

Curt was slouched, the stress of the day having caught up to him. He looked at the two officers, their body language expressing an urgency even greater than the shootout.

"Oh, great. *Now* what's wrong?"

"Gotta go, bud. Someone needs help. You're gonna go with Sergeant Calloway. He'll take you back to the jail."

"Oh. Lovely. *Jail*.... Eh, beats being shot at, I suppose." He got out and stood beside Calloway. Royce got into the driver's seat and started the engine. Screeching tires launched the Interceptor down the road.

Pam brought *Messenger* back onto her screen and began typing to Ellen. *We're coming now. Hold on.*

"So, you still feel sour about Ellen having a *Facebook*?"

"Oh, shush. Why don't you get more info out of her while we're on our way? Info about the situation. Not 'fishing and stuff'."

Pam smiled as she typed. That smile faded when she got Ellen's response. "She says the pontoon's in deep water. Middle of the lake. She says there's small boats out, but it's not safe to go out on them. The fish jump."

"That's what Holman reported," Royce said. He unclipped his speaker mic from his shirt. "All Lorenzo units, are there any boats available? I need to go to the south end of the lake."

"That's a negative, Sergeant," Holman replied. *"Boats Three and Four are rescuing stragglers over at the northeast residences. Boat One's been commandeered by the County for rescue a quarter mile south of there. We don't have any other boats available. Chopper units conducting rescues in lake's center."*

Royce slammed the mic on the dashboard. "Damn it!"

"There is another option," Pam said. "We have a chopper of our own. I happen to know a pilot."

Royce didn't bother debating. He turned the wheel and did a U-turn back to the airfield.

"If only she messaged you twenty minutes earlier. We could've gone straight there. And avoided a gunfight in the process."

CHAPTER 32

"Dashnaw to Holman. We'll be using the copter to rescue the people on the pontoon. Any updates on the resort?"

"Still a few stragglers, Sergeant, but most people are clear. Lots of casualties though. We're still in great need of ambulances."

"Dispatch is working on that. State informed me that the National Guard is being deployed. Should be seeing trucks in the next half hour or so."

"Hope they make it sooner."

Listening to the chatter on Calloway's radio in real time, without the lens of the television separating him from reality, Curt found himself having an all new appreciation for the police. He still had his issues with them, but after Royce and Pam's effort to save his life after the people he trusted tried to end it, he couldn't help but reconsider he may have misjudged them to an extent.

Royce and Pam may have been more than a little rough on him in the jail cell, but in their defense, they had just discovered their Chief's ravaged corpse. He wasn't just a Chief, but a friend. Family, practically. Their attitude was pale compared to other police departments. That aside, it was clear they were good cops. Thanks to them, he was alive. Sure, one could argue they were protecting their own skin as well, but it didn't change the fact that those guys were definitely sent to keep him from testifying.

He rested in the backseat, watching the scenery as it passed by. He saw the soccer fields and the flower shop. They passed the intersection with the half-dead tree that needed some of its branches removing.

They were headed east.

"Hey Officer?"

"Hmm?"

"Not that I'm eager to go there, but isn't the jail *that* way?" He pointed behind them.

Calloway glanced back, then at his phone. A message appeared on the screen. His eyes went back and forth between the road and the screen.

"Don't worry, kid. We'll get there."

Curt sat silently, figuring the officer was simply taking the scenic route. Maybe there were road closures on the other side due to the shootout. It made sense—*some* sense. That is, until Curt realized there were plenty of other paths Calloway could've taken. A left here. A right there. There were plenty of routes he could've used to get around the various collateral damage.

They turned south at the next intersection. Curt sat straight. In this direction came plenty of country road, trees, and few residences.

Is it just me, or is this guy going AWAY from the station?

Calloway's phone pinged again. He picked it up and typed with his thumb, keeping his other hand on the road.

"Huh. I've seen cops fine people for that," Curt said.

Calloway chuckled. He sent his message and dropped his phone on his lap.

"Yeah, we tend to be human too," he said.

The vehicle was slowing down. Curt looked down at his arms. The Sergeant had re-cuffed him, locking his wrists behind his back. It made sense at first. After all, it was proper police procedure. Now, it made him feel defenseless.

The phone chimed again. After a moment, Calloway looked at it. Curt watched his jaw clench as he read the message.

"Um, dude?" Curt said, gesturing to the road.

Calloway looked ahead and saw he was drifting into the opposite lane. "Whoops!"

Curt took advantage of the Sergeant's attention briefly locked on his task. He slipped the cuffs under his legs as quickly as he could. The chain was now under his knees. Just a little further to go. Unfortunately, he'd have to fold himself significantly to get them under his feet, which would likely draw attention.

He had no intention to escape. When he told Royce he'd testify, he meant it. However, something about this trip was off. The route, specifically this location. Calloway's increasingly fidgety motions. The eagerness to read the texts, as though they contained vastly important information.

"Must be important stuff."

"The State's giving updates on the situation," Calloway said.

"Oh. You'd think they'd announce that on the radio rather than send mass texts, considering current events. All the cops are moving frantically like ants. You'd think they wouldn't have time to stop and read texts."

Calloway didn't seem to hear him. He was watching the road intently now. The same man who spent the last five minutes driving irresponsibly was now hyper-concerned about his surroundings.

Curt looked at the streaks of sweat his palms left on the steering wheel. "Might wanna turn on the a/c."

"Uh-huh."

Now Curt was really uncomfortable. He needed to get his hands in front of him.

He looked at the phone in the officer's lap.

Come on! Whoever it is, send another text. Hurry up. Come on... The screen lit up, revealing a message bar in its center. *Yes!* The enthusiasm dissipated like a rain drop in the ocean when he saw the last four digits of the number.

9327.

"Fucking hell."

"What?"

"Uh—" Curt stammered. All doubt was gone. He NEEDED to get out of this car. Alice was paying this guy off. No wonder he was driving out into the middle of nowhere. He was looking for a place to dispose of him. That's why he was looking around. For witnesses, and for an execution zone. Probably planned to take him into the woods, shoot him in the back, then contrive a story of 'the prisoner escaped and tried to flee'.

He needed to free his hands, but knew if Calloway realized what he was doing, he'd shoot him right then. With it being his personal vehicle with no barrier, it would be an easy enough matter to say 'the inmate lunged at me, forcing me to defend myself'. No, he needed to get Calloway focused on something else.

Curt cleared his throat. "You got another text."

Calloway looked at the phone, then started typing his response.

Curt leaned forward and slipped his hands under his feet. By the time he straightened, the Sergeant was pulling up onto a dirt trail. *Make it less obvious what you're doing, why don't ya?*

This clearly wasn't a typical hustle for the crooked cop. Maybe he was fed up with working endless boring nights in a small department with no sign of rising further up the ladder. Considering his chunky build, he wasn't likely to be taken by the state, the county, or larger city departments. So why not take a couple hundred grand from a rich actress?

"Oh, lovely," Curt said.

"What?"

"Do we really have to stop here? I don't want my friends to see me in the back of this car, man!"

"Friends?"

"Yeah, today's Friday, right? We were planning to meet up over here for one of our seminars. Become one with nature. Plan the next tasks for protecting innocent animals from slaughterers who killed them for sport. Shouldn't be too far up ahead."

Calloway stopped. "Out here?"

"Yeah. Why?"

He could tell Calloway wasn't entirely convinced. Still, the tactic went to his head. The Sergeant was looking into the woods with caution. The thoughts going through his mind were so obvious, he may as well have said them out loud. *Man, I think he's lying. But if I shoot him out here, and somebody sees, I'm beyond screwed.*

Calloway backed up and turned the vehicle around. "I was just looking to do a round-a-bout anyway."

"Yeah? Here?"

"The Lieutenant asked me to check around here for, uh, any residents with twenty-footers that we could utilize to use on the lake."

Curt waited for the vehicle to pick up speed. "Oh. Interesting. Isn't he out of town on vacation?"

Fresh sweat on the steering wheel.

Calloway steered onto the country road, already in search of a new execution spot.

"Yes. He's the guy texting me. Hence I'm always looking at my phone while driving."

"Texting?! I thought the State was sending the texts."

Calloway smiled nervously, then clenched his jaw. He *knew* he was caught. His hand crept to his knee as though about to check his phone, then eased toward his pistol.

Curt lunged, throwing his cuffs over the cop's neck, then pulled back with all his might.

Calloway arched his back, eyes and mouth wide. The suppression of oxygen triggered frenzied desperation. The car whipped to the left, bumping as it hit the grass. Then came the tree.

CRASH!

The vehicle ricocheted off the tree, coming to a stop several feet away.

Curt rested against the back of the seat. He had been thrown against it during the impact. He spat a little bit of blood then checked his teeth with his tongue. There was at least one loose crown for sure.

He looked over the seat. Calloway was unconscious but still breathing. His head was slumped against the window frame, his lip cut open after hitting the upper bar of the wheel.

Curt removed his hands and dug around Calloway's belt, finding the key to the cuffs. He freed himself, cuffed Calloway's hands to the wheel, then got out of the car. It took some effort to open the driver's side door.

The Sergeant's phone had fallen by his feet. Curt grabbed it and scrolled through the messages. Sure enough, Calloway and Alice were messaging back and forth, with her promising him two-hundred grand to execute Curt Lin.

That information paled to what Curt read at the start of the conversation.

Why aren't you picking up?

Can't talk on the phone. Curt in backseat.

Where's the two cops?

I couldn't get to Dashnaw and Pam Nettie. They're taking a helicopter to the south side of the lake. Some address on Dreher Road.

Good. That's a small road. Should be easy to find him. I'll put Conrad's long rifle to use. Shoot Curt in the back. Just do it where nobody will notice. Then bring him over here. We'll say he did it…. and delete this message!

"Shit." Curt grabbed Calloway's radio. "Royce! Anybody. It's a trap. It's—" He looked at the radio, realizing it had broken during the crash.

He dialed 9-1-1 with Calloway's phone.

"9-1-1. State your location and nature of your emergency."

"Hi. I'm on… some road. One of your cops tried to kill me. He's been paid off by somebody who's planning to kill your officers in Lake Carlson."

"State your name, please."

"Curt Lin." *Oh, shit. They have me on record as an inmate— yeah, they're not gonna believe me.*

"Stay on the line, please."

"No, you don't understand. There's going to be an ambush... hello?" They put him on hold. He hung up. There was no use. They'd arrest him and question him at the station. By then, Alice would complete her evil deed.

She may have been as passionate an anti-gun activist as she was animal rights, but she knew how to shoot. Those rifle lessons during her acting career were paying off in a way she probably didn't expect.

With the radio dead and most of the cops on the other side of the lake, there was nobody to stop her.

Except me.

"Oh, come on!"

After losing the brief argument with his conscience, he got to work. First, he removed Calloway's pistol. Though it wouldn't be a good look running around with a policeman's gun, he was willing to take that risk. No way was he going to leave it with a guy who tried to kill him, even if he was handcuffed.

It only took five hundred feet of running to exhaust Curt. He stopped and rested his hands on his knees, spitting. All seemed hopeless. A *marathon runner* wouldn't run the distance in time, let alone a skinny, non-athletic vegan.

Royce and Pam were doomed. He sat on the side of the road, holding the stolen gun. *Yeah, not a good look. I'm screwed.*

The sound of tires crunching gravel drew his attention to the south. A truck was coming. Probably just some guy passing through or coming home from work. Either way, it was a vehicle.

Curt didn't like what he was about to do, but the alternative was less moral. He stood up and waved his hands frantically. The driver pulled over and rolled his window down.

"Hey, you need help—oh..." He looked at Curt's jumpsuit.

Aw, shit. I forgot about that.

Already, the guy was about to take off from the 'escaped inmate'.

Curt drew the weapon from behind him. "Ah-ah! Hands up!" The driver complied, which made Curt feel even more like crap. "Step out."

"What the hell do you think you're doing?"

"Sorry, man. I need it. No time to explain."

"No way in hell!"

"Dude... I'm pointing a gun at you!"

"The way that thing's wavering, you clearly don't know how to use it."

The man was sizing him up. He was a largely built fella compared to Curt's scrawny figure. It wouldn't even be a tussle.

Curt was shaking. This wasn't like the movies, where people simply complied with gunmen. This was the country, where people usually put up a fight even when the odds were against them.

"Come on. Out!" His attempt to add menace to his voice only made it squeakier. Now the guy was laughing.

"Not happening. Freaking criminal."

"No-no, man. I'll bring it back. I just need it for a sec."

"HA! Right!"

The shakes intensified. "For real! Without a scratch—OH SHIT!" He jumped back after accidently discharging the gun into the bed of the truck. The driver juddered, then got out of the truck, hands raised. He looked at the bullet hole in the bed, then sneered at the thief.

"You son of a bitch! If I ever find you…"

"Sorry! I didn't mean it!" Curt got in the truck and sped off, cringing as he watched the man run down the street as though to chase him.

CHAPTER 33

Time was running out. The lake had swallowed the entire bow of the pontoon and was slurping the rest up with increasing speed. Determined round shapes circled the dead machine, patiently awaiting the delivery of meat aboard.

Jacob clung to his sister and she to him.

"It'll be okay, bud."

"No it won't," he muttered. "Nobody's coming."

"Stop saying that, kid," Skip said. "Ellen made it to shore. Help is coming right now. I guarantee it."

A scream by Grace made all three of them judder. A fish had attempted to jump, only to hit the guardrail. It was the third time in the last minute she cried out, and the dozenth since she awoke. Skip had desperately tried to stir her awake since Ellen boarded the kayak, believing it would be easier on the rescue party if she was conscious. Now, he would give anything for her to pass out again.

"Grace, I know it's scary, but you need to stop."

"Easy for you to say!"

"Easy?" He waved a hand at the water. "Do I look like I'm in a different predicament?"

Grace clung to the charred stern railing. As though teetering on a fulcrum, the rear of the boat lifted higher.

The final plunge was beginning.

Jane clung to the rail with her free hand. "I'm sorry, buddy. You were right. We shouldn't have come on this trip."

Skip grabbed a firm hold on both of them, holding them close as though they were his own family.

"So, you didn't want to come aboard either?"

She looked him in the eye. "No. You?"

"Not originally. Ken tried guilting me into coming. As rich as he was, he was too cheap to bring booze."

"He wore you down, huh? At least you weren't so stupid to come on this trip because you thought you had a chance of arranging a date."

"Well…" Skip looked away.

"Well what?"

Skip watched the rising water. "I guess it really doesn't make a difference at this point."

"Just keep talking, please," Jane said.

"Maybe he wasn't the only one who had a crush on Ken," Jacob said.

Skip chuckled. The fact that this kid could maintain a sense of humor during what may be his last moments was uplifting. So was Jane's attitude. The fear was very present in her eyes, but the poor girl was doing her damnedest to keep it together.

"Not quite. I only agreed to come when…" he laughed nervously. "Well… when I learned you were gonna be on board."

Jane lifted her head. "What?"

"I know. Foolish, right?"

"No. Not at all. You want to talk about foolish. I'm the one going to my grave knowing I came on this pontoon in hopes of hooking up with Ken Lewis."

"First, you're *not* going to your grave today. Second, I'll upstage you in the foolishness by asking you out while we're on a sinking boat."

Jane managed to smile. "I'll say yes—on condition we get out of here alive."

He squeezed her hand. "Deal."

"Yuck." Jacob's humor left him as he looked at the water. "We *are* gonna get out of here, right?"

"We will, kid. I promise. Help's on the way."

"Yeah, no shit," Grace said. She was looking to the shoreline a thousand feet away. Ellen was now outside, watching from shore. Clinging to the rail, Grace stood up and cupped one hand around her mouth. "HEY YOU LITTLE TWERP! GET A BOAT AND COME GET US!"

"Jesus, Grace! Don't ask that of her. It's a miracle she made it to shore to begin with."

"There's plenty of boats. That kid can grab one and use it to pick us up."

"Most of them probably require a key," Jane said. "And Skip's right. She'll be at risk. Those fish will jump aboard and get at her, just like they did with the police."

"She'll be fine." Grace turned to shore and yelled at the top of her lungs. "KID! BRING A BOAT OUT HERE, DAMN IT! HURRY UP! WE'RE ABOUT TO DIE!"

"Grace, stop," Jane said.

"Fuck off, bitch."

So much for their supposed lifelong friendship. It was typical of Grace to get snippy during tense moments, but it was abundantly clear that when real trouble presented itself, all consideration for others went out the window.

Skip couldn't wave to the shore without sacrificing his grip on Jane and Jacob. "Ellen! Don't come out here!"

****

Ellen heard him, but it didn't matter. There was no sign of help so far. Pam had sent a message declaring they were on the way, but so far, they were nowhere in sight.

Guilt took over. How could she stand here and watch while her friends descended to their doom? There were plenty of boats nearby. She needed one with an outboard motor that didn't require key ignition.

She ran down the shore. The first neighbor had a twelve-footer, but it only had oars and no motor. They would be in the water before she made it a third of the way. The next deck was the same. Worse, actually—she saw strips of clothing near the swimming platform several yards out. The fish were fast and thorough. You didn't go into the water for more than a minute before they zeroed in on you.

It made her all the more hesitant when she finally did find a motorized boat on the third property down. The owner wasn't home by the looks of it. Lights off. No vehicles present. The only thing present was an aluminum twelve-footer with an outboard motor.

"Hurry up, kid!" Grace shouted.

Jane's voice quickly followed. "No! Don't!"

Ellen couldn't take it. She hopped aboard the boat and started the motor. The boat took off at a relatively slow speed. She pushed it up to third gear. Even then, it seemed fairly slow compared to the pontoon.

Still faster than oars.

She felt a bump on the hull. There was a grinding sound behind her, followed by something which sounded like rain.

Turning back, she saw blood and scales splattering over the water. One of the fish had run into the motor.

More thuds echoed from under the bow. Another sawing and splattering sounds.

It dawned on her. They weren't swimming into the propellor blades. She was cruising over a whole pack of them.

A few made the leap. Ellen ducked, hitting her chin on the center seat. Nursing the cut on her jaw, she sat up, only to duck again. This fish missed her, but landed in the boat. It flopped twice, clattering its jaws.

Ellen raised the oar and repeatedly drove it into its head like a javelin, crushing its skull.

More blood filled the water. The motor shook, threatening to detach from the transom. Ellen grabbed the throttle and twisted it back and forth. Up from the blood and guts came a piranha, jaws parted. It struck her forehead, knocking her backward.

"Ellen! Turn around!" Skip shouted.

His words were barely audible due to the incessant flopping of the piranha's scaly body against the boat. Ellen floundered, seeing the rows of triangular teeth snapping near her eyes. She grabbed it by the tail and flung it back, letting go before it could swing its head around to seize her.

Back on her feet, she raised the oar to crush the intruder. The simultaneous impact and pain of another fish colliding against her back drove her forward. Tripping over the seat, she came down against the bow gunwale. Her attacker landed beside her. It turned and found her ankle with its jaws.

Ellen screamed and flipped onto her rear. With a kick, she flung the piranha over the side and into the water, where it rejoined its school. She checked her ankle, finding blood leaking from a circular wound, but it wasn't anything she couldn't walk away from.

She leaned over the center deck and brought the oar down on the remaining piranha. The impact caved its body in with enough force to pop its left eye out.

The motor stalled, its blades jamming against the horde occupying the shallow waters. Her mind started to grasp the futility of her endeavor. She was only halfway between the shore and pontoon, and the fish were attacking her as if they had a personal vendetta.

She knelt against the throttle and pulled at the ripcord. Nothing. Her next attempt was halted mid-pull. Two determined piranhas, two feet in length, rose from the lake. Both hit the edge of the transom, which scraped their undersides and drew blood. As soon as they hit the water, the rest of the pack converged. Scales and fins were torn free. The piranhas bit back in a brief attempt to defend themselves, but the pack had the power of numbers and were powered by the scent of fresh blood.

The piranhas were loyal to their brethren. Until blood was drawn.

Ellen watched the chaos unfold. It only took a few seconds for the fish to tear the wounded members to bits. Immediately, they turned their attention back to the twelve-footer.

There were dozens at minimum. They were all over the boat, waiting along the surface.

Ready to strike.

Their threatening glares were eclipsed by a vast shadow. A heavy downdraft hit Ellen. She looked up.

Like angels from Heaven, her father and Pam descended in the department helicopter.

He's gonna be pissed at me for coming out on this boat.

****

"Why the hell is she out on that boat when she was on shore?!"

Pam kept her eye on the instrument panel as she lowered the chopper. "You know Ellen. She was obviously trying to help her friends." She steered the chopper in a tight circle to gauge the situation. The pontoon would be completely underwater in two minutes at most. Additionally, they could see the fish gathering around the smaller fishing boat. "It's your call. How should we do this?"

Royce opened the fuselage door and pumped his company shotgun. "Take us near Ellen. I'll clear the water, then board her vessel. You bring the chopper by the others and tell them to climb aboard."

"Aye-aye, Sergeant."

She lowered the chopper until it was a few feet over the water. Royce opened the fuselage door and pointed his shotgun at the water near Ellen's boat.

"Get down as far as you can, honey!"

Ellen crouched low and folded herself. The sight of the shotgun muzzle made it clear what the plan was.

Royce unloaded into the water. Buckshot formed a dozen tiny streaks under the water, resulting in a new blood cloud followed by the floating bodies of dead fish. Pam carefully maneuvered the chopper around the boat, allowing Royce to pump lead into the pack.

The bloody water simmered as the dead were fed upon by the others.

Royce held the shotgun by the barrel and knelt at the edge of the fuselage. "Alright. Take me down."

Pam brought him as close as possible. She immediately had to adjust, for the downdraft forced the boat to the side.

Realizing what was happening, Ellen sat up and drove both oars into the water. She rowed against the air current, keeping the boat as steady as possible. The chopper settled eight feet overhead.

"Watch out, kid!" Royce said. He let himself drop, landing perfectly upright in the front seat. "Shit! Damn! My ass is gonna feel that for a while."

"Dad! What about them?" Ellen pointed at the pontoon.

"Pam's gonna get them. Right now, I need to get you to shore." Royce loaded some fresh shells into his shotgun and moved to the stern. He fired four shots into the horde below, then handed the weapon to Ellen. "Remember how I showed ya?"

"Yeah." She shouldered the weapon and aimed it away from him. On multiple occasions, she had been the subject of scrutiny among her peers about being trained in firearms at such a young age. As far as she was concerned, those kids could go to hell. Shotguns were not her favorite weapon. Too much kick. However, in this situation, it was the most ideal weapon to use against a tight group of targets.

Royce yanked on the ripcord twice. The propellors spun to life, spitting bloody water and guts. He turned the boat around and pointed it to shore.

"Just hang on… WHOA!" He saw the group of fish gathering on the port side, ready to jump. A loud *crack* and the onslaught of buckshot sent all four fish spiraling backward like hockey pucks.

Ellen caught her breath, the kickback having nearly knocked her over the seat. She pumped the shotgun. "They're everywhere."

"Not for long," Royce said.

"You have a plan to kill them?"

"Yeah. It's called 'get everyone out of the water'. With nothing to feed on, they'll turn on each other." He pushed the throttle to third gear and watched the shore get nearer.

****

"Yes! Yes! Yes!" Skip said as the landing skates drew near. He lifted Jane and Jacob over the guardrail. With the bow beginning to angle straight down, they were literally standing on the stern rail.

"Watch yourself, Jake."

"Yes, sis."

"I don't get it! Why don't they have anyone coming down on them drop ropes, or whatever they're called?!" Grace said. "Why are they getting so low?"

"You're seriously complaining?" Skip said. "This isn't the Coast Guard. These choppers are for reconnaissance and general patrol. Not water rescue. They have boats for that."

The chopper came down next to the stragglers. The pontoon's fall accelerated. Water climbed over the guardrail, swallowing the boat whole. The group were literally standing in the middle of the lake, ankle deep in water.

"Go! Jump! Get aboard!" Skip shouted. He lifted Jacob and threw him through the open fuselage entrance. Jane was next, then Grace. Skip was now knee-high and sinking fast.

Jane turned and reached down. "Grab my hand!" Skip clasped hands with her. Jacob knelt by her side, grabbed his wrist, and pulled.

The chopper lifted, hoisting him from the water as the piranhas converged. A few jumped at him and missed. One managed to get ahold of the sole of his shoe, only to be kicked free by his other leg.

With a pull by his crush and her brother, Skip was aboard the chopper. He slammed the fuselage door shut and rested against the seat.

"WHEW! Talk about perfect timing, Officer!"

"Sorry we didn't get here earlier," she replied.

"Pam? Is everyone aboard?" Royce asked.

"Yep! Everyone's safe!"

"Pam? Thanks for the lift!" Jacob said.

Pam looked back. "Don't worry. It's all over now."

"Where's Ellen?" Skip said.

"She and her dad are on shore. I'm gonna find a spot to land and let you guys out."

A series of thank yous followed, even from Grace. Safety brought back normalcy to her senses, and a realization of how quickly she got selfish when things got tough.

"I can't believe we're safe."

Pam pulled up on the joystick and breathed a sigh of relief as she watched Royce and Ellen step on shore. Had they arrived a minute late, it would've been disaster for the whole group. Most of all, she was overjoyed to see Ellen safe and sound.

Had she been killed or severely injured by those things... Pam couldn't bring herself to even imagine it. It was a moment that made her realize that she didn't just like that kid. She had a fleeting love for her. Almost a motherly love, or at the very least, a big sister type.

Once the chopper was set down, Pam's first plan of action was to give Ellen the biggest hug ever.

Thud!

"The hell was that?" Jane said.

Pam looked around. She knew the sound of a small projectile impact. Another one echoed through the hull. And another, this one higher. The fourth one resulted in smoke billowing from the rotor. Alarms blared in the cockpit.

The engines were failing, the rotors quickly losing speed.

"Strap yourselves in right now!" she said. The group followed her instructions and got in the seats. Pam twisted the joystick in an attempt to steer the chopper over land. Crash landing was inevitable. Better to land on shore than in water teeming with hungry fish.

More thuds hit the chopper. More emergency lights appeared on the panel. The tail rotors were failing.

The shore was still a few hundred feet away and the chopper was falling rapidly. Pam was forced to weigh her options within a split-second. Getting to shore was impossible. She needed to get as close as possible.

The chopper twirled in midair like a leaf in autumn. With each rotation, she studied the shoreline for the safest area to crash land.

There!

Roughly seventy feet south of Royce's position was a floating swim platform.

"Hold on!" She steered the chopper to the south and braced for impact.

****

"Oh, Jesus!" Royce said. His mind was warped between figuring out the source of those gunshots and figuring out a way to help Pam.

There was nothing he could do but watch as the chopper hit the water. The rotor blades snapped on impact. Like shrapnel from a grenade, they soared through the air, shredding vegetation and splintering any real estate unfortunate enough to be in their path.

Royce forced Ellen to the ground and held her there. Once the metal storm ended, they rose back to their feet. The chopper was in seven feet of water, the cockpit angled up. The tail had broken off, protruding from the water like the end of a busted tree branch.

"Pam! Jane!" Ellen screamed.

"Come on."

They ran down the shoreline.

"Jane! Jacob!" Ellen shouted.

"Ellen, STOP!" Royce didn't give her a chance to obey. He grabbed her by the shirt collar and yanked her back. Ellen fought initially, unsure why her father would hold her back at such a moment. When she saw the woman approaching with a rifle aimed at them, she understood.

Ellen didn't know who this woman was. Royce did.

"Alice Kirkman, you psychopathic bitch!"

CHAPTER 34

Alice Kirkman held her breath, keeping her sights on the cop. It was the only way she could think of to steady her heart rate and keep the gun from shaking. She was jittery from the devastation she had just caused. She had been on set to witness several spectacular special effects during her career. She had seen buildings crumble, vast stretches of land go ablaze, simulations of tsunamis in giant pools, and cars crash in explosive impacts that seemed impossible for any stuntman to live through.

The chopper crash was real, as was her understanding of the acts she had just taken. Despite her hate for people like Royce, she never thought she'd go to such extremes to follow her beliefs. Though unpleasant, she would do it again in a heartbeat.

The mission was almost over. All she had to do was take care of this cop. The only aspect that caused hesitation was the question of whether she would off the kid. The cop, no problem. That hesitation only lasted a few moments. It was the greater good that mattered. How many young animals were lost in the food industry and sports? What was one life compared to the millions of eggs that were scrambled for breakfast every morning?

With that in mind, Alice was at peace with her actions.

She was surprised how natural the weapon felt in her hands. She generally hated firearms, generally because she believed they were the primary tools used to slaughter wildlife. She had attended a few gun control marches, though she mainly focused her efforts on animal rights. Still, she made a point to post on her twitter about the evils of the Second Amendment and those who believed it applied to present day firearms. Those thoughts extended to her firearms instructors, many of whom walked away from various productions after she initiated heated arguments on the subject.

The training held up. It took four shots to hit the swash plate, but considering it was a moving target at a fair distance, she felt rather impressed with herself. She felt the weight of what she had done, but only in the sense that she needed to wrap up loose ends. Remorse had no part of it, not even as she pointed the weapon at Sergeant Dashnaw and his kid.

If only the guy had actually gone fishing yesterday like he said he would during their encounter at the grocery store. She would not have needed to go to such lengths to keep her name cleared. She'd be out of town, reading about Lake Carlson on the internet.

Good riddance to all the fishermen in this town. To all the hunters. Everyone who saw humankind as the only species worth protecting.

With time, she would hopefully revive her career, obtain new wealth, and fund more projects. There was always a producer in need of some talent. Surely, her looks hadn't faded enough to keep her from leading roles. Certainly not her acting ability.

More genetic experiments would lead to the protection of more wildlife. No animals would be harmed by people again. She was one person waging a large war, but it had to start somewhere. Might as well start with Lorenzo, Michigan.

Keeping the gun pointed at the policeman, she watched the lake in her peripheral vision. How ironic she ended up at this spot of all places. She was only five years old when her family moved away. Yet, the memory of that water was as clear as though it were yesterday.

She remembered those summer mornings when she'd come out to the dock. Her mother was a fashion designer and always dressed Alice up in style. It made her feel cool to look like a cowgirl, a princess, or a rock artist—until she got to kindergarten. Kids, even at that age, were vicious creatures. Especially the boys. The teachers did their best, but even they cast judgement from time to time. Alice had no friends. She spent her playtime at school reenacting scenes from television with dolls and action figures, resulting in more judgement.

There was nobody to seek comfort with. Mother was always seeking talent jobs whenever she wasn't planning protests for rallies held by her political opposition. Back in those days, there was no internet. Everything was face to face. Such a situation left Alice to turn to animals for companionship. Mother didn't want to own a pet. 'Animals are supposed to live out in the wild, not under the oppression of humans.'

Following that strict belief, she spent much of her time at the dock, feeding the fish swimming below. Over time, she recognized a particular one with a missing right pectoral fin and a few missing scales. Somehow, the bluegill had suffered damage, from being placed in a live-basket.

Being a creative young girl, Alice named the fish Leftie. Over the months, she fed Leftie whatever she could find, including flakes from the pet store. Whenever she went to the dock, Leftie was always there. From a five-year old's perspective, it seemed like Leftie was waiting for her best friend to visit. As an adult, Alice understood that the fish had simply been conditioned to feed along her dock. It didn't matter though. For a young kid, friendship was important. Being as it was not available through people, she found it in this little bluegill. Over time, Leftie grew into a ten-inch long adult.

She'd lay on the dock, flicking flakes into the water, while talking to Leftie about her sorrows. Sometimes, she'd stick her toes in the water and giggle as the bluegill nipped at them as if they were little worms. A little panfish with hardly any intelligence provided something for young Alice that nobody else could provide.

A connection.

Looking further north, Alice could see the dock where her neighbor used to fish. He was a factory worker who always had a cigarette in his mouth. Every afternoon, she'd watch him fish off the dock after he arrived home. Many times, she told him to be nice to the fish, which only triggered a laugh. Day after day, she'd watch him haul a few bluegills and bass out of the water and imprison them in a bucket or basket, where they waited the agonizing fate of being cut open. He wouldn't even put them out of their misery first. She remembered watching their little bodies spasm as the knife sliced the meat from their bones.

A chill swept over Alice as she recalled that fateful day. It was a Friday afternoon. She arrived home from school and immediately ran to the dock. Goldfish flakes in hand, she was ready to feed Leftie, only to see that she wasn't waiting. She tossed a few flakes in, but her friend did not come up from the water. It wasn't uncommon for Leftie to not be there immediately upon her arrival. However, she *never* missed a feeding. Once the flakes hit the water, it took a minute at most for her to arrive. Ten minutes later, there was no sign of her.

That was when Alice turned her attention to the neighbor. He was kneeling on his dock, knife in hand, and a struggling fish on his cutting board.

She approached his dock just in time to see the knife slice into the fish's body. As it attempted to flop off the board, she saw the stub where Leftie's right fin used to be.

"No! No! You're killing my fish!"

"Sorry, kid. Not your fish. My dinner. I'll let you have a fillet, though!"

Her crying had no effect on him. He sliced her best friend into bits, revealing her skeletal body, organs, and intestines. The gills continued to attempt to pump oxygen into her bloodstream as she was tossed into the newspapers.

Alice's one and only friend was dead, all for the enjoyment of this murderer. How many other fish suffered the same fates all for the 'sport' conducted by other murderers? How many deer had been gunned down? How many birds blasted out of the sky?

Petitions did nothing. Protests only riled up the opposition. Politicians were useless. As the years went on, Alice understood that the only way to make a change was to take action herself.

Now, all that stood in the way of that was this cop.

Royce held still. Alice had the eyes of a hungry predator. The slightest movement could trigger a violent response. His shotgun was in his left hand, held by the barrel. He fought against the temptation to shoulder it and blow her damn head off. If only her weapon wasn't already pointed at him.

"Toss it into the water," she said. The rifle lowered to Ellen's height. Royce bitterly threw the weapon into the water, keeping his other hand steady. Alice tilted her head in the direction of his Glock. "And that too. Left hand. Slow. No tricks, or your daughter will pay the price."

"I thought fishermen and hunters were the murderers."

"You are. And murderers should be put to death without remorse."

"They're *fish*!" Ellen said.

"All God's creatures," Alice said. "I thought you people were all about God."

"Leave it to an obvious atheist to use such punchlines whenever they're convenient," Ellen said.

"Shh!" Royce slowly pulled his Glock with his left hand, keeping the other high above his head. After tossing the weapon into the water, both hands were up. "Now what?"

"Into the water."

"You're planning on feeding us to your pets? Fair enough. You obviously want to keep me from spilling the beans about your involvement in all of this. One question? How do you plan on getting to Curt? You might kill me, but you still have that loose end. Believe me, he's more than eager to let the world know of your psychopathic scheme. And with my death as a connection, you're guaranteed to get the death penalty, lady."

Alice smiled. "Trust me. Curt's not an issue. Your man Calloway was a great help with that."

Royce swallowed. *Calloway, that fat useless prick. She bought him off. No wonder they were able to get the fish into the lake without anyone noticing. He kept the night patrols AWAY from the water.*

"Enough talk. In the water now."

Royce stepped in front of his daughter, serving as a human shield. "Go to hell." He took a deep breath and awaited the shot. Alice would gun him down. In the time she needed to chamber the next round, Ellen could get a running start down the road.

Alice leveled the rifle. "Alright. Have it your way."

****

Within two seconds of the crash, the lake had completely filled the interior of the chopper. Panic struck the fuselage, as all four civilians struggled to make their way up to the fuselage door.

Pam was underwater, still strapped in her seat. Her head had cracked the window during the crash. Had it not been for the taste of lake water, she would have passed out.

She coughed and saw the air bubbles floating to her right. As she was taught in the Marines, when underwater after a traumatic situation such as a crash, simply follow the air bubbles to get a sense of direction. Right was up. She climbed over the co-pilot's seat, opened the door, and found fresh air.

"Officer! Help!" Jacob said.

She knelt by the fuselage door and took him by the hand. The attempt to hoist him nearly resulted in both of them tumbling over the side. Keeping herself balanced was a battle in itself.

Skip pulled himself out of the fuselage and knelt at the edge, helping Jane and Grace out. He looked to Pam and saw the blood trickling from a cut on her hairline.

"You okay, Officer? That doesn't look good at all."

"Hurts like a bitch," Pam said.

"What happened?" Grace shouted, back in hysterics. "How could you just crash like that? What kind of shitty ass helicopter is this?!"

Skip put a hand on her shoulder. "Grace..."

"Shut up. She crashed the chopper..."

His gentle touch became a firm grab. "Grace. Shut. Up." He cupped her mouth for good measure, then looked to the shoreline.

Jane put both hands to her mouth and gasped.

Pam followed their gazes to the shore. It took a moment to identify the situation through her hazy vision.

There, less than a yard away from the waterline, was the reason for their crash. Alice Kirkman stood with a magazine-fed bolt-action rifle pointed at Royce and his daughter.

Pam's vision was hazy, but she could recognize a firing stance from a mile away. Alice was about to execute Royce and Ellen.

She drew her Glock and fired.

Alice jerked to the side, her gun firing high. Pam resumed firing, her shots going wide. Had it not been for that splitting headache and dull vision, Alice would have five holes in her chest.

The eco-terrorist fired back. Her shot went wide, allowing Pam to take more careful aim. Adrenaline worked in her favor. She centered her iron sights on the target. Alice had backed up to a tree inadvertently and was fumbling with her bolt action. She wasn't used to being in a real firefight.

"Gotcha, bitch." Pam began to squeeze the trigger.

Pain soured through her hand as a pair of jaws clamped on her palm. Her bullet zipped to the side, followed by several more as muscle tension kept the trigger depressed.

Like a servant protecting its master, the piranha clung to her hand. Blood trickled into the water, stirring the rest of the nearby pack.

****

Alice exhaled sharply, then smiled. It was as though her precious fish knew they were helping her. Those people on the chopper wouldn't last long. Right now, she needed to focus on the priority.

The cop and kid were sprinting down the shoreline.

"Go! Run!" he shouted to his kid.

Alice sprinted after him, but quickly realized she wouldn't catch up to them. She shouldered her rifle and fired repeatedly.

She heard a yell. A moment later, the cop went down.

Damn. I'm a natural at this.

He wasn't dead. She could see the blood soaking his right pantleg. But he was immobile. Finishing him off would be a simple matter. And thanks to the fact that his kid was running to his side, it wouldn't be hard to finish her off either. With all the cops concentrated on the north end of the lake, she'd be gone by the time they realized what happened.

The crumbs of humanity were completely gone. She not only felt virtuous, but powerful. Nothing was more empowering than the sight of her enemies at her mercy.

She aimed down at the officer and squeezed the trigger.

Click.

"Damn it." The mag was empty. *No worries. Only a minor delay.* She ejected the mag, then reached for another as she approached the two.

****

"Goddamn! Get off!" Pam shouted.

Skip reached over at her and smacked the fish with his bare hand, knocking it away. The fish joined the rest of its group. Like flies buzzing around a corpse, they swarmed the fallen chopper.

Fins thrashed along the surface as many attempted to slither over the fuselage.

Pam emptied her mag into the group. Like the head of a hydra, whenever one fish floated dead on the surface, two more seemingly arrived to take its place. Pam looked at her Glock. The slide was locked back. With the mag empty and the rest of her bullets used during the vehicular chase, she was unarmed.

The determined fish began making their leaps. Pam spun on her heels and fell, narrowly dodging one that whipped by her head.

The others went into a frenzy as many more piranhas jumped at them. One struck Skip square in the chest, driving him backward. Jane grabbed him by the shirt with both hands and pulled back before he reached the edge. The fish fell from his torso with a piece of his shirt in its mouth.

Skip stomped down repeatedly until its head was crushed. After kicking the thing back into the water, they watched the miniature feeding frenzy.

From that festering water came another deranged predator. It went for Jacob, only taking a snippet of his hair before splashing down behind him.

The next one, however, found its target.

Nobody realized Grace was overboard until they heard the splash. She didn't scream.

She couldn't—the fish had sunk its jaws into her throat. All she could do was reach for someone to pull her up. Skip outstretched his hand but his reach fell short.

Ribbons of flesh came off Grace's face. Her white eyes and teeth seemed brighter in contrast to the red, bald, skinless face. Within seconds, the piranhas stripped the muscular tissue away, revealing the cheekbones.

They could do nothing except look away. Unfortunately, that only led to another horrible sight.

Royce Dashnaw had fallen face-down on the shore. Ellen was pulling on his arm, trying to get him to his feet. Behind them, Alice Kirkman approached.

Pam shut her eyes and cursed herself for wasting the last of her bullets on the piranhas. *Please, God. Let it be over quick.*

****

Royce could barely move his leg. The bullet had dug deep into his hamstring and likely severed a tendon. He could only get limited motion from it.

Ellen tugged on his left arm. "Get up, Dad!"

"No, sweetie!" He looked over his shoulder. Alice was ten feet away, fresh magazine in hand. She slammed it home and worked the bolt. He yanked his arm free and pushed Ellen away. "Run, Ellen! Run! Do as I say!"

Alice chambered a round and angled the muzzle at his head. "Ha! Is this how cops feel when they gun down unarmed people? Can't deny, in this case, it feels kinda good."

A honking horn and roaring engine drew her attention to the driveway. The truck bounced along the uneven ground as it raced off the road onto the beach. Right for her.

Alice moved to the left, but the truck only followed her. She fired a shot at the windshield, but it did nothing to slow the truck. She threw her hands over her face and screamed. That scream was cut short by a thunderous impact that knocked her off her feet.

The next sound was that of her landing in the water.

Royce propped himself up on his good leg and watched the aftermath. Alice was only in twelve inches of water, making her easily visible. She was still alive, though badly mangled. Her left shoulder was very visibly dislocated, the arm itself broken in several places, as were many of her ribs. She pushed herself out of the water with her good arm and watched the driver step out of the vehicle.

Blood and teeth spat from her mouth. "Curt?!"

The young man caught his breath, amazed but also somewhat disturbed by his actions.

"I always thought people like *him* were the fascists!" he said, pointing at Royce. "I guess you proved me wrong. You're a disgrace to the movement. Have fun with your pets."

Alice looked to and fro at the dozens of fish, genetically altered thanks to her funding. This relationship held no meaning to them, for they lacked emotion. Despite her many visits to the lab, they did not remember her face, nor did they understand the reason of her affections.

Like Leftie, they only came to her for food.

Alice was pulled in two dozen directions at once. Teeth sawed through her hands and fingers. Several more closed in, drawn by the scent of blood. Many closed in on her left arm, tearing the meat from the broken bones. With everything around the fracture removed, those tugging on the fingers were free to run away with the entire arm, pursued by many others who nipped at the stump.

Clothing was torn free, revealing all of Alice's upper anatomy for a split-second before the fish shredded it.

Hair and fabric drifted away. Intestines uncoiled as piranhas ran away with them as they would a nightcrawler. Cheeks were torn to bits, revealing teeth and cheekbones.

The last thing she saw were the teeth of one of the piranhas before they clamped down on her eye and pulled it from the socket.

Royce held Ellen close, forcing her to look away from the carnage. Curt was wobbling in place. It was his first time seeing the piranhas do their nasty work.

"Damn! GodDAMN!" He turned away and was met with a hug from Ellen.

"Thank you!"

"Oh! Uh, it's alright, kid." He took Royce's hand and helped him up. The officer balanced on his good leg and pressed one hand to his bullet wound.

The two men looked each other in the eye and expressed their mutual respect with a nod.

"Where's Calloway?" Royce asked.

"Taking a nap. I cuffed him to his car. I have his phone, in case you're wondering what happened."

"Alice proudly announced it. Hang on to that, though. It'll come in handy when we prosecute that son of a bitch." Royce looked at the truck. "I suppose you had to take drastic measures to get here."

"Yeeeeeah. I, um—"

Royce tapped him on the shoulder. "Don't worry about it, man. I owe you my kid's life."

"Dad?"

Royce looked to the chopper. It was a hundred feet away and surrounded by piranhas. The four people standing atop were huddled in its center to avoid any leaping fish.

"How do we get them out of there?" Ellen said.

"Just call for help. Maybe get a boat out here?" Curt suggested.

"Won't get here fast enough," Royce said. "There's too many fish and they're hungry as hell. They'll pick them off before we get to them. We need to commandeer one of these boats."

"I already tried," Ellen said. "The big ones need ignition keys, and I can't find them. The owners are either dead or not home. All that's available is the twelve-footer."

"Driving through a tight swarm, we might as well just dive in and serve ourselves up." The frustration and intensity made his leg throb, which flared his temper. "Damn it! If only we had something to kill those fish in one swift stroke."

"What about an explosion?" Curt said.

"Yeah!" Ellen said. "There's gotta be something we can use to make a bomb, right? Plenty of gas grills and propane tanks around."

"No. They're too close. We'd risk killing them in the blast. It's not like *Predator* where all you need is a hill or a tree trunk to save you."

The mention of that movie took Ellen back to last night's viewing.

"You see that electrical discharge before it goes off? Maybe there's more to the bomb than a simple blast. Maybe it uses intense electrical impulse, like a massive bolt of lightning, to fry anything in sight."

"Wow...and I thought I watched this movie too many times," Ellen said.

"I thought talking about the lore was part of the fun."

"I have to agree with your dad on this one," Pam said. *"Not sure I agree about the electricity thing. Electrons scatter off oxygen and nitrogen molecules, so an electrical blast would break apart in a short distance. It's not like water, which contains salts and metals. So, no, an electrical blast would not have worked unless Arnie was in a lake."*

She looked up at the power cable. "Dad? What about that?"

Royce studied the cable's position. If it were to come loose, it would fall near the waterline.

"That might work, except they're standing on a steel helicopter," he said. "We'd just zap them."

"Not if they got on the floating platform," Curt said. "Electricity doesn't go through wood. Even if it's wet, the underside is rubber. They should be safe enough from any major electrical current."

Royce gauged the distance between the chopper and the platform. Maybe twelve feet. If only they had a bridge...

The boat!

He hobbled to the twelve-footer and pulled it near the dock. Leaning over the side, he started the engine then pointed the bow to the chopper.

"PAM!"

"Don't come out here, Royce! They're everywhere!" she shouted back.

"I know! Get to the platform! Use the boat as a bridge. I'm sending it to you." He adjusted its position then let go. In that same moment, a fish leapt out of the water and grabbed his shoulder. "Son of a mother!" He smacked the piranha repeatedly until it fell back into the water.

The boat continued on its course, leaning slightly to port. The fish attacked it from below, stalling its engine. Momentum pushed it the rest of the way.

Royce tensed as the boat moved further left. "Come on! Get there…" Pam and Skip knelt down and reached. Their fingertips found the edge and managed to pull it close. "Yes!"

They adjusted the boat to put it between them and the platform. Jacob was the first to cross over to the platform. Then Jane. Skip and Pam went together, the latter still a little off balance from the crash.

The platform wobbled as each one jumped aboard. Tiny dorsal fins coursed around them. The piranhas were insatiable in every extent of the word. Over a half-dozen people devoured in this area alone in the last hour, and they were still starving.

Royce limped to the rear of the dock and looked at the juncture where the cable connected to the post. Climbing was not an option, thanks to his injured leg. There was no ladder around. Ellen could climb like a monkey, but there was no way in hell Royce would risk her safety by having her mess with a high-voltage cable.

"Damn it. If only I could shoot that thing down."

"Where's your gun?" Curt asked.

"In the lake. So is Alice's rifle."

"Hang on." Curt ran to the truck, reached inside, then returned to the dock. In his hand was a Glock 19. "Took it off the crooked Sergeant."

Royce snatched the weapon and took aim. "Better stand back. You too, kid!" He gave them a count of five to get by the truck, during which he gave another glance to the platform. The piranhas were attacking, the survivors swatting them away.

He pointed the weapon and fired. A thousand sparks flew through the air. The cable detached and fell into the inlet, landing right on the waterline. More sparks soared like fireflies as thousands of volts coursed through the lake.

All at once, the hundreds of fish in the nearby vicinity were seized by its current. Their spasming bodies gave the lake the appearance of a rainstorm without the rain. Over the course of the next few seconds, the spasming stopped.

Royce collapsed on the dock and watched the bodies floating across the lake. Ellen ran up to him and threw her arms around his neck.

"You alright?"

"I'm alright, hon. It'll all be alright now. They're dead." He looked to the platform. Pam, Skip, Jane, and Jacob were breathing a collective sigh of relief.

"You did it, Royce!" Jane shouted.

He gave a thumbs up. "Is everyone alright?"

"What's left of us," she replied.

"They're doing better than I am," Pam said. "At least they're not gonna have to suffer in a hospital bed."

"Better on one of those than on this lake," Jacob said.

Royce reached for his phone. "Let me call the right people. We'll get you out of there."

CHAPTER 35

Thirty minutes after the electrical surge, EMS and electrical workers arrived on site. The power was shut off and the survivors safely brought to shore. Despite the insistence of the paramedics to transfer him to the hospital, Royce demanded to wait until Pam was tended to. Once she was ashore, he allowed them to load him onto a stretcher and wheel him to the ambulance.

Jacob walked to Ellen's side, gasping after seeing her father's bloody pant leg. "Will he be okay?"

"Yeah, he'll be fine," one of the paramedics said. "He'll be in the hospital for a week."

"A lot of people will," Jacob said. He looked back at Jane. She was seated next to Skip on a private porch while paramedics tended to both of them. "Once she pulls herself together, I think she'll be infatuated with him."

Ellen smiled. "You say that like it's a bad thing."

"It's not. I like him. He's cool."

"Like you," she said. He looked at her. A compliment from Ellen Dashnaw? This truly was a weird day. "Thanks for what you did on the boat. That was quick thinking."

"Oh, that!" With everything that happened, he literally did forget about the trick with the fishing line. "Had a good teacher."

"Damn right you did." She closed her eyes and inhaled deeply. Never before did she feel such an appreciation for the gift of life. "Hey?"

"Yeah?"

"I know Jane will be busy. I'll take you to that *Thor: Love and Thunder* movie if you want?"

"Really?"

"Yeah. Just don't be surprised if I cringe during the whole thing. And *you're* buying the popcorn."

"Deal," he said with a smile.

Ellen gave him a hug, then trotted off to see her dad. As she approached, another cop car arrived. Officer Holman stepped out, his foot heavily bandaged, his uniform indicative of the hell he went through on the north end.

"Jesus, Sarge! You alright?"

"Perfectly fine," Royce said. "The people who did this have already been put to justice. If those damn fish did anything helpful, they saved us taxpayer dollars in court costs."

"Damn straight," Holman said. He turned to his left and saw Curt standing by a tree. "What about him?"

Royce shook his head. "Cut him loose."

"Wait. What?"

"He's good. Let him go. It's my call."

Holman nodded. If Royce said Curt was good, then he was good. "Speaking of calls, we're gonna need a new Chief. I don't think the Lieutenant has a good shot. The department needs a good leader. Maybe, once you're up and walking again…"

Royce shrugged. "I don't know. This town is gonna be forever changed after today's tragedy."

"Which is why they need someone who cares about this place to lead it," Holman said.

"I agree," Pam said. "The Mayor will go for it. Especially with all of our endorsements."

"Things went bad today. They'd be even worse if you hadn't made the calls you did," Holman said.

"You guys aren't gonna let up on this, are ya?"

Ellen practically danced in place. "You gonna come to the hospital with us, Pam?"

"She'll have to," one of the paramedics said. "She has a bullet injury and probably a concussion. She's going to be staying overnight for sure. If you're worried about your daughter, sir, the hospital has expandable sofas for her to sleep on."

"Works for me," Ellen said. "Hey? Can you and Pam share the same hospital room? They have semi-private ones. You can keep the curtain open; that way you can see each other."

"I'm all for that!" Pam said.

Royce smiled and leaned close to Ellen's ear. "I know what you're doing, little smart aleck."

"Like I can't hear you." Pam laughed. "Maybe this will convince you?" She leaned forward and planted a kiss on his lips. The touch of her lips shocked him more than Alice's bullet.

"It… has an effect."

Pam leaned on the rail. "A good one, I hope, Chief."

He sat up and kissed her back. "Does that answer the question?"

"I'd say it does!" Ellen said. Royce chuckled and hugged them both. Ellen raised a fist, gloating. "All my idea!"

Royce squeezed her tighter. "Very true. How'd you get to be so smart?"

"I take after my dad."

Check out other great
Sea Monster Novels!

Michael Cole

CREATURE OF LAKE SHADOW

It was supposed to be a simple bank robbery. Quick. Clean. Efficient. It was none of those. With police searching for them across the state, a band of criminals hide out in a desolate cabin on the frozen shore of Lake Shadow. Isolated, shrouded in thick forest, and haunted by a mysterious history, they thought it was the perfect place to hide. Tensions mount as they hear strange noises outside. Slain animals are found in the snow. Before long, they realize something is watching them. Something hungry, violent, and not of this world. In their attempt to escape, they found the Creature of Lake Shadow.

C.J. Waller

PREDATOR X

When deep level oil fracking uncovers a vast subterranean sea, a crack team of cavers and scientists are sent down to investigate. Upon their arrival, they disappear without a trace. A second team, including sedimentologist Dr Megan Stoker, are ordered to seek out Alpha Team and report back their findings. But Alpha team are nowhere to be found – instead, they are faced with something unexpected in the depths. Something ancient. Something huge. Something dangerous. Predator X

Check out other great

Sea Monster Novels!

Robert J. Stava

NEPTUNES RECKONING

At the easternmost end of Long Island lies a seaside town known as Montauk. Ground Zero on the Eastern seaboard for all manner of conspiracy theories involving it's hidden Cold War military base, rumors of time-travel experiments and alien visitors... For renowned Naval historian William Vanek it's the where his grandfather's ship went down on a Top Secret mission during WWII code-named "Neptune's Reckoning". Together with Marine Biologist Daniel Cheung and disgraced French underwater explorer Arnaud Navarre, he's about to discover the truth behind the urban legends: a nightmare from beyond space and time that has been reawakened by global warming and toxic dumping, a nightmare the government tried to keep submerged. Neptune's Reckoning. Terror knows no depth

Bestselling collection

DEAD BAIT

A husband hell-bent on revenge hunts a Wereshark... A Russian mail order bride with a fishy secret... Crabs with a collective consciousness... A vampire who transforms into a Candiru... Zombie piranha...Bait that will have you crawling out of your skin and more. Drawing on horror, humor with a helping of dark fantasy and a touch of deviance, these 19 contemporary stories pay homage to the monsters that lurk in the murky waters of our imaginations. If you thought it was safe to go back in the water... Think Again!

SEVEREDPRESS

🐦 @severedpress
f /severedpress

Check out other great

Sea Monster Novels!

Matt James

SUB-ZERO

The only thing colder than the Antarctic air is the icy chill of death... Off the coast of McMurdo Station, in the frigid waters of the Southern Ocean, a new species of Antarctic octopus is unintentionally discovered. Specialists aboard a state-of-the-art DARPA research vessel aim to apply the animal's "sub-zero venom" to one of their projects: An experimental painkiller designed for soldiers on the front lines. All is going according to plan until the ship is caught in an intense storm. The retrofitted tanker is rocked, and the onboard laboratory is destroyed. Amid the chaos, the lead scientist is infected by a strange virus while conducting the specimen's dissection. The scientist didn't die in the accident. He changed.

Alister Hodge

THE CAVERN

When a sink hole opens up near the Australian outback town of Pintalba, it uncovers a pristine cave system. Sam joins an expedition to explore the subterranean passages as paramedic support, hoping to remain unneeded at base camp. But, when one of the cavers is injured, he must overcome paralysing claustrophobia to dive pitch-black waters and squeeze through the bowels of the earth. Soon he will find there are fates worse than being buried alive, for in the abandoned mines and caves beneath Pintalba, there are ravenous teeth in the dark. As a savage predator targets the group with hideous ferocity, Sam and his friends must fight for their lives if they are ever to see the sun again.

Made in the USA
Middletown, DE
01 July 2022